The
Queen Bee

WORDSWORTH ROMANCE

The Queen Bee

PHYLLIDA BARSTOW

WORDSWORTH EDITIONS

First published by Macdonald & Co (Publishers) Ltd

This edition published 1994 by
Wordsworth Editions Limited
Cumberland House, Crib Street, Ware,
Hertfordshire SG12 9ET

ISBN 1 85326 508 X

Printed and bound in Denmark by Nørhaven

Chapter One

I wouldn't have chosen Rosie as the person I most wanted to die with. After only a week of her company I felt she could be relied on to cause the maximum fuss and embarrassment to everyone within earshot of the Pearly Gates. But it didn't look as if I was going to get much choice.

As the pea-green lorry hurtled towards us out of control, on a bend of the Grand Trunk Road from Udaipur to the Khyber Pass, I felt first terror, then rage, and then – oddest of all – a definite sensation of relief, as when at the last moment of a nightmare you give up, let go, or turn to face whatever you've been running away from. Fate, I thought, having struck at all my family, had at last made up her mind to clobber me, and this time she was going to make a job of it.

Rosie and I, with Stewart Royal, our guide and driver of the clapped-out minibus Rosie had hired, had left hot, dusty, swarming Delhi at nine that morning, heading north for Kashmir. All the oriental world and his wife, plus cows, goats, camels and buffaloes seemed to have chosen that bright November day to take a stroll on the Grand Trunk Road, and after about the hundredth narrow squeak I'd given up advising Stewart to drive slower, and seen the futility of stamping my feet against the back of his seat in an effort to add to our braking power. It was now just after three, and I fet hot, thirsty, dusty and rather tired.

But when I saw the pea-green lorry crabbing across the crown of the road, heeled well down on its right back axle, nearly broadside on to us, my lethargy vanished. Flashing mirrors on short chains dangled from its front bumper, and the bodywork was a shrieking, clashing riot of gaudy stencils. I could even see a twinkling nose ornament on the face of a fat

1

woman jammed in beside the driver.

I screamed: 'Look out, Stewart! *Look out!*' but there was nothing Stewart could do to prevent the crash.

A huge hand seemed to thump me between the shoulder-blades, and I catapulted into the front seat on top of Rosie. I couldn't have chosen a softer landing.

Just before we overturned, I saw the lorry career past us and go straight over the edge of an embankment. As it toppled, bundles and sacks and bodies spilled out of it, all the way down the slope to a stream at the bottom. Then our minibus was on its side, and I was trying frantically to get out.

It's a horrible feeling – the sort of panic that grips you when you can't find your way to the surface after diving into a murky pool and going too deep. You know the sky is still there above you, if only you could tell which way was up. As the minibus stopped spinning, I scrabbled for the window, but found it blocked; I could hear someone sobbing and battering at this window, and only when I tried to call to them for help did I realize that I was making the noise myself.

Suddenly, under my hail of kicks and blows, the back door burst open and I fell out into the road. The minibus was upside down, the roof crushed in, and figures had started to scurry towards us from a row of shacks not far away. They looked like anxious brown ants.

Quite a lot of Rosie was sticking out of the upper window, but I couldn't see Stewart. I grabbed handfuls of soft, white, spongy arm and shoulder and pulled as hard as I could. She didn't budge.

'Rosie,' I said, and I heard my voice all high and hysterical, 'come on, Rosie. Help me! You've got to get out!'

It was grillingly hot. I thought at any minute the petrol tank would blow up and that would be it. I couldn't see what to do. Rosie was so floppy, so heavy.

Then a hard hand gripped my shoulder. 'Let go,' ordered a man's voice. 'Come away.'

I struck at him blindly. I couldn't leave Rosie and Stewart to fry. 'The door's locked. Inside. I can't open it.'

'Get out of the way, then.' He shoved me aside, jumped on the

2

crumpled bonnet, and kicked in the windscreen.

'Sandy!' he shouted. 'Give me a hand. There's two more in here.'

Another man ran to join him and together they lugged Rosie out through the windscreen and carried her to a gleaming white Land Rover parked in the shade at the side of the road. I propped her up on a kitbag I found in the back while the men went back for Stewart. Rosie's head lolled as if her neck was broken. She was breathing very loud and fast through her mouth – almost snoring – and I knew I mustn't think about Bill. My brother Bill. That was another time, another place, forgotten, dead and buried. But no matter what I told myself, then and now ran together and mingled in my mind like badly-mixed paint. Undercoat running into topcoat. I'd thought the whole thing was dry – five years dry – but I'd only to touch the paint to see how fresh it still was.

Our rescuers came back, carrying Stewart. He looked a mess: blood from a split lip pouring down his bright Madras cotton shirt, and both eyes swelling fast. But at least he was alive.

It was a squash in the Land Rover by the time they'd salvaged our luggage, and all round both cars was a tight ring of Indians, staring at point-blank range. A boxer must feel like this, I thought, fighting off claustrophobia, hemmed in by bodies and unable to escape.

Sandy climbed into the driver's seat and slammed the door. 'What now, Nick?' he asked. 'No good waiting for the cops, ennit?'

'Useless,' agreed Nick. 'Drive to the British Hospital and we'll dump the casualties.'

Did I count as a casualty? I didn't much care either way. I crouched on the back seat, propping up Rosie, who flowed out of her bucket seat on to mine like a thick, soft eiderdown, content to let someone else make decisions.

Our rescuers had their heads bent over a map. I thought they looked an odd pair. The one called Nick was short and dark and thick-set, with broad shoulders stretching his faded denim shirt. His curly black hair grew low on his collar and curved neatly into the nape of his neck. A square guy, I thought; solid and

3

square. He had the wide cheek-bones and tidy, chiselled features I associated with *ski-lehrers* – the type of face you're apt to find decorating the other end of an Austrian bottle-opener. His voice was as calm and matter-of-fact as if he was discussing a menu instead of clearing up a messy road accident. I guessed he'd never been rattled in his thirty-odd years.

In contrast, the one called Sandy, in the driver's seat, seemed nearly as shaken as I was. He was a shrimp of a man, thin and wiry and rather older than Nick, perhaps thirty-five, I thought, with a jockey's sharp, wizened features and thinning, slicked-down, gingery hair. His movements were quick and nervous; his freckled and nicotine-stained fingers shook on the steering-wheel.

Nick took off his sun-glasses and turned to smile at me, and I saw that his eyes were an unexpected light blue – the colour that can look either guileless or mad – strangely out of place in that tidy, conventional face.

'Take it easy,' he said. 'Don't worry. The old girl'll be all right if we get her to hospital as quick as we can. The other chap's not so bad, in spite of all that blood. Try not to let her roll about too much.'

Sandy engaged the clutch gently and we moved off.

'Keep her steady,' insisted Nick.

'I *am*.'

'Good.' He didn't sound convinced, though, and leaning over the seat, he rearranged Rosie, draping her arm over my shoulders so that I became a human coat-hanger. 'There, that's better.'

He either ignored or was oblivious of the fact that it was far worse for me. 'Watch the bumps, Sandy,' he warned. 'No sudden jolts.'

'OK,' said Sandy. I thought he was doing wonders, threading a skilful path through the tightly-packed bicycles and bullock-carts on the outskirts of a town.

'What about the – the people on the lorry?' I asked, shivering. It was all very well for us, getting the hell out.

'Nine lives apiece,' said Nick cheerfully. 'Don't worry; Sandy and I saw exactly what happened. You won't have any trouble.'

4

This seemed unduly sanguine. I foresaw nothing but trouble. No car, injured driver, nowhere to stay the night . . .

'It wasn't even our car – '

'Eastravel bus, wannit?' said Sandy without taking his eyes off the road. 'From that dump in the Qutab Minar road?'

'Yes,' I said, surprised that he should have identified the wreck so easily.

'This bloke one of their drivers?'

'Yes.'

'Then who's the old girl?' asked Nick. 'Your mamma?'

'Heaven forbid! No – I don't mean that, exactly, but we're not related at all. We're just – well, travelling companions. We were going to Kashmir.'

'Just the two of you?'

I sighed and braced myself, foreseeing further questions. It would probably save time and trouble if I did all my explaining at once. I wondered where to begin. It seemed a long time, though it was barely a month, since I'd battled my way into Alan Devereux's office for the purpose of handing him my resignation.

Alan was then my boss, lord and master of Devereux Designs, the firm he had built from scratch to challenge the textile giants on their own ground. I'd joined his organization three years before, on the strength of winning an art-school design competition, but I'd hardly been face to face with him since the day he hired me. He was only about twenty-five then, but he'd managed to avoid the whizz-kid label by cultivating a deliberately middle-aged appearance with a sweeping chestnut moustache, a spreading paunch decorated with a gold fob-watch-chain, and a thoroughly senior, infuriatingly pontifical manner to go with them.

Alan's parents had flown into the side of a mountain when he was six, leaving, so the girls in my department told me in awed tones, half a million in trust for him. It had grown a good bit by the time he came of age, and his careful trustees had yelped when he proposed to blue a large hunk of it on some derelict textile mills. They needn't have worried. Alan had the Midas touch, and making money breed money was truly his greatest.

pleasure.

So for three years I'd been happy enough working like a well-disciplined, well-oiled cog in my own little section of the Devereux machine, sharing a flat with my sister Anna, who was all that was left of my immediate family. It was she who'd advised me to talk things over with the boss before quitting. As she reminded me, Alan had said at the end of our first interview: 'I want you to be happy. People work best when they're happy, I've noticed. So come and see me if you're got any problems. I mean that.'

So when I couldn't face my problem any more, Anna made me take it to him.

I hesitated, looking at the black head and the ginger one in the front of the Land Rover. There was absolutely no need for me to go into details about falling in and out of love with Johnny Marris.

I was a fool; he was a four- (if not three-) letter man, and when his pretty, pregnant wife came to our flat to beg me to leave him alone, I felt sick. I hadn't known he was married. The worst of it was that I couldn't stand bumping into Johnny in and around Devereux House after that. I decided to resign.

'Miss Granville to see you, sir,' said the blue-rinsed dragon who guarded Alan's door, showing me in. 'Don't forget you're lunching with Sir Thomas,' she added severely, as if warning me to get it over quick. 'One-fifteen at the Savoy Grill.'

'I won't forget,' said Alan, making a token hitch of the behind from the chair before sinking back to the swivel chair and leaning his elbows on the shining acreage of desk. 'Silly bitch – her, not you,' he went on, not bothering to lower his voice though the door had hardly clicked shut. 'Bosses me around, or would if she could. Still, at least she's not *glamorous*. Sit down, Charlotte, and tell me what's on your mind. No, on second thoughts, don't tell me. I know just what you're going to say, and I don't want to hear it. You just listen to me instead.'

I sat obediently, waiting for my moment to get a word in edgeways.

'It's no good running away, Charlotte. You've had a fair bit of trouble one way and another, I know, what with your parents, and poor Bill . . . It's been a miserable time for you and I admire the way you've faced up to it. We've kept your nose to the grindstone, and believe me, you're coming on very well. We're delighted with your work and I don't want to lose you – or, come to that, lose Marris. I had enough difficulty luring him away from Courtaulds in the first place.

'Now about this latest business, I grant you that he's every kind of a knave and a fool, but you haven't been too brilliant yourself, have you? Can't you call it a draw? Put it down to experience and forget it, but don't for Pete's sake walk out on us because of a lovers' tiff. That'd be too ridiculous.'

'But – '

'No buts. You've been messing around with those Japanese prints for *months* now. Oh yes, I know just what goes on in that cosy little department of yours. It's high time you pulled yourself together and tried something new. Right, then,' he said, glancing at his Rolex Oyster. 'That's settled, my dear. I'm so glad to have talked it over with you. Go away and think about it and if you ever find anything worrying you, *anything at all*, do remember I'll be only too happy to sort it out for you.'

He leaned back, stroking his moustache and clearly considering the interview at an end. But I'd battled my way past a receptionist, two secretaries, a P.A., a right-hand man and a Girl Friday as well as the blue-rinsed dragon, and I wasn't going to be dismissed without a hearing.

'The trouble is, Alan,' I said rather diffidently (I hardly knew him but one couldn't say Mr to someone only two years older than oneself), 'it's no good telling me to think about it. I *have* thought. I'll have to leave. I don't really want to and I'm sorry; you've been very kind to me . . . '

'Leave Devereux?' Alan's Leander-pink jowls drooped in petulant surprise. 'Haven't you listened to a word I said? You can't leave – it'd finish you. You may think you're trained and you're beginning to get a name and a reputation, and you could manage on your own, but you'd be wrong. You're not a natural free-lance, dear: you can't sell yourself. You need the Devereux umbrella. It wouldn't be fair on your sister, either.'

I stared. I'd never mentioned Anna's troubles in the office for

7

fear of being swamped with sympathy.

'Oh yes, I know all about your sister,' said Alan. 'I think it's splendid the way you look after her. But she's a very powerful reason for you to stay with us. I'm right in thinking there are just the two of you, aren't I? No useful aunts or cousins?'

'No.'

'It would be hard on Anna, then, if you threw up a well-paid, secure job which gives you plenty of time at home, and had to start tramping from pillar to post trying to sell your stuff. The insecurity would soon tell on your work.'

He was right and I knew it. I only work well when I have no worries. That was the bliss of the Art Department I was proposing to leave. The designs I produced were all that was required of me. No anxiety about printing, packaging, marketing. One day the design would be on my drawing-board, the next (it seemed) I would recognize it in a shop, discreetly tagged and labelled *A Charlotte Granville Exclusive by DEVEREUX*. Sometimes it took me several minutes' thought to identify the original, because when I drew my sketch, I'd had no idea what it would eventually decorate. That was someone else's job.

I said, 'I know; but you see it's him or me, and Johnny doesn't want to leave.'

'And he's got a wife and kids to support,' said Alan dryly. 'Well, I agree that of the pair of you, you're the easiest to shift. But shift is all it'll be, see?'

The buzzer on his desk rang. He pressed a button, said: 'All right, all right. Tell him I'm stuck in a traffic jam,' and turned back to me. 'What a nuisance you young females are! You'd think no one had ever had an affaire go wrong before. But I suppose I'll get no decent stuff from you until you're happy.'

He thought for a moment, tugging his moustache, then said rapidly: 'You need a change. You've been stuck in that ivory tower long enough. Time you came into the market-place and did some haggling.'

'Haggling?' I said in alarm.

'Right. The best place to learn to haggle is India. (Or anywhere east of Suez, for that matter, but in India you'll be most use to me.) I'll send you to collect this year's – I mean next

8

year's – orders of material from our Indian suppliers and arrange transport home for it.'

I began to bleat, 'But I don't know the first thing about – '

He cut me short. 'Nonsense, girl. Rubbish. I expect you've been shopping? That's all there is to it. Shopping in very large quantities. The stuff's all ordered, anyway. You have to see it's delivered.'

'D'you need to send anyone, then? I mean, can't they simply put it on a plane?'

'Not as easy as you'd think. Not quite. But the experience will do you good – broaden your horizons. It may even give you some new ideas. I'll arrange domestic help for Anna while you're away, or rather my secretary will, so don't try that as an excuse, and I'll go and see her every week. How's that?'

He paused, then tossed in the carrot: 'If you don't make an utter balls-up of this, I might – I just might – put you in charge of the Exotic Textiles Department of *Junk* when you come home. They need a bright girl.'

This was a cunning bribe. *Junk* was Alan's newest and dearest baby: a kind of ornamental oriental supermarket where very rich people bought their friends beautiful, useless wedding presents and poor people yearned through the plate-glass. Long before the business with Johnny, I'd applied for a job in *Junk* which I'd seen advertised in the Devereux house magazine, but the manager had turned me down because I wasn't an expert on oriental materials. Since then I'd read quite a lot of Chinese and Indian history, hoping for another chance.

The buzzer rang again. 'OK, OK,' he shouted; then to me, 'It'll be hard work, mind. I want you to bring back everything I ask for. Don't be put off. You're much too easily put off, you know.'

I knew.

Alan added, bustling to the door: 'When you've checked off everything on my list, you can take a holiday. Take a month. I believe the Taj Mahal is worth seeing.'

The Land Rover purred through the spicy-smelling dusk. In the front seat the men waited patiently for me to speak. I took a deep

9

breath and plunged in.

'I met Rosie in Delhi, you see, just a week ago today . . . '

Chapter Two

I'd been wilting by the hotel swimming-pool, trying to find a place that was both shady and protected from the soot dropped from the laundry chimney, when I first noticed the statuesque blonde who turned out to be Rosie, doubly insulated from the sun's damaging rays by a wide-brimmed hat and the largest of the pool's umbrellas.

She'd had the hotel staff fairly leaping around, bringing iced drinks and intriguing-looking envelopes delivered by special messenger, towels wrung in Eau-de-Cologne and tinsel-wrapped sweetmeats. Then a speck of soot was ass enough to land on her fat white arm, and I watched a virtuoso display of outrage that brought even the habitually supercilious young hotel manager to smooth the blonde's ruffled feathers. She was evidently a valued client.

One night she sailed over to ask if she might share my table in the restaurant, and I was glad to say yes.

She'd calculated her intrusion nicely: I was beginning to long for company, and everyone else in the hotel seemed to belong in a party. Talking business with Indians was a strain on the nerves, as Alan had warned, and I was near the end of my tether.

Although it was late October, the beginning of the cool season, New Delhi seemed to me like an oven. For the fortnight I'd been there, stropping up our suppliers and ordering materials that never got delivered, I'd tried to gallop through the work and visits, the cups of tea and interminable bargaining, in order to finish the day's work by eleven in the morning. After that it was simply too hot to think. It was so difficult to pin the merchants down. You'd talk, look at samples, agree a price, quantity and date for delivery, and part the best of friends. On the agreed date, nothing would turn up.

You'd go back; start again from scratch. This time you'd harry them a little; ring up a few times, and be assured that all was going well. Yes, yes, memsahib, all would be ready in time. Only it wouldn't be.

At first I couldn't believe it. Time and again I was on the point of cancelling the orders and storming out, but I realized that every other merchant was liable to be just as bad. Besides, Alan wanted his stock. He'd said, 'Try not to lose your temper, and don't forget to oil the wheels.'

So I oiled, and bribed, and threatened in the politest of tones, and bribed some more, and suddenly obstacles would vanish and my order would arrive at the hotel.

Each bolt of silk, bale of cloth-of-gold, shadow-work or batik I acquired in this way was a battle that left me wrung out. I could quite see why Alan didn't communicate with his Indian suppliers by letter. The six weeks he'd allotted me began to seem far too short to collect all the goods he'd ordered and, worst of all, I'd been stuck in New Delhi all the time, with the rest of the mysterious sub-continent tantalizingly out of reach.

When the stately blonde began to talk of Kashmir, with its mountains and lakes, birds and brilliant flowers, I felt a sharp longing to leave this noisy, smelly, hot, frustrating city and go with her. She was making a sentimental journey to visit her husband's grave.

'I go every year,' she told me, and easy tears welled up as if to order in her round, china-blue eyes. 'I put flowers on his grave – just a cairn, really, in the rocks above a little river. Marigolds. He was so fond of marigolds. He used to say if I hadn't been a rose, he'd have liked me to be a marigold.'

I swallowed my nausea and pinned a bright, interested expression to my face.

This year, it appeared, she'd run into difficulties. A German tourist had had his throat cut and money stolen on a solo trek into the mountains above Srinagar, the capital of Kashmir. His embassy had raised a stink, and the Kashmiri Tourist Board had put a ban on foreigners junketing about alone.

'They don't realize it's different for me,' she said peevishly.

'Why is it?' I could think of no one more likely to arouse the murderous cupidity of a mountain robber than a fat, fair, foolish, rich, middle-aged widow.

'Of course it's different. Utterly different. I don't drift off into the blue like that silly German boy. Mine's a proper expedition: I take a guide, porters, ponies, the lot. We could see off any bandit.'

'What if your own men attacked you?'

'Me?' She looked outraged. 'My own men? That's a ridiculous idea. I *know* them. I've lived here all my life. I know Indians backwards.'

So did the British officers at the time of the Mutiny, I thought grimly. So did the men who devoted their lives to the Indian Civil Service. They got kicked out just the same.

But it wasn't worth arguing with Rosie. I soon found it was like fighting a wall of foam rubber, which gave way and then sprang back into shape the moment you released it.

'Tell me more about Kashmir,' I said. 'It sounds marvellous.'

'Oh, it is. I can't describe how lovely it is. You feel so different in that clean, clear air – so strong and invigorating. Charlotte, my dear, you can't leave India without seeing Kashmir.'

'I'll have to,' I said rather gloomily. 'I've only got a f.w weeks, and the orders I'm taking back to England are nowhere near ready.'

Rosie fiddled with her *tandoori* chicken, pushing it about her plate. 'You didn't believe me,' she said slowly, 'when I said I understood Indians.'

There seemed no point in denying it. I didn't.

'Well, I'll prove it to you. And if I do, you come with me to Kashmir. One good turn,' she said archly, 'always deserves another.'

'How d'you mean?'

'Give me a list of the goods you need, and I'll have the whole lot here by tomorrow evening. How about that?'

Folie de grandeur, I thought. Aloud I said awkwardly, 'It's most awfully kind of you to offer to try, and it's not that I don't believe you or anything, but it just can't be done. You see I spoke to Baldev Singh today – he's sort of a middle man – and

13

he said the bulk of the material I've ordered will be ready in a week. That's optimistic, of course. I bet it'll be more like three.'

Then I got a taste of the foam rubber. I might not have spoken, so little notice did she take.

'Baldev Singh,' she said musingly. 'Isn't that the little export agency in Sundar Nagar?'

'That's right. D'you know him?'

'Would you think it impossibly interfering of me if I called on Baldev Singh tomorrow on your behalf?'

'Not a bit. But look, I don't want to put you to a lot of trouble, and really I don't think it'll do any good. He's only the middle man, you see. He collects the stuff, but he doesn't make it.'

'Tomorrow evening then,' she said. Smiling sweetly, she picked a large, silver-coated sweetmeat from the tray held by a hovering waiter, and gestured for another white-coated boy to pick up her bag and fur wrap. She rose, and I too got to my feet, though I was only half-way through my curry and hoping for litchis to follow.

'Don't hurry,' she said kindly. 'Finish your meal. I'm sorry to rush, but I'm expecting a telephone call of some importance.'

Hands materialized behind her, helping her get clear of the table, easing on her stole.

'Shall we plan to dine together tomorrow?' she asked. 'I may have some good news for you.' I nodded, and she switched off her smile and sailed like a galleon for the double doors.

Silly old cow, I thought indulgently, tackling my curry again. What does she think she can do? I wasn't at all sure that Alan would approve of my letting a stranger stick her oar in. It can't do any harm, I argued, trying to convince myself. Anyway, I was sick of Delhi and the glib procrastination of the merchants I'd had to deal with. I called for another glass of the thin, straw-coloured liquid that passed for lager, and meandered through the rest of my meal. I was pretty sure I'd never see Rosie again.

I was wrong.

At seven next evening, while I was brushing chlorine out of my hair before dinner, the bell-boy brought a message. Mr Baldev Singh was below with a number of parcels for me.

Would I please come down to the hall to take delivery?

I couldn't believe it, but I went.

If I hadn't wrangled with Baldev Singh almost every day for a fortnight, I might not have recognized the stocky, parcel-laden figure waiting dejectedly under the fan in the deep-carpeted foyer. Even his turban seemed to droop. At our last meeting he had been offhand to the point of insolence, his moustaches vibrating as he swore I was rushing him. Now he looked half-cowed and half-resentful; I was reminded of an egg-stealing Labrador I'd once seen tricked into eating an eggshell filled with mustard.

'Miss Granville, I have with me your goods. Please to sign for delivery,' he said hurriedly, coming to meet me with evident relief and thrusting pencil and order book at me. None of the usual glib chit-chat about London, where he hoped to visit his houseful of relations living in Westbourne Grove off the bounty of the Welfare State.

'*All* my order, Mr Singh?'

'Indeed yes, all. Please to sign.'

'I'll just check it against my own list.'

I tore open the parcels while Baldev Singh fidgeted and muttered. It was true: he'd brought everything.

'And your bill?'

He fished it from an inside pocket and waited impatiently while I checked it, doing slow sums converting pounds into rupees and back again. Nothing wrong there, either. By now I was so used to the unexpected obstacle, the hidden snag, the taxi-meter that mysteriously 'broke' *en route*, the bill that close inspection showed to be multiplied instead of added, that I couldn't believe all this honesty.

'Mr Devereux will be very pleased. I'll tell him how helpful you've been.' I felt suddenly sorry for the cocky, garrulous little man. What could Rosie have said to change him so?

'I am not doing any more dealings with Mr Devereux,' said Baldev Singh flatly. 'I am not taking any more his supplies.'

I was astounded. 'What's the matter, Mr Singh? What has happened?'

He hesitated, glancing over his shoulder towards the recep-

15

tion desk, where an American family was immersed in time-tables, trying to fix up transport to Agra. Then he said hurriedly, 'It is on account of Mrs Honeywood, I tell you. She is not – '

He broke off and stared over my shoulder.

'Not what, Mr Singh?' I turned to follow his gaze. Rosie appeared behind the American family, heading for us. I waved to her.

Baldev Singh vanished. One minute he was there; the next I was standing alone, hock-deep in parcels. What Rosie was or wasn't I'd never know.

'*Honeywood*?' interrupted Nick from the front seat. 'Did you say Honeywood?'

'That's right. Don't say you know her?'

'No, but it rings a faint bell,' he said slowly. 'I know – wasn't a chap called Eric Honeywood murdered by bandits in the mountains around the time of Partition? I vaguely remember reading about it.'

'*She* says he walked over a precipice. They were trekking and he got up to pee in the night and fell down a cliff. Anyway, he's dead.'

Rosie stirred and groaned. It was a struggle to keep her upright. 'Are we nearly there?' I asked. It seemed hours since the lorry ran into us.

'Not far now,' said Nick. 'Go on. So kind Mrs Honeywood helped with your shopping.'

'Yes.' I didn't add that she had nearly driven me mad in the process, and seriously jeopardized the previously good relations between Devereux and its Indian suppliers. One and all had reacted like Baldev Singh: flung the goods at us and bolted. I had gained a splendid collection of rich and rare materials, now safely cached in the strong-room at Claridge's, and lost Alan half a dozen friends. It was odd that Rosie, who spoke so gently and looked so cuddly, should produce this violent effect.

'She speaks Hindi, then?'

'Hindi, Urdu, Pushtu, Gurkhali – you name it, she speaks it. It's all gobbledegook to me, of course, but she fairly rattles away in them all. She really gets a shift on people, too.'

On me, as well. Half-way through our whirlwind shopping together I'd tried to back out, thanking her for her help, and saying I'd manage the rest on my own. By now I felt extremely uneasy at having allowed her to muscle in at all, and the thought of what Alan would say when he found all his merchants refusing to deal with Devereux any more was beginning to haunt my dreams.

It was no good.

'My dear child,' said Rosie, 'you can't possibly manage alone. They'll cheat you in fifty different ways. I simply cannot imagine what Mr Devereux was thinking of, sending you out here with no experienced person to guide you.'

'I'll manage,' I said stiffly.

'And let your firm suffer? Don't be foolish, dear. No Indian will respect Devereux Designs if he knows he can cheat them. Haven't I shown you what they're like?'

'Yes, you've been very kind, and I'm awfully grateful. I really am. But I do want to buy some stuff on my own; I've been relying on you far too much.'

'Nonsense, dear. I'm relying on you as well, you realize. I want you to come with me to Kashmir. Didn't I tell you the Tourist Board is insisting on travellers joining a party this year? All because some foolish German got himself killed. If we finish your shopping tomorrow, there'll still be a couple of weeks before you're due home.'

She had the whole thing taped. 'I've ordered a car and driver to take us to Srinagar – that's the capital of Kashmir – and our guide and porters are expecting us. Please, Charlotte, don't let me down at the last moment.'

After all her help, I felt I couldn't. We left two days later.

'Here we are,' said Sandy. He swung the Land Rover through some gates and stopped in front of a Prudential-style Gothic pile with BRITISH HOSPITAL inscribed in large gold letters over the front door. It was nearly dark. The swift dusk had fallen as we drove.

17

Now I was reacting from the shock. Hands and knees were shaking and I felt utterly jellified. Nick took charge.

'Leave this to me,' he ordered, plonking me down in a sort of sea-green box of a waiting-room, typical hospital decor the world over. 'I know hospitals.'

There was no one else in the waiting-room. I sat and let myself shake.

After an age, Nick looked in to report that Sandy had booked us into a hotel, and both Rosie and Stewart would live, but they'd have to stay in hospital. She was still unconscious, but otherwise OK; Stewart had escaped with nothing but cuts and bruises.

'What about you?' asked Nick. 'D'you want a doctor to check you over?'

'I'm fine,' I said through chattering teeth. I was, too. By some lucky chance I'd escaped without so much as a scratch. I just couldn't get control of my nerves.

'You'll have to come with us.'

I sat and looked helpless. This had always been one of my party tricks; it's not difficult when you're only five foot three and skinny. At school they used to send me to the doctor every time I forgot to rub lipstick into my cheeks to give them a healthy natural glow. I could always sham sick, to the fury of Anna, who couldn't.

'I – I can't abandon Rosie.'

'Why not? They'll look after her. You've done your bit.'

'Well – '

'You're shaking,' he said, noticing at last. 'Delayed reaction. Come on; what you need is a stiff drink.'

Bonelessly, spinelessly, I went. He put a thick arm, hairy in its rolled-sleeved shirt but none the less comforting, round my waist and frog-marched me down the dark streets to a sleasy-looking hotel.

Sandy was parked in front of it, locking the Land Rover with great care and a variety of keys. 'Steal anything not bolted on,' I heard him mutter. He waved at the heap of suitcases he'd extracted from the vehicle, and a swarm of stringy little boys swooped on them and staggered into the hotel.

'Not exactly five-star,' said Nick, 'but it'll do.'

Considering its run-down appearance, the hotel wasn't bad. I washed and changed in my penny-in-the-slot of a bedroom, and within minutes Nick was hammering at the door with the prescribed drink.

'How marvellous,' I said. I'd had no alc except that thin beer for over a month.

'Sock it back,' he advised, pouring me a second four fingers of *Black and White*. 'Medicinal.'

'Thanks. *Just* what I needed.' The whisky hit my tonsils with its warm, familiar glow, and I felt things were looking up.

At dinner, Nick did the talking. I realized that all his questions in the Land Rover had been a deliberate ploy to keep me from agonizing over poor groaning Rosie and mangled Stewart.

He was, of all things, a travel agent. That was why Sandy had recognized the Eastravel minibus. But theirs was a very different kind of travel agency: Grand Mogul catered for the old, the rich, the distinguished – luxurious rubber-necking in the grandest of styles. Nick was a director, younger son of the boss; apparently it was very much a family business.

'I've heard of Grand Mogul. "See India and die happy," ' I said, quoting Stewart.

'Not only India. Persia, Afghanistan, Nepal, Bengal . . . Not Tibet, I must admit. I haven't been able to fix up a tour of Tibet. But we're planning a route through China, and possibly Mongolia as well.'

'Surely there isn't much to see in Mongolia?'

'Depends what you're looking for. Most of our travellers are interested in archaeology. We spend half our time persuading them not to buy genuine manuscripts of the Mogul period printed in Amsterdam in 1970, don't we, Sandy?'

Sandy grunted, his attention still on his plate. It seemed to me there was some kind of antagonism between him and Nick. I could feel it spark now and then like an electric current.

It flared when Nick, at the end of our dinner, offered me a lift on to Srinagar.

'Not a lot of room in the car,' said Sandy quickly.

'Not a lot of Charlotte, either. Three can easily get in front, and that leaves the whole of the back for luggage. What have you got? A couple of cases?'

'Only one. I've left the rest of my stuff in Delhi. But look, I don't want to crowd you – '

'The more the merrier. I mean it.'

Sandy looked mutinous. 'Your father gave me those orders, Nick; I'm not going against them.'

'What orders?'

'Don't go packing more than two into those Land Rovers, he says. Two plus the luggage's the limit in this heat.'

'Balls,' said Nick. 'That only applies to the short wheel-bases. These long ones can take eight. I've seen *ten* in a Land Rover in Afghanistan – and all their kit.'

I wasn't going to be the bone between these two dogs.

'I'd better stay here and wait for Rosie. It may only be a day or two before she can travel.'

'Don't be an ass,' said Nick. 'Take no notice of Sandy. My father only meant that rule to apply to the paying customers. Well, you're a hitcher, and I'm Management: we can do as we like. You can't hang about this dump for days on end; you're sure to be raped or have your money stolen.'

'I can look after myself,' I said with dignity. 'Besides, Rosie – '

'She'll survive without you. They said she was only shocked.' He grinned wickedly at Sandy. 'Perhaps she'll be all right tomorrow and we can squash her in as well.'

Sandy's mouth twitched, but he said no more. I wonder how long he'd worked for Grand Mogul, and if Nick made a habit of pulling rank. I was attracted to Nick, but I wasn't at all sure that I liked him.

I pushed back my chair. 'I'll decide in the morning, when I see what kind of a night they've had. Anyway, thanks for the offer.' I smiled at them impartially.

'That's right, sleep on it. We won't be off before eleven; right, Sandy?'

'Six hours' driving,' grunted Sandy. 'Depends if you want to stop for lunch.'

'Eleven o'clock, then. Sleep well,' said Nick.

I glanced back at our table before pushing through the chain curtain into the foyer. The dark head and the ginger one were close together, bent over a map. Clearly the argument had been dismissed. It wasn't hard to guess who had won.

Chapter Three

My room had an overhead fan but no air-conditioning, so I left the fan running all night. In spite of this, the air felt thick when I awoke: it was like trying to breathe through a gauze mask, and I had a nasty fantasy that the whirling blade might break loose from whatever moored it to the ceiling, and spin down on the bed, cutting off my head in one easy movement.

Once I'd thought of this horror, a long lie-in was impossible. I dressed in sandals and a cotton shirt-waister and went into the fresh morning streets in search of the hospital. It was just after seven and beautifully cool, but the hordes of people walking and bicycling to work moved with the usual absent-minded languor that made them such a menace to cars. Each man looked as if he had been checking over the hundred names of Allah, and was worried sick because he could only remember eighty-six of them.

Rapidly I acquired the foreigner's trademark – a posse of small boys with shaven heads and penetrating voices. I like children, but these miniature touts are the bane of sight-seeing in India. They stick like hookworms. It hadn't take me long to learn to act like a deaf mute as soon as they attached themselves; trying to buy them off was worse than useless.

I found my way back to the hospital with no difficulty. My retinue took fright at the gates – perhaps they had painful memories of hospitals – and I reached the open front door unescorted. I went into the cool, tiled hall, and looked around; there was no reception desk, just a number of doors opening off the hall.

An old man was sweeping the tiles, very slowly. He didn't look up when I asked him where I could find Dr Mohan Singh, who had apparently taken charge of Rosie and Stewart.

I took a deep breath, ready to repeat the question at full blast, but luckily for any sleeping patients, before I got my East-of-Suez bellow off the ground, a door opened behind me and fat, white-coated Dr Singh waddled through, the light from the door glinting on his gold-rimmed spectacles.

I thought he looked tired, but he knew at once who I was.

'I am glad to see you, Miss Granville,' he greeted me. 'Before you visit your friend, I hoped for a short word.'

I didn't like the sound of this. 'Something wrong, Dr Singh? Don't say she's worse. Is it her heart?'

Overweight equals heart trouble: simple equation.

He was smiling reassuringly, shaking his head. 'No, no. Do not be afraid. Mrs Honeywood's heart is in good condition and she makes good progress.'

'Then what – ?'

'She is not an easy patient,' he said sadly. 'Believe me, not easy at all. Already she wishes to travel: she demands to leave hospital and continue her journey today. And I am telling you this would not be wise. Not at all. She has suffered a shock. With concussion it is essential to have absolute rest, absolute quiet. Then the body can throw off the shock. To travel today would be extremely hazardous, I am telling you. I would not like the responsibility of discharging her.'

'Of course not,' I said soothingly. 'I didn't imagine she'd be fit to travel today. It doesn't matter a bit.'

'Then I beg you to tell her this. She will accept it better from you. To me, she was very angry. She was insisting that you have urgent business in Kashmir.'

Poor little man. He had clearly heard the rough edge of Rosie's tongue, and I admired him for sticking to his guns and keeping her in bed. Nine doctors out of ten would have been glad to be rid of the old termagant.

'Business?' I said. 'Oh, lord, it's not all that urgent. It can quite well wait. Anyway, I've been offered a lift to Srinagar,' I said, making up my mind to accept it whether Sandy liked it or not. 'There's no reason for Mrs Honeywood to leave because of me. I'll tell her so.'

He looked ridiculously relieved, and his spectacles twinkled as he smiled. The old gas-bag must really have thrown her weight around.

'Thank you, Miss Granville,' he said. 'In these cases of cerebral shock, it is never wise to hasten the recovery. I am glad that you understand.'

We shook hands, and he summoned a little Indian nurse with arms as thin as bent twigs in their starched elbow-cuffs, who escorted me to Rosie's room. She opened the door and I stalked in with measured tread, feeling like the champion of all oppressed housemen, and ready to slap Rosie down if she showed any tendency to get up.

Rosie sprawled in the neat white high-legged bed like a great overblown Hybrid Tea, in a froth of salmon pink nightdress with a riveting cleavage. Dearest, I thought, irresistibly reminded of my mother's gardening catalogues. Dearest in a rather passé condition. Or perhaps Lady Sylvia 'free flowering to a fault, Very Sweetly scented.' Blue Grass battled with hospital disinfectant and won by a short head.

'Rosie,' I said severely, 'I hear you're making a nuisance of yourself. That poor little doctor's scared stiff of you. It's not his fault. He can't let you out till you're OK.'

'They don't know what they're talking about. There's nothing wrong with me,' she protested, but her voice gave her away. The fruity contralto was a shadow of its usual self. She went on breathlessly: 'All this nonsense about cerebral shock: I saw through that straight away. They can't fool me.'

Oy-oy, I thought. People who think they're all right after a conk on the coconut usually aren't.

'Nobody's trying to fool you, Rosie,' I said peaceably.

'Yes, they are. They want to keep me here and get all the money they can out of me. I know their cunning ways. I've seen it all before.'

She struggled up to a sitting position on her pillows, blowing like a stranded whale.

'Take it easy, Rosie. You're much too weak to get up. Just lie quiet and rest. Dr Singh won't keep you here a moment longer then he has to, I can promise you that.'

It didn't seem quite the moment to upbraid her for using me

as a stalking-horse for her wish to leave.

I went on: 'You've certainly chosen the best place to stay. The hotels are grotty beyond words.'

'How did you manage last night?' she asked more calmly.

'Nick Jameson and Sandy Smith – the men who picked us up – got me a room at the local flea-house. Can you remember the crash at all?'

She shook her head. 'But the doctor told me you were with two Englishmen.' She didn't ask any more about them, and I guessed that her brief effort to exert her will-power had tired her. Being a captive audience in hospital is exhausting, Anna had told me, and indeed I remembered dimly from my own appendix removal how difficult it is to tell your healthy, hearty visitor to push off after five minutes.

I said, testing the water, 'They've offered me a lift to Kashmir. There's nowhere much to stay here. Shall I go on ahead and take up your booking at the Excelsior? I'll wait for you there.' And get my shopping done before you arrive to scare the pants off all the merchants, I added to myself.

Rosie considered, staring at the half-drawn window blind. I felt the room was too plain for her: I should at least have brought flowers.

'It might be best,' she said at last. 'But do *promise* me you won't go off on any wild expeditions. I'm so looking forward to showing you round. It's so important to see the sights with someone who really *knows* and *cares*, not one of these dreadful touts who call themselves guides.'

'Of course.'

'There are one or two little things I'd like you to do for me before you go.' I was relieved to hear the natural bossiness creeping back into her voice. 'I'll write a letter for you to take to my guide – a nice young man called Khurram Mohammed Beg. He'll wonder what's happened to me. I'll tell him to keep the ponies and porters on standby for another week.'

This sounded a bit too grand for me. 'Won't that be expensive?'

She went on as if I hadn't spoken: 'Then there are various bits and pieces I'll need here. Soap: I can't bear this Indian Lux. It's

25

made under licence, but it's more like sandpaper than soap. Get me the proper Yardley's Lavender. There's bound to be a European chemist if you ask around.'

Soap: Y. Lavender, I wrote on the back of an envelope.

'Toothpaste: get Macleans or Signal if you can. I'm not fussy.'

Not half, I thought, scribbling away.

'Two pairs of cotton sheets – these ones on the bed might be made of sacking – and you'd better get four pillow-cases. I them changed at least twice a day. Got that? Oh, and the last thing's one of those frozen Cologne sticks. I find them quite refreshing. Now, if you'll get me a biro and some writing-paper . . . '

My relief at the way she'd accepted the need to stay in hospital was only a faint memory by the time I had, with Sandy's help, attended to her shopping and left her, pen in hand, composing a letter to her Kashmiri guide to explain the change of plan. Ten to one I'd be asked to deliver it, I thought, returning to say good-bye and give her the good news that Stewart had already discharged himself and hitched a lift back to New Delhi.

Sure enough, her letter lay on the single blanket, signed, sealed, and tucked in its little white envelope, and sure enough she'd decided that her unpaid postman was to be none other than lucky old me.

Chapter Four

It was dark before we reached Srinagar. All morning we crawled over the dusty broken ground of the Jhelum Valley, inching forward like a cumbrous white beetle, but once we met the sharp gradients of the Himalayan foothills, the Land Rover came into its own.

From the high perch of the front seat, the views were spectacular: range after range of snow-capped peaks, like American frosting on chocolate cake; tumbling jade-green torrents cutting through gorges so sheer and narrow that at times we were shut in, unable to see the sky. The powerful engine laughed at the slopes, unlike Stewart's minibus, which had groaned and laboured over the smallest incline, but the hard springs of the Land Rover faithfully transmitted every jolt in the road from wheels to seat to passenger's backbone, and after six hours of it I was longing to lie down.

Sandy, crouched dourly in the back among the suitcases, fairly radiated disapproval, but at least he suffered in silence; Nick seemed perfectly happy, and I hoped that, when in charge of a party of paying customers, he wasn't as tough on them as he was on himself. Surely not: business would suffer.

The other drawback to the vehicle was the noise. Exchanging views and information at the top of your voice for several hours at a stretch is peculiarly exhausting, and I soon got to the stage of limiting my conversation to exclamations only.

Lights twinkled ahead as we rounded a sharp curve and began to swoop down into a valley.

'Srinagar – we've made it!' called Nick above the whine of the transmission. I had an impression of pointed roofs across a street so narrow that the Land Rover's wheels spanned from gutter to gutter, cobblestones shook me rigid, and lattice windows with intricately cross-hatched shutters threw patterns of light across our path.

We seemed to be in a main thoroughfare, and soon there was the dark gleam of water on our left, while the houses gave way to pretentious hotels festooned in fairy-lights on our right.

'Rosie booked rooms at the Excelsior,' I shouted back. 'Will you drop me there?'

The hot bath and soft bed which the name seemed to promise were wonderfully alluring.

Even in the dark, I could feel Nick turn to stare at me.

'You can't stay in a hotel!'

'Why on earth not?'

'Because the houseboats are one of the best things about Srinagar. Didn't Rosie tell you?'

'She said they give you gut-rot.'

'Silly woman. They're out of this world. You can stay on ours, we've plenty of room.'

'Thanks, but I'd rather go to a hotel. Look!' I shrieked, 'There it is: Excelsior.'

Nick kept going. 'Stop!' I shouted.

'I said you can stay with us,' he said coolly.

'I don't want to. Don't be such a bully. I want to stay at that hotel.'

He was going too fast for me to jump out, and anyway I didn't fancy losing my luggage. 'Sandy,' I begged, 'make him stop.'

Sandy muttered unintelligibly. I guessed he was saying that as far as he was concerned I could stay where I liked or indeed take a running jump into Lake Dal. But he wasn't going to tangle with the boss.

'Relax,' said Nick, in a tone nicely calculated to madden me. 'I really do know what I'm talking about. You'd far better stay with us. None of these hotels is very suitable for a girl on her own; I've never stayed at the Excelsior, but it looks about fifth-class.'

'Rosie always stays there.'

'Perhaps she has a low ceiling of comfort, unlike me and Sandy. Do give the houseboat a try.'

'All right,' I said grumpily, cross with myself for giving in and with him for steam-rolling me. Let there be so much as one creepy-crawly in my room, or a single twinge of gut-rot, and I'd be off to the Excelsior like a shot, I swore silently.

'Good girl,' said Nick, and I ground my teeth.

He stopped the vehicle at last. Water gleamed like dark silk beside the road, and I saw that we were parked alongside a wooden landing stage. Frost bit through my cotton frock, and hastily I pulled on a quilted nylon jacket. We'd had such a lovely fug in the Land Rover that I hadn't noticed how cold it was outside.

At the bottom of a wooden ramp, the graceful shapes of punts with canopies over them jostled on the rippling water. Nick gripped my elbow and guided me down the ramp with a firmness that suggested he thought I still might dodge back to the Excelsior. Sandy was chattering away to an Indian, more animated than I'd ever seen him.

'This is our *shikara*,' said Nick, manhandling me towards the nearest punt. I didn't know if he was referring to the boat or boatman, but I gave a gracious sort of nod and stepped lightly aboard. The floor of the punt was soft and unexpectedly bungy, and my chilly poise disintegrated as I measured my length on to foam cushions. I heard a slight snort behind me, but Nick managed not to laugh out loud.

Kneeling for safety, I discovered that the whole boat was lined with foam rubber, an idea Oxford punts might well adopt. I wriggled forward to the front; Nick stretched out amidships, and Sandy crouched with the boatman. A shove from the punt-pole, and away we glided in perfect silence under the star-studded black velvet of the sky. I adore going in boats, and suddenly felt absurdly happy: to hell with that soft bed and hot bath. Though tired and far from petal-fresh, I was enjoying myself.

I needn't have worried anyway. The houseboat had a bath. It stood proud and splay-legged in the middle of a large cabin, and it had steeply sloped sides and complicated wastepipe arrangements: the sort of bath you'd find in a Scottish ducal stalking lodge, quite unknown to modern plumbers.

The rest of the boat had just the same Edwardian air of faded grandeur. Antimacassars were draped on every red plush chair in the salon, along with yellowing photographs in silver frames, signed by previous visitors to the *Convolvulus*, who raved about its charms and the excellence of its cook in faint, spidery handwriting. The dining-room was highly polished, but its floor was a waiter's nightmare of uneven boards and holes cunningly positioned to trip the server.

I explored, my spirits rising like a hot-air balloon. There were three double bedrooms, my single small case looking battered and trivial on the luggage-rack of the grandest, and a rickety staircase that led to the upper deck.

A buzz of activity on the long, low, narrow craft moored alongside us caught my attention.

Nick joined me at the rail. 'Who're they?' I pointed at our neighbours.

'That's Mr Songali and his family. He owns this boat, you see, and rents it to us. His wife cooks for us, his daughters do all the cleaning and laundry, and his son Ahmad waits at table and runs errands for us in the *shikara*. I'll introduce you to them all. But first, wouldn't you like to wash and change?'

'Gosh, yes.'

'Go ahead, then, but don't hang about. I've ordered dinner in half an hour. Sandy's gone back with the boat; he wants to see some friends. We won't wait for him.'

Nevertheless I took my time over my bath, and fiddled my shoulder-length hair into an unnecessarily elaborate knot before sauntering into the salon. I was beginning to see that Nick was perpetually in a hurry – it must be the result of riding herd on rich old tourists with a tight itinerary.

As I entered, Nick uncoiled like a spring from the red plush "Madeira, m'dear", spindle-shanked chaise longue that took up a whole side of the Edwardian state-room. His light-blue eyes flicked rapidly up and down my dragon-green silk culottes, a Devereux Exclusive.

'Worth waiting for,' he said, ushering me briskly into the dining-room. He ate like a tiger, packing away the mounds of rice and chicken with speed and economy, and fired by his example, I relaxed my usual vigilance on food east of the

Bosphorus. I was hungry, too.

Sandy didn't appear, although there was a place laid for him, and I found it a relief not to have him breathing disapproval down my neck. Ahmad Songali, a rosy-cheeked boy of about sixteen, served our food and left quietly, after placing a bottle of apricot brandy on the table between us.

Nick smiled at me in the candlelight. 'You'd better tell me your dark secret.'

'What dark secret?' I was instantly on the defensive. Surely he didn't know anything? He couldn't.

'Every career girl has a dark secret lurking in her back-ground,' he said easily. 'Or why would she be a career girl?'

So it was just a gambit; I felt unreasonably disappointed; he'd obviously used it so often before.

'Male chauvinist,' I said, imitating his tone. 'Why shouldn't a career girl simply enjoy her job?'

'Sorry, I put that badly. I'll start again. What I meant was: here we are, two strangers on a mountain-top . . . '

'Lake.'

'OK, lake. Lake on a mountain-top, in the most beautiful place in the world. We've had a goodish dinner and a goodish drink, and I'd like to feel you were happy, but I know you aren't. If I can do anything to help . . . if it even helps to tell me about it —'

'Thanks,' I said. 'But no. You're right in a way, but I don't think talking about it does any good.'

'Have you tried?'

'No,' I admitted, and my treacherous mind was saying, Go on, tell him; you're longing to tell him. What harm can it possibly do? Think of a pressure cooker: all that steam building up into pressure that'd blow the lid off if there wasn't a safety valve. Talking is a safety valve. Pressure's been building up in you for years now. It's why you can't work properly. It's why you had that rotten affaire with Johnny. All because you didn't dare talk and get it out of your system. But now's your oppor-tunity: here, like he says, away from everything . . .

I heard my voice asking, 'Promise you won't laugh?'

'Nobody's troubles are funny.'

'It sounds ridiculous when I put it into words.'

31

'What does?'

'Fear.' I stopped, appalled at myself. Now I'd started I'd have to finish. 'I'm afraid of the world – of the modern world. I'm scared stiff of machines: aeroplanes and lawn-mowers and battery-operated carving knives. And cars. Particularly cars. My brother was killed in a car crash and that's when I started to be scared. At first it was only cars, but now it's getting worse and I feel sick if I see a circular saw working, or hear a printing press; I actually feel sick and shake. Some people get vertigo from heights, but with me it's machines, and as I happen to be living in the twentieth century there's no escape from them. I know they'll get me in the end no matter how much I run and dodge and try to outwit them . . .'

I stared at him across the candle-flame. There wasn't a hope that he'd understand. I should never have tried to put into words the absurd panic that gripped me at the sound of an engine, the horror I fet on seeing a train, a roundabout, a steam-roller. The dining-room seemed to have shrunk to a dark cave, where the twin lances of flame reflected in Nick's eyes were the only points of light. The brandy burned in me, urging me to talk, get it all off my chest.

'Go on,' I said miserably. 'Laugh. Even I can see how ridiculous it sounds.'

'I don't feel a bit like laughing,' he said seriously. 'I only wish I could help. Have you asked a doctor for advice?'

'My GP suggested tranquillizers but they were completely useless. I felt stupid as well as scared with them inside me.'

'What about your boss?'

I thought it over. What did Alan guess about me?

'He just thinks I'm a bit odd,' I said finally. Odd because I'd asked for a room which didn't face on to the street, and always walked home although there was an Underground station right opposite our flat.

'The worst of it is that I can't tell anyone without making myself sound absolutely bonkers. Sometimes I'd dream I'd told someone how I felt and when I woke up I wouldn't know if I had or not.' I was silent for a moment, then I said: 'And now I have.'

Nick said reassuringly, 'Don't worry about me. I'm told all

32

sorts of odd things. People on our tours – rich and old and lonely, most of 'em – they talk a lot.'

Strangely, I resented being lumped with all these lonely old chatterboxes. I suppose everyone likes to think his problems are special.

I said stiffly, 'I'm sorry. I'm not usually so talkative. It must be the brandy.'

Nick laughed. 'Don't be so prickly. I'm glad you told me, otherwise I'd have been sure to put my foot in it sooner or later.' He held the brandy bottle up against the candle. 'Look, that's taken a fair caning; we'll blame the booze for any soul-searching we've done.' He sloshed a little more into my glass. 'Now tell me about your sister.'

So I smoothed down my feathers and talked about Anna, who'd been keen on skiing and fishing and riding and the great outdoors, quite different from me, until her horse put his foot through the Helsinki Steps in a novice one-day event and somer-saulted on top of her. She and I shared a ninety-nine-year lease on a flat in Mecklenburg Square – ground floor with gar-den – and she whistled round it in her wheelchair keeping house while I brought home the bacon.

'Won't she be lonely while you're away?'

'I very much doubt it. She's got lots of friends – droppers-in, you know. And Alan promised to keep an eye on her for me, too.'

'Decent of him. What about your parents?'

'They've split up. Daddy lives in Cornwall now. Both he and Mum have remarried, and we don't see much of them. Mum's got a sheep station in New Zealand. She keeps asking us to come and stay, but it costs a bomb to get there.'

'I know.' He drained his glass. 'They'll be bringing our coffee any minute. We'd better make a move.'

Chapter Five

In the stately Edwardian drawing-room, Mr Songali himself brought us coffee. He was a tall, thin, courtly old man in a robe of striped brocade so elegant that it rather dimmed the glory of my culottes. His English was excellent.

'In the month of Ramadan,' he explained, refusing coffee, 'we eat when darkness falls, and must eat again before dawn. Then no more until the next sunset. When I was as young as you, I would drink coffee at any hour, but now no longer.'

'It keeps you awake?'

'Yes, Miss Granville.' He smiled at me. 'I wake and worry. Aaii! That is a bad way to spend nights.'

'So fine a houseboat,' said Nick, 'and yet you have worries?'

'Three boats, sir,' he said proudly. 'Yet all have worries at this time.'

Nick didn't move, but I could sense his alertness. 'Particularly at this time?'

Mr Songali's hand patted the air gently, as one would slow down a passing car. 'I did not speak to alarm you, sir. My worries are my own. Tourists should see only the smiling face of Kashmir.'

'We'll drink to that,' said Nick with, it seemed to me, slightly overdone heartiness, but when Mr Songali had left us he said: 'I hope to God the old boy's right.'

'About?'

'Saying his worries were only personal.'

'You think they're more than that?'

Instead of answering, he asked: 'How much d'you know about the political situation here?'

I smothered a groan. Once I had a boy-friend who was trying to make the grade in politics, and he was a Class One banger-

34

on. I don't know if he put me off politics or politics put me off him, but at the end of our whirl I was off them both for keeps. One's own country's politics were bad enough, but other people's were the ultimate knock-out drop as far as I was concerned.

I said quickly, straight from the fourth-form Geography primer: 'Kashmir has common frontiers with Pakistan, China, Tibet and Russia. It belongs to India, but – ' I began to improvise as memory ran out – 'there was a bit of a kerfuffle before it opted for Congress, that's to say, India; rather than the Muslim League which would have made it part of Pakistan, in 1947, when the country was divided.'

Highly delighted with myself for this succinct résumé of the country's affairs, I sat back, took a gulp of scalding coffee, and prayed that it wouldn't encourage Nick to give me a blow-by-blow account of Indian politics *since* Partition.

'That's roughly it,' said Nick. I made no comment, and he must have mistaken my silence for fascinated eagerness to have the gaps filled in, because before I could put him right, he was away.

'At the time of Partition,' he went on, and I groaned and yawned inwardly, 'Kashmir was ruled by a Sikh Prince called Sir Hari Singh. You know about Sikhs?'

I nodded hastily. I didn't want him starting any farther back. I'd mugged up a good deal of Indian history to impress on Alan that I'd be a knowledgeable assistant for *Junk*, but my researches had stopped short in the nineteenth century. All the causes leading up to Partition had seemed such a tangled mess that I hadn't the strength to sort them out.

Besides, I did know a few things about Sikhs: they were a sort of cross between Hindus and Muslims, but different from both; they never cut their hair, carried wicked-looking swords, and were slick, shrewd businessmen. Most taxi-drivers I'd met in New Delhi seemed to be Sikhs.

'Right,' said Nick. 'So you know that the Partition line divided the Punjab, the great grain-growing area. It was completely arbitrary, of course. Sir Cyril Radcliffe was given five weeks in which to divide the sub-continent – an appalling job, very nearly an impossible one. There were bound to be injustices. Here, in Kashmir, for instance, Hari Singh was a Hindu, but most of his subjects were and still are Muslim. So the question was, which of the new countries should Kashmir accede to: India or Pakistan?'

'Pakistan, I suppose, if most of them were Muslims . . . '

'Well, Hari Singh didn't see it that way. In fact, he wouldn't make up his mind at all. Lord Mountbatten himself went to tell him he'd simply got to decide. Hari Singh made all sorts of excuses, and finally said they'd discuss it on the last day of the Viceroy's visit to Srinagar. But when that day arrived, he went to bed with a tummy-ache.'

'The Viceroy let him get away with *that*?'

'Well, yes. I suppose he was pushed for time and fed up to the back teeth with Nehru and Jinnah and all the rest of the quarrelsome politicians. Anyway, the next thing that happened was that a pack of Pathan tribesmen from the hills tried to force Hari Singh's hand by invading Srinagar. They got quite a bit of loot, but that was all, because at the first sign of trouble old Hari Singh quickly acceded to India and shouted for help.

'Indian troops were brought up double-quick, the tribesmen beaten off, and what's called the Ceasefire Line established.'

'Where's that?'

'Not far from here. Up beyond Gulmarg, where I'm hoping to build a hotel one of these days.'

'So we,' I said, thinking it out, 'are in the Indian part of Kashmir.'

'That's right. The other bit's ruled by the Azad Kashmir Government, supported by Pakistan, occupied by Pakistani troops. Oh, and to complete the picture, the UN keeps "observers" on the Ceasefire Line.'

'What a mess!' Power politics in this remote mountain paradise – it hardly seemed possible.

'So you see why I don't like to hear Mr Songali, who's an astute old bird and, like me, keen on tourists, saying that he wakes and worries. It worries me, too. Any kind of trouble always hits the tourist trade.'

'Have your firm got a lot of money tied up here, then?'

'Not yet, but we hope to have. I'm seeing Mr Chaturvedi, Minister for Tourism, tomorrow morning. He's quite a bright boy, according to Sandy, who keeps his ear to the ground, and I'm hoping we can do a deal. The Tourist Board's putting a mint of money into developing a ski resort at this place I told you about – Gulmarg. It means "Valley of Flowers" and it's the prettiest place. I must take you there. They've built a fantastic new road and ski-lifts, and now all they want is some good hotels.'

'I see. You'd build the hotels?'

'I will – or rather I'll advise my father to – if the political situation looks stable, but only if. We'll see. I'd really like to build my own chalet there while I'm at it. It's a marvellous place. You look right across the valley of Srinagar, across the lake, up to a mountain called Nanga Parbat. It's one of the highest peaks in the range.'

'Sounds as if Grand Mogul gives you a pretty free hand,' I said with a touch of envy.

'My father feels this will be *the* playground of the 'seventies, so he's prepared to shell out. He's doing much the same in Zambia — building hotels for tourists. My brother Sam's out there now.'

What a lovely, free, nomadic life! 'Is Sam married?' I asked.

'Yes, he is,' said Nick rather curtly. C'mon, give, give, I thought; but he said no more.

'What about Sandy? Where does he fit in?'

'Oh, he's the local expert. He's been our man in Kashmir for several years.'

'What's the matter with him?' I asked bluntly. 'Why doesn't he like me?'

A curiously evasive look crossed Nick's face. I was reminded of Anna's horse making up its mind to refuse a jump. I could see him trying out and rejecting several answers then, to my surprise, the horse decided to take the fence.

'He's in a bit of a mess emotionally, too.'

'Like me?' I tried not to sound prickly.

'Yes. Poor old Sandy's in love with the wrong person. She's a Kashmiri girl called Leila, daughter of one of those tribesmen I told you about – the ones who looted Srinagar in

37

1947.'

'Hardly her fault,' I said indignantly. 'Or Sandy's.'

'Oh, nobody minds about her father,' said Nick hastily. 'That's all water under the bridge. No: her wretched brother's the snag. Says Sandy's not good enough for his sister, I gather. He's proud as hell, though he's nothing but the owner of a down-and-out tourist trap near the Nishat Bagh. Sandy's pretty determined, though, and I fancy matters have reached a stalemate.'

'What's he called?' I asked, recognizing the name Nishat Bagh from the address on Rosie's envelope.

'Khurram Mohammed Beg.'

I stared at Nick.

'But that's Rosie's guide. Look.'

I rummaged in my bag and pulled out the letter.

'Common enough name, I suppose,' said Nick, examining it. 'But no, you're right, it's the same chap. Nishat Treasure Palace: that's him all right.'

Together we stared at Rosie's bold black letters on the cheap envelope.

'Shall we open it?' said Nick, running his fingers tentatively under the flap.

I twitched it away and stuffed it hastily in my bag, shocked to the core. My family thinks reading someone else's letters is a slightly blacker crime than cowardice in the face of the enemy. 'Certainly not.'

Then it occurred to me that the horse had refused after all, or at least run out. I faced him at the obstacle again.

'That's all very interesting, but it doesn't exactly explain why he dislikes *me*. I'm not crossing him in love.'

Nick looked resigned. 'Not exactly subtle, is our Sandy? It's not you personally, I assure you. It's only your body – your *bulk* – he's objecting to.'

I considered the two things inseparable. 'What's wrong with my body?' I demanded belligerently.

Nick laughed. 'I love the way you rise. Most rewarding. No; the only thing wrong with your body is that it takes up space in the Land Rover – space which Sandy would like to reserve for

Leila. He wants to get her to elope with him. Deeply romantic at heart, is Sandy.'

'He had me fooled.'

'I said we would spirit her away in the Land Rover if her brother still wouldn't budge about their marriage. Simple as that. But until that time, I've told him to stay clear of Khurram, and I advise you to do the same.'

I relaxed. 'Then for heaven's sake tell Sandy I'm going to fly back. I don't want a solid frost until Rosie turns up. You might have explained the situation before.'

'If I had, you'd have stayed in Amritsar with Rosie, right?'

'I suppose so.'

'Well, for some odd reason, I wanted you along.'

His hard brown hand closed over mine where I had left it carelessly lying about on the back of the "Madeira m'dear" chaise longue. I wondered if my cabin door had a lock. I hoped so. Then I wondered if I really hoped so or if I only hoped I hoped so.

Through the haze of brandy fumes only one thing was really clear to me, and that was that it was time for bed.

I found Sandy easier to handle on his own. We left Nick next morning grilling his well-muscled torso on the top deck of the houseboat, awaiting a visit from Mr Chaturvedi, the bright boy from the Tourist Ministry.

'Join me,' he invited, but I shook my head. My skin is treacherously fair and I have to get used to sun in minute doses.

'It's prettier to be white.' Sour grapes: I'd have loved to be rich mahogany bronze like him.

He grinned. 'If you're through with your sight-seeing by lunch time, come back here and I'll take you fishing. I've only fixed up one appointment today.'

'Fishing in the lake?' I visualized myself drifting in the softly-padded *shikara*, complexion protected by the canopy, trailing a lazy fishing-line.

'No, it's a river called the Lidder; it's got some smashing trout. We can hire rods from Mr Songali.'

'Great.' I'd never fished, but it looked easy enough, I thought. 'I'll look round the town this morning, and be back here about one.'

'Fine. Sandy'll show you the sights. Enjoy yourself.' He closed his eyes.

Sandy was tapping his tiny toe with impatience, already seated in the *shikara*. I sensed his annoyance at being lumbered with me for the morning because Nick was busy, but remembering last night's revelations about the state of Sandy's poor heart, I resolved to be nice to him.

Lowering myself cautiously aboard, I installed myself on the cushions with rather more grace and control than I had the first time. We sped across the still, shining water to the jetty.

'What d'you want to see?' Sandy's manner was definitely brusque.

'You're the expert,' I said, soft-soaping away. 'You choose.'

He didn't actually smile, but the tight line of his mouth relaxed a little and he glanced quickly at his watch.

'Right. First thing we'll take a look round the Nishat Gardens. A – a friend of mine sometimes walks there about now, and it's one of the sights, anyway.'

He set off at a great rate along the road that skirted the shore, reeling off guide-talk in a flat, rapid monotone.

'Nishat Bagh, the famous Mogul pleasure-garden carved out of the hillside by Asaf Khan, father of the famous beauty, Mumtaz Mahal, who married Shah Jehan, who built the Taj Mahal to her memory when she died in childbirth with their thirteenth child.'

'When was that?' I asked to stop him.

'Nishat Bagh? Oh, 1620s, I reckon,' he said in his normal voice. 'It was during the reign of Jahangir, who built the Shalimar Bagh, the other famous garden here. He wasn't too chuffed when Asaf Khan, who was only a lousy subject, after all, built his own pleasure-garden. Anything you can do I can do better, y'know. There was a chappie in France made the same mistake, showing off to one of the Louis' – I forget the fellow's name – '

'Fouquet, wasn't it?'

'That's right. I'll have to work that into my patter. Mind you, most of the types I bring here know it all already. They just want to see for themselves. I don't have to tell them much.' He paused. 'I like the Nishat Bagh best, myself. It's not so grand, but more natural-looking than the Shalimar. See what you think.'

The sun was scorching through my cotton dress, with that clear, dry feel that you get in the mountains, blessedly different from the heavy heat of Delhi. As in a fairy-tale, we came to an iron gate set in a high wall. Sandy paid a hoary ancient who was snoozing on a three-legged stool, opened the gate, and stormed up a flight of worn steps.

I followed, panting, wishing he'd slow down; and entered Fairyland. Never had I seen flowers from so many seasons blooming at once. Brassy marigolds dominated, as usual, but the roses, planted in blocks of solid colour, gave them a run for their money. Pansies, forget-me-nots, dahlias, and chrysanthemums lined the paths in a luxuriant jumble; the turf was close-mown and brilliant green with an invitingly soft, thick texture. From where I stood, the garden rose steeply, with the hills sheering off to the far end in a magnificently theatrical backdrop. Stately plane trees – the golden *chenar* Rosie had talked of – reared graceful arms to the heavens.

Truly an Emperor's pleasaunce, I thought, slowing down to admire individual flowers.

A shadow rose from the flower-bed, making me jump. A gardener, turbanned and barefoot, holding out a dew-fresh bloom in defiance of a black-lettered notice forbidding people to pick flowers. What a charming gesture, I thought, accepting it with conscious grace.

'Baksheesh?' he murmured.

Would I never learn? I groped crossly in my bag and gave him a coin. Now I was stuck with the flower and it looked as if I'd picked it; nowhere to stow it except in my hand, and that meant I couldn't use my camera, which was a two-handed job.

Sandy was well ahead by now, quartering the flower-beds like a pointer after grouse. I quickened my pace to catch up, dropping the flower as unobtrusively as I could.

41

I came up to Sandy, panting from the climb, and found him sitting on a stone bench with a fine view of the garden, but he wasn't making use of this vantage-point. Instead, he stared at the ground as he dragged morosely on a cigarette.

'Can't you find your friend? Bad luck,' I said, sitting beside him in spite of his deliberately uninviting attitude. He looked as if he could do with some good news for a change, so I said, 'I meant to tell you before: I shan't be travelling back with you in the Land Rover. You can stop worrying there won't be room for Leila.'

He smiled reluctantly. 'Nick told you, then?'

'I asked him why you were so stand-offish.'

'Sorry,' he said. He took a last drag and threw away the cigarette. 'I didn't mean to be – you know.'

'I know. Forget it.'

We sat now in more companionable silence, then he said: 'Truth is, I feel a bit down. That brother of hers, he won't let up. I've been on at him now for a couple of months, but it's no good. He won't hear of me marrying her, and she won't go against him. Daren't.'

'D'you think she'd be happy in England? Your job must take you away a lot.'

'Happy as a sandboy,' he said scornfully. 'My old ma, she'd think the world of her. Leila's a lovely girl – and clever. You never saw the like of her paintings. She can draw anything she's a mind to, but she's never been taught. It's all come natural to her. She wants to go to a proper art school. She's got a dozen or more girls working for her here in Srinagar – they do the donkey work. They turn out some beautiful things between them, but it's a crying waste to keep her cooped up in this dump.'

'Does her brother sell her work, then?'

'Not him. Doesn't seem to know the value of it. His shop's just full of junk; I don't know how he makes a living at it, besides being away half the time I come here.'

Junk. I felt oddly excited. If Leila's work was that good, perhaps I could buy something for Alan.

'Will you take me there?' I asked. 'I might find something I want.'

'It's full of junk, I tell you.'

'Still, I would like to see it.'

'Suit yourself.'

He rose and started to slouch down the slope. 'How far?' I called after him. Even if Sandy was indifferent to the heat, I wasn't going to walk miles under this blazing sun.

Without stopping, he jerked a thumb towards the wall of the garden. 'Right here,' he shouted back. He waited till I caught up then said more quietly, 'Do me a favour. Don't tell the guv I took you.' So it was the guv now, instead of Nick.

Intrigued as much by Sandy's sudden assumption of inferior status as by his desire to keep something from the boss, I asked, 'Why on earth?'

'Never mind why.'

'Oh, OK, then. Have it your own way.' I decided I wasn't really interested in their private squabbles.

He nodded, satisfied. 'Come on, then.'

The shop was a grotty little clinker-built shack between the wall of the Nishat Bagh and the backyard of the Excelsior Hotel. We stood in a narrow, dusty room with fly-blown windows and a rough trestle counter, and I wondered if I was wasting my time. Shelves full of papier-mâché bric-à-brac in gaudy reds and greens looked as if they hadn't been moved or dusted in years. The place had a forlorn, sullen ugliness which promised little of interest to the buyer for Devereux Designs.

A door creaked open behind the counter, and Khurram Mohammed Beg glided through.

He was tall for an Indian, slender and boyish. A whipper-snapper, I thought immediately. He doesn't look like my idea of a guide; he doesn't look *responsible* enough. Khurram's smooth pale oval face was dominated by strongly marked arched eye-brows, thin black crescents over heavy-lidded eyes. A pencil-fine moustache drooped on either side of his mouth, oddly old-fashioned. It took me a moment to place the memory which nagged at my brain – I'd seen this face in old Persian paintings.

He wore a dirty collarless shirt and scruffy grey flannels girded with a sort of pyjama cord, and looked at us without enthusiasm.

43

'Khurram,' said Sandy, 'this is Miss Charlotte Granville. She buys material for Devereux Designs, and would like to see some samples.'

Khurram's unfriendly expression didn't change; it was clear the mighty name of Devereux cut no ice in this neck of the woods.

I said in an undertone, 'Go on.'

Sandy pitched in manfully and did his stuff. I heard my own name again, and Leila's. Khurram lounged against the counter, staring at, or rather through me, as Sandy ploughed on in Urdu or Hindi or whatever Godforsaken dialect he'd chosen. When he ran down, Khurram nodded coolly and dismissed him. I nearly laughed to see him: it reminded me so much of my grandmother's quiet, unemphatic, 'That will do, Florence,' if the parlourmaid showed signs of wanting to talk as she brought in the tea-trolley.

Sandy left without a backward glance, and I felt a small degree of panic. Poltroon that I am, I longed for Rosie's support. She'd have known how to snap this insolent boy into helpfulness. Perhaps I should have waited till she came. I remembered her letter and opened my handbag.

Khurram spoke in very good English, only faintly sing-song. 'I regret I have nothing to show you, Miss Granville. My sister works only for pleasure. Her pictures are not for sale; Sandy did not understand this. Here I have woodwork, ivories, papier-mâché – ' he gestured towards the pathetic shelves.

I handed him the envelope. 'Mrs Honeywood asked me to deliver this.'

The languor dropped from him as if he'd brushed against a live wire. 'A letter from – from Mrs Honeywood! She gave it to you? Where is she?'

'She's in hospital in Amritsar, I'm afraid. We were travelling together and a lorry ran into our car. I expect she explains in the letter what she wants you to do.'

A moment ago I'd been wishing Rosie was with me. Now, it seemed, the mention of her name was enough. Khurram stared at the envelope, then tore it open with feverish haste as if terrified of what he might find in it. I turned to go.

44

'Miss Granville, forgive me . . . ' He was calling me back. He darted from behind the counter and plucked at my sleeve. 'I didn't know you travelled with Rosie. If you leave, she will be angry. But when you came here with Sandy, I thought something different. Come, all is changed now. We must speak together.'

He'd certainly changed his tune, though I didn't quite see why. This one sounded much more promising to my ears. God bless Rosie, I thought, following him out of the dingy shop, down a dark passage and through a badly-hung door into the blinding white concrete dazzle of a courtyard.

Here things looked in better repair. A fountain played in the centre of a square of grass bordered with marigolds, which bent their heads forward to catch the sparkling drops of water.

The contrast between shop-front and private apartments became even more marked when we crossed the courtyard and went up a short flight of stairs to Khurram's office.

By now I was used to the dark cubbyholes with threadbare carpets and lights of minimum wattage which masqueraded as offices for Indian businessmen. Most of the Devereux suppliers seemed to spend their working hours in Stygian gloom, but not so Khurram Mohammed Beg. The room was white-walled and bathed in sunlight; a Kashmir carpet glowed underfoot, with rich reds and blues stretching from wall to wall. I felt I ought at least to remove my shoes. Here and there large cushions were scattered in a kind of rough circle, while a low table of beaten brass held coffee-making materials. The tall windows with rounded tops gave the room a curiously mosque-like effect, but the view they afforded over the courtyard and fountain was a great improvement on the squalid back-alley which the shop itself overlooked.

Not bad, I thought, sinking on to the nearest cushion in response to Khurram's invitation. Not bad at all. Why on earth does he bother with that crummy shop?

Chapter Six

'Tell me of Rosie,' said Khurram, seating himself on another cushion and crossing his legs in a neat, long-practised way. 'For over a week I have waited for news. Is she badly hurt?'

He really cared, I saw with surprise – or if he didn't he was putting on a first-class act. He jumped up again and paced the carpet, clenching and unclenching his thin, nervous fingers. I played down the accident.

'No, luckily it's nothing serious, but the doctor said she must rest a few days.'

'A few days . . . ' he muttered. 'That is bad, very bad. A few days may be too late.'

'Too late for what?'

'Rain, snow, who knows? Too late to travel in the mountains. We must hope the doctor soon lets her go. And you, Miss Granville – ' he looked at me with interest for the first time – 'you, too, will travel with us? There are many fine sights in the hills for you to see, oh yes . . . ' he seemed to be enjoying a private joke, but I smiled politely, judging that the climate had now thawed enough for me to talk business.

'Certainly I hope to come with you, but first I have to finish the work that brought me to India. I'm hoping you'll be able to help me now you know I'm a friend of Rosie's.'

The cold mask clamped back on his face. 'Sandy should not have spoken of my sister's work. It is not for sale.'

This was ridiculous. 'But that's why I bothered to deliver the letter personally,' I said indignantly. 'If I'd known you were going to be so obstructive, I'd have sent it through the post. Oh well, there's no point in my staying. I'll have to see if the Tourist Board can suggest someone to help me.'

I got up, pleased to see that he was beginning to look anxious again.

'But you will come in the hills with Rosie?'

Aha, I thought. He doesn't want to lose his customer after all. Keep up the pressure.

'I'm afraid not,' I said with a coldness to match his own. 'Business before pleasure, as I'm sure you understand. I'm not just here on holiday.'

He was silent, the black eyes boring into me, sizing me up. At last he seemed to reach a decision.

'Because you are a friend of Rosie, I will show you my sister's pictures.'

'Show only?'

'We will see. Come.'

I followed him into an adjoining room stacked with boxes and crates. Against one wall hung bundles of rugs and carpets, and propped on a corner shelf was a stack of what looked like rolled umbrellas with bamboo handles. Khurram picked one at random and held it at arm's length, so that the material unrolled in a rich cascade from the bamboo support. Hardened as I am to lovely textiles, I had a job not to gasp.

It was a wall-hanging, a silken picture about four foot long by two foot wide in a natural off white background embroidered with a riot of colour. It had a deep border of flowers, stylized poppies and cornflowers, each graceful twirling stem linked with its neighbour's, and alongside the flowers but separated from them by a sort of balloon outline – like the speech of people in cartoons – were black hieroglyphics; no doubt a text from the Koran making some witty crack about the unwisdom of letting elephants fight, because there, in the centre panel, were two elephants locked in mortal combat, reared up on their hind legs and hell bent on doing one another in.

I bent to examine it closer. It was a work of art, no doubt of it, but I couldn't really believe Khurram's sister had made it. The silk looked new enough, the colours strong and vivid, yet it was a period piece in some ways. The elephants were not modern animals – they were the wrong shape, the work of an artist who'd never seen a photograph or studied anatomy. The trunks were absurdly thin and segmented neatly, the bodies as barrel-

47

like as a prize baconer's. Most give-away of all, they had hocks like a horse instead of an elephant's forward-bending hind knees.

Yet for all their anatomical faults, their creator had splashed them across the silk with wonderful certainty. Their almond eyes flashed, their trunks snaked wickedly above their over-large ears. I was entranced.

Khurram watched me, assessing my reactions.

'See this, also.'

He held up another picture, four smaller panels this time, with a narrow border of golden leaves. Three portraits of men in rich clothes, one with a hawk on his wrist. The same bird, enlarged, in the fourth panel. It was like a huge page from someone's photograph album.

'Your sister did all this?' I couldn't believe it. The wall-hangings looked as if they really belonged in some museum, but I was crazy to acquire them. Alan's eyes would fairly drop out of his head: it would be the scoop of all time.

Khurram nodded. 'My sister and her women.'

'They are very fine. But the clothes are old-fashioned, aren't they?' I said, feeling my way. 'Where does your sister get her ideas – her subjects?'

That made him think. 'From old books,' he said at last.

'Your books?'

'Books of my family. She looks at books and then she draws, and her women make the embroidery. It passes their time.'

I bit back my women's lib. No sense in antagonizing him, but the arrogant waste of such creative talent made me shake with suppressed fury. Anyway, we were getting closer to a deal. This must be the moment to stress my friendship with Rosie, since her name had such an effect on him.

'Have you known Mrs Honeywood long?' I asked.

'Many years.' He waved a vague hand.

'She says you're a wonderful guide,' I oiled.

'It is true, as you will see when we journey into the mountains.'

'*If* I manage to buy what I want before you set out.' I sighed. 'Otherwise I shall just have to stay here in Srinagar. Good-bye,

48

Mr – ' I hesitated. Which name should I use? I couldn't cough up all three *and* keep a straight face.

'Khurram,' he supplied. He watched me carefully as I got up, smoothed my skirt, remembered to grope behind me for my bag. He was fingering the last of the scrolls he had shown me. I moved briskly towards the door. 'Don't worry, I'll find my way out. Thank you for showing me those lovely pictures – it's a pity you won't sell them, because I'd give you a very fair price.'

'Wait, Miss Granville,' he said softly. 'Like Rosie, you are a very determined lady. I understand why she made you her friend. I cannot see you disappointed.'

I waited, holding my breath.

He went on: 'Come tomorrow at ten, and you shall meet my sister. Together you can choose what you wish to buy.'

'You took your time.' Sour as PLJ, Sandy was propping up the sun-baked wall of the Treasure Palace.

'I thought you could use a few minutes chatting up your girl-friend,' I said. Khurram's sudden change of front had left me walking on air. 'Where to, now?'

'Back to the houseboat if you want to do any fishing. It's past one. We've had the sight-seeing for today.'

'Sorry, Sandy.' I was getting plenty of cheek-turning practice today. 'It took longer than I expected, but I think I've got what I wanted. He was a bit sticky at first, but it was wonderful the way you broke the ice for me.'

Nick was grilling his torso again on the sun deck, I saw with envy. If I'd lain in the sun a quarter of the time he had I'd have been as sore and raw as Steak Tartare. The Minister for Tourism had come and gone; I wondered if Nick had put on a shirt in his honour, but before I could ask about this, he said: 'Chaturvedi's given me a list of places you'll find the sort of materials you're looking for. I wrote them down – here.'

He'd scrawled them on the back of an envelope, and it was a surprise to see his writing: it was so like my own. Handwriting's supposed to show your character, and we couldn't have been more different.

'Oh, thanks. That'll give me something to work on.' I glanced through the list, but there was no mention of the Nishat Treasure Palace and I felt a tiny spurt of triumph. Not even the Minister for Tourism knew what treasure that run-down shack concealed.

'*Mañana*,' said Nick. 'Time enough for more work. We're going fishing right now. Ahmad's been packing a basket of goodies, and here's your kit.'

He picked up and demonstrated a neat little split-cane rod, about eight-foot long, a net which collapsed over its handle at the touch of a button, and a khaki canvas satchel containing a clear-lidded plastic box of brightly-coloured flies, empty pockets lined with mackintosh in which to carry the miraculous draught of fishes, a flat tin box of nylon casts, tweezers, scissors, a tube of anti-midge, and a curious heavy hunk of horn, about eight inches long.

Though I fancy the image of myself as a hothouse bloom, there are times when I feel the attraction of complicated sporting equipment. 'What's this?' I asked, fingering the hunk of horn. You could see why it was so heavy: the middle had been hollowed out and filled with lead.

'That's a priest; useful for giving the *coup de grâce* if you hook one that's too big to kill the usual way.'

'Usual way?'

'Some people bonk them on the nose with a stone, but I always stick my thumb in their mouths and bend their heads back until their backbone cracks. It's quickest, and you get much less flapping about.'

Sickers. I said quickly, 'You do the fishing; I'll be absolutely happy just lying on the bank and watching.'

'Don't be so wet. I've bought you a licence now, and you might as well use it.'

I wasn't going to descend to a prep-school wrangle. I said haughtily, 'Of course, if you really want me to . . .'

'Splendid. Then let's be off.'

Sandy drove us round the edge of the lake and up a bumpy track that reached back into one of the tributary valleys. The day was hot, golden, and still. I had a marvellous feeling of freedom. Free from work, from traffic, towns, haggling, worry . . . Free even from Rosie's chatter; I hadn't realized how glad I'd been to get away from that.

Corn stood waist-high in fields the size of pocket-handkerchiefs scattered with the scarlet splash of poppies and ringed with copper-bronze plane trees. When we reached the river and Sandy switched off the engine, the silence was so total that my ears seemed to hum with it.

I offered no resistance as Nick put up my rod, tied on cast and fly with complicated knots, and plonked me in the river, which was more like a wide brown stream, and came half-way up my borrowed waders. He spent a few minutes showing me how to cast, flicking the line back over my shoulder with a count of one, two, three, and across the water on *four*. Kid's stuff, I thought, dreamily watching the sparkling ripples. Nothing to it. I looked round to see where Nick had disappeared to and felt a sudden alarming tug at my rod. My heart seemed to slow and then race like a badly-set watch.

'Nick!' I yelled. 'Come back! I've caught a whopper.'

He was there in a flash, taking the rod from me, pulling gently, then harder, then pulling out yards of line from the reel and flicking carelessly forward.

'What are you *doing*?' I asked, dancing about on the bank. 'You'll shake it off.'

He laughed. 'It's not a fish at all, I'm afraid. You've hooked the bottom. If I'm not careful you're going to lose the fly. Blast!'

The line flew suddenly into the air, minus fly.

Nick swore, tied on another, cautioned me against casting too near rocks, and disappeared again. Chastened, I concentrated on casting into the middle of the stream and removing the fly from the water before it could tangle in the sedge and rushes at the bank. The line kept giving exciting little jerks, and at last I traced these to my satchel, which hung down low enough to catch on the butt of the rod.

I hitched it out of the way, pulled out more line with a flourish, as Nick had done, and gave a firm, authoritative cast.

Straight and true sailed the line, straight and true sailed the fly. I watched in narcissic admiration which turned to rage as I saw my beautiful cast overshoot the river by several feet. Too late I tried to snatch it back. The barbed fly had hooked itself firmly into the opposite bank.

'I told you not to use a lot of line.' Nick's voice behind me was decidedly unwelcome.

'You didn't,' I said hotly.

'Well, I meant to. Never mind, it was a lovely cast. You're getting the hang of it.' He retrieved cast and line at the expense of another fly. I dropped the net on the grass and resignedly offered him my fly-box again; he chose a mangy object like a moth-eaten mosquito.

'Why not that greenish chap?' I objected, pointing to a handsome fly with viridian hackles and a tail fetchingly striped in Arsenal colours.

'Too bright on a day like this. And heaven knows where I'd get another to replace it when you hook it into the bank', he said dampingly. 'You stick to these little brown numbers if you want to catch fish.'

I was no longer sure that I did. I'd had about enough of this tiresome casting and its attendant worries.

Right, I thought, watching Nick stride away downstream, that's the last time I ask you for help. As soon as you're out of sight I'm going to give the blasted rod a rest and have a kip in the sun. But annoyingly this time he remained just at the edge of my vision. I let the line float idly, waiting, and watched a flock of goats escorted by a red-skirted moppet ford the river a hundred yards or so above me. She waved, and I took one hand off the rod to wave back.

Suddenly a tremendous jerk, quite different from anything I'd felt before, nearly snatched the butt from my other hand. At the same time the reel screamed, while far out in the water, much farther downstream than I had imagined my fly to be, something silvery started frantically jumping and splashing.

Instinct told me to jerk the rod upright. Thrilling currents were running up the line into my hands. The reel abruptly stopped pulling out, and very cautiously, my heart thundering, I began to reel in. Tick-tick-tick-tick, tick, tick, tick tick . . . There was a definite drag on the line, but no more of

52

that frenzied wriggling. Don't say I was on the bottom again . . . ?

I hesitated, wondering whether to call Nick but reluctant to cry wolf for the third time. Another strong pull immediately convinced me that this was Leviathan, not the bottom, and glancing up at the rod point I was concerned to see it bent in a tight U, with the line plunging almost vertically into the water. The top section of the rod wasn't much thicker than a drinking-straw; I was doubtful if it could stand much of this strain.

Just then the fish jumped clean out of the water, making my heart jump in imitation. It looked sleek and powerful, too strong for the puny rod, as it hit the water again and raced away. Once again the reel screeched in protest; there was nothing for me to do but stumble downstream after the fish, keeping the line as taut as possible.

Mr Songali's second-best waders weren't up to this kind of treatment, and both instantly sprang leaks as I slipped and stumbled on the sharp rocks. Warily I reeled in more line, determined not to let the fish reach the tumbling foamy water and broken rocks at the end of the pool. If he snagged the cast round a rock, I was sure it would snap. The fish seemed tired now; the deep steady drag against the reel was my only indication that there was something on the line.

Nearer I reeled him, nearer – I could see the long dark shape below the surface of the water. I fumbled at my belt for the long-handled net, then cursed aloud. I'd taken it off and put it on the bank when Nick put on the new fly. Now what was I to do?

Gingerly I backed upstream again. I could see the net lying on the grass. Just a few more steps, easy does it . . . Leviathan gave a desperate tug which upset my balance on a sloping rock. Clutching the rod I fell forward, and icy water closed over my head.

A glacier must have fed that river; the cold nearly stopped my heart. I realized at once that unless I could kick off the water-logged waders, pulling me down as effectively as concrete boots, I would drown. I couldn't move my legs at all, though my head was only just under water and my empty flailing arm kept breaking surface. My right had seemed welded to the rod; I'd forgotten how to unclench my fingers.

My lungs ached and red mists swam in front of my eyes. The current felt like a great hand pulling me down. I fought against it, then suddenly realized it was a hand – Nick's hand – and instead of dragging me into the water it was trying to pull me out. My head broke surface and I drew a deep, gasping breath. Next moment, iron arms had gripped me in a fireman's hoist. Floundering and spluttering, with those damned leaky waders still flooding water down my legs, I was cast on to the bank like a stranded fish.

I lay there feeling utterly at peace, with the hot sun baking my back and Nick murmuring romantically, 'You clot; you utter, idiotic, brainless little clot. Why didn't you call me? What on earth made you hang on to the rod? No, don't talk. I thought you were a goner.'

I stood a few minutes of this before pulling myself together and sitting up, after which we both quickly withdrew into our shells and smoothed our ruffled feathers and things were normal again. On the bank lay a fair-sized fish – not precisely a monster of the deep, but definitely no minnow.

'Is that all I caught?' I asked in some disappointment.

'Quite a decent fish,' said Nick reprovingly, measuring it in handspans. 'About four pounds, I guess, and foul-hooked.'

'Foul nothing. I did it exactly as you said. There was no suggestion of foul play,' I said indignantly.

'Keep your hair on,' he said, laughing. 'All that means is that he didn't bite at the fly; it simply hooked him while he was swimming about minding his own business, so no wonder he fought like a tiger. See where the hook is?'

He demonstrated with a finger crooked into the angle of my jaw, where my gills would be were I a fish. The touch of his warm, strong, slightly rough hand on my wet skin sent a delicious shiver through me.

Minnow or monster, that fish was the best I've ever eaten. We grilled it over a fire on the bank, hung by the gills from a forked stick, and ate the deliciously charred, pink-fleshed fragments

54

messily in our fingers.

'It was a ferox, a cannibal trout,' said Nick, tossing his section of backbone into the fire. 'Look at his savage teeth.'

'Must you?' I said. He and his mates might even now be nibbling at me. 'I hope that poor girl has some more clothes,' I added.

The lady of the nearby cottage had eagerly sold Nick her daughter's quilted cotton jacket and trousers for the princely sum of four rupees. They were clean, though smelling faintly of goat, and remembering my mother's adage – so useful when caught short in male company: 'If he's a gentleman he won't look, and if he isn't, it doesn't matter,' I had changed brazenly and thankfully out of my own sopping garments right there on the bank of the river. When I completed my Kashmiri-style toilet, I found Nick not only being a gentleman but also holding at bay half the village, who wanted a share in the peepshow.

The disappointed voyeurs at last drifted away, and we gorged on my catch, lying on our backs in the sun.

I said idly, 'What bliss it must be to travel with Grand Mogul. Sport organized from Dover to Dacca. I don't think I've ever caught my own lunch before.'

'Better than Prunier's?'

'Much.'

'You deserved it after that ducking. The last woman who fell in the river here gave me an earful for not telling her the rocks were slippery – silly bitch.'

'D'you often bring people here?' I asked jealously, disliking the idea of the common herd trampling my scene of piscatorial· triumph.

'Not many. We don't have big groups of travellers, anyway. That would spoil it. We make our clients pay through the nose, but once they've signed the cheque they know they'll enjoy themselves. They can cross the world from top to bottom and side to side and feel they're honoured guests all the way. You needn't laugh: it's perfectly true.'

'I'm not laughing. I know just what you mean. It's the feeling you very definitely *don't* get with Eastravel. But I suppose, however nice you are to your travellers, they get the same bureaucratic delays and restrictions as everyone else. That's what's nearly driven me round the bend, trying to arrange export for all these materials. Half the time the officials behave as if you're a crook, and the other half they're showing you what crooks they are themselves.'

'Only one thing for it,' said Nick. 'Travel with GM in future.'

'What? Pay you *and* the customs men. No, thanks.'

'No,' he said patiently, 'that's what I meant. We don't get these restrictions and delays. Our jeeps sail through the frontiers as if they weren't there. Believe me, it's worth it. Cuts out all the bribes, for a start.'

'How on earth do you swing that?'

'Not a question of swinging. It's mutual self-interest. My old dad's spent years persuading the important smells in each country that what they want is rich tourists. Not the hitch-hiking teenagers who haven't a bean to spend anyway. But rich tourists won't be messed around. They refuse to queue. So the frontier guards are instructed by their masters to go easy on our jeeps and buses. They glance at our papers and wave us through, easy as kiss your hand.'

'Perfect opportunity for smugglers,' I said, half joking. 'Don't you spend twice as much baling out your couriers?'

I sensed rather than saw him sit up. 'You couldn't be more wrong,' he said coldly. 'Smuggling is the one pitch-black unforgivable crime in G.M.'s book. All these concessions I've been telling you about are because the countries concerned trust Grand Mogul. Anyone who abuses that trust is out on his ear.'

This hobby-horse was evidently very high indeed. I said pacifically, 'How did you get on with Mr Thingummyjig this morning?'

'Chaturvedi? Oh, fine. I think he got the message. I dangled the carrot of a vast investment in front of his nose, and he nearly choked trying to swallow it whole.'

'You'll get your hotel?'

'With any luck. You must come and help me choose the site.'

'I'd love to. I'm going up to Gulmarg as soon as Rosie arrives, that is, if Khurram – '

The name had slipped out before I remembered Sandy's

warning. Nick pounced on it.

'Khurram Mohammed Beg? The chap we talked about last night?'

'Yes,' I said sulkily.

'You went to see him today? Oh, give me strength! Didn't you hear a single word I said last night? I told you to steer clear of Khurram Mohammed Beg: I don't want Grand Mogul to get a name for associating with people like him.'

How dare he boss me around? I stood up, fairly shaking with rage. 'I'm not Grand Mogul, dammit! I'll do what I like. Of course I heard you last night; I thought you were being pretty neurotic then, but this is plain ridiculous. You can't tell me what to do and who I should or shouldn't talk to, so get that right out of your head. If I want to visit Khurram, buy material from him, do anything I like with him, I shall, and you can't stop me.'

I picked up my rod and basket, annoyed to see that my hands weren't steady.

Nick said more calmly, 'If you do, you'll ditch my hotel.'

'I'm simply not with you.'

'Use your loaf, sweetheart. You and I arrived together. Right? We're sharing a houseboat; we're spending the day fishing together. So in the eyes of Mr Chaturvedi, we belong together.'

'We don't.'

'Try explaining that to him. If you go getting all pally with someone the Government distrusts, i.e. Khurram, just when I'm in the middle of some rather dodgy negotiations with said Government, don't you see you're liable to rock the boat?'

'Khurram doesn't look interested in politics,' I said scornfully. 'You're seeing Reds under the bed.'

Nick gave a short, exasperated laugh. 'You sound like my little niece. "But, Mummy, that kind man with the sweeties doesn't look like a kidnapper." She's only seven. I thought you were a bit more – ' He didn't say more what, and probably just as well as I might have sloshed him.

'There are thousands of shops in Srinagar. D'you have to go straight to the one I've warned you against? I can see it's a matter of principle to fight any advice you're given, but . . . '

That did it. I'd been about to agree there were plenty of other shops when he added that fatal rider.

'Sorry, Nick. You seem to have got this out of perspective,' I said as calmly as I could. 'Why should I buy second-rate mass-produced stuff when I can get beautiful handworked original tapestries? I'm not interfering in politics. I just want to do my job as well as I can, and if that means buying from people you happen to dislike, it's just too bad. Anyway, there's an easy way out for both of us.'

'Which is?'

'Stop sharing a houseboat.'

'My dear girl,' he managed to make the endearment sound insulting – 'the last thing I want to do is drive you away. Besides I'm afraid the damage is done.'

'Not at all. Tell Mr Chaturvedi just why I've moved out, and you'll be in the clear.'

We glared at one another. I felt a tearing disappointment that the day had to end like this. The sunset was reddening the surrounding peaks, the gurgling river slid peacefully past us; only man was vile.

'Promise me you won't take it out on Sandy,' I said. 'I made him take me there.'

He hesitated, watching the Land Rover crawl up the valley road towards us. 'I can't promise that,' he said rather grimly. 'It's what I was talking about – a breach of trust. You don't understand how things work out here. You don't know the time of day. And I don't think on present form that you ever will.'

Chapter Seven

'Never a hasty temper show
Or strike your little friend a blow,' I sang in the bath to the tune of
L'Amour Est Enfant de Bohème.
'Far better wait till you are cool,
And then half kill the little fool'.

The soft, scented water sluiced the soap and irritation off me,
and I emerged in a better mood. Annoyed as I was to find Nick
so opposed to my dealings with Khurram, and rude and bossy
as he had undoubtedly been, I felt it was not worth leaving the
comfort of the *Convolvulus* in a huff. *Far* better wait till you are
cool . . .

I liked Nick; I fancied him quite a bit, too, which – my sister
Anna would have said – was a step in the right direction. I'd
been right off men lately, ever since the squalid business with
Johnny. Anna used to laugh at me from her wheelchair. 'How's
the love life?' she'd ask. 'Got any torrid pulsating passions to
thrill me with?'

When I said no, she'd make her eyes huge and round. As soon
as *she* got out of that chair, she'd say, she was going to make
Fanny Hill look like an under-sexed iceberg. She knew as well as
I did how slim were her chances of ever getting out of that chair,
but we didn't talk about that.

Drying myself, I took Nick to pieces and reassembled him in
search of the vital ingredient. It couldn't be his looks – I preferred strong silent blonds – though he was certainly strong
enough. I remembered those steely arms fishing me out of the
water like a drowned rat, with no more effort than if I'd been
one.

Not looks, then: could it be his lovely nature? The answer
would have been Yes any time in the past forty-eight hours, but

since our quarrel by the river I wasn't so sure. Picking us up off the road at Amritsar had been definitely Good Samaritan stuff, well over and above the call of duty, not to mention bringing me to my destination and saving me from a watery grave. Ten out of ten for character – until tonight.

Then there was Sandy. I could see for myself how Sandy was pushed around; it looked suspiciously like a habit.

I put a mental question mark against the lovely nature, and fell back on that old favourite, animal attraction. This has the advantage that one is traditionally helpless when it crops up; it constitutes an excuse for the most reprehensible behaviour.

My father and mother had such strict, regimented, seen-and-not-heard childhoods themselves that they leaned over backwards to give Anna and me our heads, and sent us to a school so co-educationally progressive and syllabically permissive that we escaped teenage motherhood more by luck than good management.

It took us years, after leaving school, to work out a reasonable moral code, and mine was never anything to write home about. It's such an effort to think everything out for oneself; sometimes I even envied children who'd been forcibly propelled along the straight and narrow from the word go.

Anna, I knew well, was all for the positive approach. If I fancied Nick, it was up to me to do something about it. Kicking my sodden clothes into a corner of the bedroom, I went out to meet the boys, all fresh make-up and shining hair and sweetness and light.

Socially, the evening was a success: no quarrels, clashes, or tempers. But sexually it was a frost. Sandy was there all the time to cramp my style, and though Ahmad strummed plaintive love-songs on a lute, and candle-light glowed seductively through brandy glasses, the love interest never got off the ground, and Nick was so hearty and brotherly that I fancied he was adopting this new personality especially to annoy me.

At midnight, when I went to my cabin, I went to the trouble of leaving the bedside light to throw a flattering aureole over my sleeping profile, but fell heavily asleep before anyone turned the handle of my unlocked door.

60

The light looked small and silly, shining in competition with the sun, when I woke. Nine-thirty, and the boat was silent. My appointment with Leila was at ten. The wretches, I thought, dressing at furious speed, to go off without waking me. I might have slept till lunch time. I whistled up a cup of coffee, and commandeered Ahmad and the *shikara*.

'Where's Mr Jameson this morning?' I asked as we glided over the glassy water towards the jetty.

'Mista going today in Gulmarg.'

'And Sandy?'

'Sandy going with Mista.'

'How far is it?' I wanted a look at this village. I couldn't imagine an Alpine-style ski resort existing in the same country as the town of Srinagar, whose planning belonged to the Dark Ages. Narrow streets and gutters running with sewage above fairytale pointed roofs and cross-hatched lattice windows leaning so close together that lovers living on opposite sides of the street could certainly clasp hands and probably even kiss above the traffic. I found it fascinating yet oppressive, and longed for the clean hills we'd seen from the banks of the Lidder River.

Ahmad was frowning as he calculated. 'Two half hours,' he said at last.

'You mean an hour?'

He tried again. 'Two hours and half.'

'By car?'

'No, miss.'

'How long by car?'

'One hour.'

I left it at that. Communication was too painful, and we were nearing the shore. I told Ahmad to bring the boat back at eleven o'clock, holding up fingers to be sure he understood, then took a taxi to the Treasure Pavilion.

Khurram was in the front of the shop, looking languid and oriental. The short, fat, sleek Indian talking to him stopped abruptly as I entered, and looked me over carefully.

'Good morning,' said Khurram. 'You have come to talk of our trip to the hills, Miss Granville? Good. Very good. May I present to you Mr Ram Sirdar of the Srinagar police?'

The fat man shook my hand.

'You see,' said Khurram dryly, 'I have good friends in high places.'

The fat man shifted uncomfortably. I wondered what Khurram meant. Was Ram Sirdar breaking bounds or the law? A crumpled rupee, if that was the Indian equivalent of a bent copper?

'You stay long in Srinagar, miss?' asked Ram Sirdar in slow English.

Khurram intervened before I could answer. 'Miss Granville comes with Mrs Honeywood. She does not stay in Srinagar.'

Ram Sirdar visibly relaxed. He said, 'I wish a pleasant journey for you. Which is your hotel?'

'The Excelsior,' I said on impulse.

Khurram opened his mouth as though to contradict me, then shut it without speaking.

'Good. Excelsior very nice hotel. Good-bye.' Ram Sirdar ducked me a little bow and waddled out.

As the door clicked shut I asked Khurram, 'What was all that about?'

'Please?' He substituted a puzzled frown – not altogether convincing – for the smile on his smooth pale face.

'Why do the police want to know about me?'

'The police want to know everything. So – ' the smile returned – 'I tell them everything. They are happy when tourists spend money in Kashmir. And now Leila is waiting. Please to follow.'

We crossed the flowery courtyard and climbed some stone stairs to the room above. It was more of an atelier than a studio, a long, light, airy room with a high ceiling.

A dozen or more women and young girls dressed alike in quilted blue cotton – the same as my four-rupee suit – knelt or squatted at looms and embroidery frames, chattering softly while their fingers flew over many-coloured strands of wool. They worked in pairs, stopping from time to time to consult the pattern spread between them.

As we entered, the flutter reminded me of a deep litter hen-house suddenly opened; black eyes flashed towards us, veils

62

were twitched into place, hands stopped in mid-knot while their owners questioned, assessed, summed up, and returned to their work.

I would have liked to stop and look at the weaving, but Khurram was beckoning me forward towards the girl who sat on a raised dais at the far end of the workroom, thumbing through a heavy book on a lectern. She might have been posing for a portrait, so studied was her position. She was tiny, slender and doll-like, with a cream-pale oval face framed in two glossy black plaits and the same finely arched eyebrows as Khurram's. Her tilted eyes watched our progress up the room.

Her stillness was somehow queenly: the whole tableau made me think of a medieval princess among her ladies, whiling away the hours and years till her prince came riding up. Was Sandy that prince? He hardly seemed to measure up to the role. 'She's a lovely girl,' he'd said, and I'd conjured up a picture of a bouncing, robust peasant-type, square-built and rosy-cheeked, the sort of girl I thought would appeal to a bag of nerves like Sandy. I certainly hadn't expected the fragile perfection of the figure at the end of the room, and when the smooth-carved features broke into a smile, I was as much surprised as if an ivory statue had come to life.

Khurram, who'd been muttering softly to her, switched to English and introduced me. I pushed away my impulse to curtsey or salaam, and instead took the fragile, bird-boned hand, loaded with rings, that she held out to me.

'My brother tells me you like to see my work. I am happy,' she said. Her voice was high-pitched and lilting, perfectly suited to her doll-like appearance.

'Your silk-pictures are beautiful. I hope you'll be able to make some for my firm to buy,' I said carefully, inhibited by Khurram's veto on selling her work. I wished he'd push off and leave us to it: I was sure we'd get on better without his basilisk eyes watching every move we made.

Leila darted a mischievous glance at Khurram. 'Always I tell to sell my pictures. This is what I like, for my pictures to be known in many countries. You see, I would make a better man of business than Khurram.'

63

Khurram muttered something sharp, and her smile faded. She drooped like a chastened puppy. Damn the boy, I thought.

'Does it take you long to make a picture?'

She shrugged delicately. 'My girls can work fast when I give them a picture, but just now they work at their carpets. That is their normal labour. The pictures are for pleasure: very pretty, not useful. If I am happy,' she said softly, 'I make many pictures.'

The implication was clear. If she wasn't happy, work stopped. I didn't think she was too happy now.

She turned suddenly to Khurram, who was staring with those flat black eyes of his, like a snake watching a bird.

'Go now, Khurram,' she said imperiously. 'We have work to do. We cannot choose designs while you sit and stare. Go, I say.'

To my surprise and delight, he obeyed. As the door closed behind him, Leila said matter-of-factly, 'Khurram has many crazy ideas and of pictures he knows nothing. It is better to be alone.'

I couldn't have agreed more. Clearly she was boss on her own ground.

'Come.' She moved to the broad shelf that ran the length of the window like a working surface in a dream kitchen, and flipped open a heavy looseleaf folder. Its spine was tortured almost to breaking point with the bulk of papers crammed into it. Side by side, elbows on the table, we began to go through it.

I enjoyed that hour. Once I knew a child – my father's groom's daughter – who was so musical that if you asked her what a police siren sounded like, she would sing the exact note. Leila's work had the same instinctive quality. There were fine, precise, detailed studies in pen and ink side by side with boldly smudged crayon sketches; geometric futuristic whorls and swirls of colour which might have belonged to the galaxy sequence in '2001', closely followed by a series of stylized birds and flowers that belonged to the sixteenth century more than the twentieth.

She was amazingly versatile. I felt that, given the equipment, she would be equally at home in oils, sculpture, metal-work, or any medium you could name. But she was hard to please.

Time and again she flicked over a page I wanted to linger at, clicking a disapproving tongue.

'No good, that one. Bad, no good.'

'Show me.'

'No, no. You will see only the best.'

I asked who had taught her to draw.

She shook her head. 'I copy always. I learn through copying. Khurram brings me many books, also Sandy.'

She opened a sliding door below the working surface, and showed me rows of art books, the high, stiff back of Berenson among them. No wonder her work was so varied, if she copied from that lot.

'Which is your own style?' I asked.

'My own?'

'Yes. Something original, not copied.'

She didn't understand. 'It is best to work from originals,' she said, smiling.

'Yes, but that's still copying . . . '

She looked wounded. 'You don't like my copies?'

'Yes, I do,' I said hastily. 'I like them very much.'

'Good, then you will choose.'

So I chose, and looked, and changed my mind, and at last decided on three designs for her girls to translate into embroidery. That'd be enough to show Alan what she could do, and shouldn't run me into too much trouble from the Customs men.

One picture was of a goat rearing up on its hind legs as it nibbled the branches of a tree; the second an arrangement of flowers, poppies and the copper chrysanthemums, wide as soup plates, I'd seen next door in the Nishat Bagh. The last was loveliest of all – a group of majestic plane trees set about with the silvery slender poles of Kashmir poplars.

'You live in a beautiful country,' I said, tucking the cardboard folder I'd brought under my arm, ready to go.

'Beautiful to you. A prison to me.'

'Why?'

'Because I am a prisoner.' Her soft voice was suddenly harsh and shaking. Tears weren't far away. 'You come, you look, you say, "Yes, it is beautiful." See the *shikara* on Lake Dal; see the temples, the mountains, the flowers in colour. Then you go back to great cities and studios and galleries and museums. I read of them in my books. But I must stay and draw and dream. Now even Sandy cannot meet me in the Nishat Bagh.'

'D'you really want to leave here? Go with Sandy?'

'Of course I want. But Khurram will not allow.' She shook her plaits until they flew. 'He wants me to be a queen.'

She was so tiny, so delicate, I could understand Khurram's over-protective attitude, though there'd been a certain toughness in her dismissal of him which made me think she knew she was the brains of the outfit all right. But it was impossible to imagine Leila battling in the rough and tumble of a modern city. I hated cities myself, and I'd been brought up to it. She wouldn't begin to know how to cope. I tried to put this thought into words that wouldn't hurt.

'You're safe here,' I said. 'You belong. It may not be exciting, but you don't know how cruel cities can be. Cruel and lonely. You'd be lost. Your brother doesn't know much about pictures, you say, but he looks after you. But Sandy – ' I hesitated. I didn't want to knock Sandy, but I felt in my bones that he wouldn't be much of a shoulder to lean on.

'Sandy is good,' she said confidently. 'Sandy can drive a car. He will show me real museums, real artists, not just books.'

'Sandy's only a driver. A working man.' How could I explain that because Sandy drove a car, that didn't make him a magician nor a millionaire? 'You wouldn't be safe –'

She interrupted passionately, her tilted eyes sparkling with tears: 'No, no! Here I am not safe. With every day that passes, the safety grows less. The danger is here, Charlotte. I may call you Charlotte? You do not understand.'

First Nick and now Leila. I felt tired. How could I understand something they wouldn't explain?

She looked small and defenceless. 'I am afraid,' she said very softly. Her women were eyeing us, wondering what I was saying to upset her.

'Is there anything I can do?' I asked, doubting it, but her face lit up with a brilliant smile.

She called something to her girls, and one ran to the window,

66

peered out, and called back.

'You will take my present to Sandy?'

Cupid's messenger. 'Of course.'

'I did not know how to give it to him. My brother must not know. That is very important.' She looked solemn.

'OK,' I said. 'How can I get out without seeing him?'

'I show you. But first, the message.' She recited, 'Tell Sandy that I pay for my journey.'

She took me down a staircase I hadn't seen, gliding fast and furtively along a thin dark passage smelling of fish and cats, and through a small door let into a wall. I blinked as I recognized the flamboyant colours of the Nishat Bagh. So this was how she used to slip out to her rendezvous with Sandy. At the door she thrust the untidy parcel she was carrying into my hands.

'For James-son,' she murmured, and was gone like a wraith, slipping back into the shadows and pulling the door shut behind her.

I stared at the blank face of the garden door, alone in the still, baking morning. Jameson. The parcel was for Nick, then; not a present for Sandy. How odd!

Never mind, I thought. The wall-hangings were as good as mine, the morning was beautiful, my skin was standing up well to the unaccustomed doses of sun, all was right with the world.

I wandered happily past the luxuriant flowerbeds, sniffing a rose here, a tobacco plant there, happy and relaxed. Reaching Shah Jehan's pavilion at the edge of the lake, I sat on the stone bench inside it and pretended I was a Mogul emperor, lord of millions, mulling over the proportions of the Taj Mahal and wondering whether to sack the architect. I was enjoying this fantasy when a breathy, gushing voice spoke below me, almost, it seemed, beneath my feet.

'Darling boy,' it said, 'was that wise? Once she's seen them she may smell a rat. She's a silly little thing, I know, but we shouldn't take risks.'

I grinned and peered over the balustrade. Rosie hadn't wasted time in giving poor Dr Mohan Singh the slip. But who was the darling boy? Don't say she'd picked up another hippy with a hard-luck story?

Whoever it was, was pitching it hot and strong, but keeping his voice down. I could hear a soft, continuous mutter. I dithered: should I go to the rescue? No. She had to grow up sometime. It wasn't in her nature to stalk silently past touts; she couldn't resist talking to them, and once a conversation had started it was always the devil's own job to break it off.

She turned and began to climb the flight of steps. Her companion followed, still talking hard. They were bound to pass the pavilion. I picked up my folder and Leila's untidy parcel and was about to step out to greet Rosie when I saw the man with her. It wasn't a tout or hippy. It was Khurram Mohammed Beg.

Blast, I thought. Leila didn't want him to see the parcel and I could rely on the ever-curious Rosie to ask what I'd bought. There was nowhere in the bare little pavilion to hide it while we talked.

My folder? I tried to shove the parcel inside it, but the loosely tied string came adrift, and the parcel's contents fluttered to the floor.

Rosie and Khurram were approaching. I heard her say, 'I know it's a perfect pest, but we'll have to. We can't leave them without a queen too long . . . '

They were close now. I scrabbled frantically at the loose sheets of paper, shuffling them together anyhow. They were small, pale-blue pages, the size and shape of a small block of writing paper. Funny present, I thought. I couldn't see them very well. It was shady in the pavilion, and I was still wearing my dark glasses, but I seemed to see a faint white circle traced on each page. Was Leila trying her hand at pop-art? I stared at a page I had just picked up, momentarily forgetting Rosie and Khurram. Surely, that white circle was a ring of letters?

Then I got a shock. I was holding the page face down, and as I turned it over I saw it was headed OBSERVATIONS. Towards the lower edge of the white circle was written RENEWALS, and beneath that, in case one should fail to get the message, RENOUVELLEMENTS.

I was getting the message now, loud and clear. There was no need of a magnifying glass to show me the close overprinting of

68

white letters on the pale-blue background. DOMOFGREAT-
BRITAINANDNORTHERNIRELANDKINGDOMOF-
GREAT . . .

I was holding a sheaf of copies of page 5 – the renewals
page – of a British passport. Leila's passage money.

Chapter Eight

Anger brought the blood flaming to my face; I felt hot all over. Why had she dumped these on me? I stood flattened against the rough wall of the little old pavilion, praying that Rosie wouldn't halt there, wheezing, after climbing the steps, and flush me from covert.

She walked straight past, not five feet away, still deep in talk. The rest in hospital must have done her good, I thought, staring in relief after her retreating back. If she could still chatter after a steep uphill pull, her wind must be better than I'd have expected from her figure.

They were gone. Keeping a tight grip on Leila's beastly little papers, I slipped down the steps and out to the white road that bordered Lake Dal. I walked furiously, taking a masochistic pleasure in the sweat that soon started to trickle down the furrow of my spine. I put a mile between me and the Nishat Bagh before I stopped to rest.

Then I opened the folder and stared again at the incriminating pale-blue pages, comparing them with my own passport. They were excellent forgeries: all they needed was a purple stamp and scrawled signature from the Chief Passport Officer and, I thought, they would pass anywhere.

I remembered Leila saying she preferred to work from originals and wondered who had been so kind as to supply the original for this little lot. Sandy? No wonder her brother had hounded him from the house.

My anger boiled up afresh as I remembered who had tried to make sure I never met up with Leila and her brother. Nick. His holier-than-thou pi-jaw about peace in Kashmir and playing ball with the authorities when all the time he was involved with this dirty racket.

I was well aware, too, why I was so shocked and furious. I wasn't a passport officer. If Indians wanted to risk buying forged passports with the hope of making an illegal entry to Britain, it was their own look-out. No; I was angry because I had liked Nick – had even fancied him a bit – and now my idol proved to have feet of the very muddiest clay.

What should I do? Take the pages to Khurram, and tell him how his sister was being exploited? No; he might well turn nasty, and that would be the end of my lovely wall-hangings. He might even ask how I came to be acting as go-between.

It was lucky for me that Khurram had put a stop to those idyllic meetings in the Nishat Bagh. Leila wouldn't be able now to tell Sandy that she'd given the forgeries to me to deliver, and he'd probably think she hadn't finished work on them. Nick would imagine that he'd scared me away from the Treasure Palace; my lip curled. It took more than a bawling-out from an opinionated, black-visaged gorilla like him to scare me off my lawful business.

Nevertheless, caution warned me not to risk a confrontation with Nick; I resolved to change my place of abode, and the touter the sweeter. No revelations until I was safely out of the Grand Mogul orbit, because if there should be any rough stuff aboard the *Convolvulus* I might easily come off second-best.

I was back at the jetty before I realized it. There sat patient Ahmad, cross-legged on the sun-baked boards, rolling dice with two other mahogany-faced boatmen.

I waved, and he brought the *shikara* alongside with a smoothly practised swirl.

'You going in boat, miss?'

'Yes, please.'

He looked worried. 'Mista say he come two o'clock.'

I glanced at my watch: heavens, it was already a quarter past one. I'd better step on it.

'Take me back now,' I said. 'I want some things from the boat. Then you can return for Mista.' Lucky Ahmad, I thought; nothing to do all day except skim across the shining water from boat to jetty and back again. I wondered if he ever got tired of it.

I packed in a hurry, decided not to leave a farewell note, but tucked a hefty tip for Mrs Songali into the corner of my dressing-table mirror. Thanks to her cooking, my tummy was still in perfect order, and I hoped she'd be the one to find the money.

Ahmad rowed me back to the jetty in disapproving silence: he must have guessed I was about to do a flit. A dozen men rushed up to hail a taxi and haul my solitary suitcase into it. Fearful that it would drive off with my all, I hurried up the steps after them. Ahmad followed. I wound down the window, leaned out, and pressed five rupees into his hand.

'Tell Mista that I have to meet my friend at the Shalimar Hotel,' I said very clearly.

'Shalimar. Your friend. Thank you, miss,' he repeated, grinning again.

'Good-bye.'

'Good-bye.'

The driver revved his engine and we crawled away. I let him go three-quarters of the way to the Shalimar Hotel before asking him to drop me at the Excelsior instead. His abstracted expression never changed, but when he finally stopped at my destination I found he was sharp enough to demand nearly twice the fare Sandy and I had spent on virtually the same journey.

I was beginning to enjoy haggling, and beat him down briskly. He drove off, muttering, and bag in hand I sauntered into the gloom of the Excelsior lobby.

A horrid smell of primitive plumbing was the first thing I noticed; dead flies lay in heaps on the reception desk and more lively ones buzzed happily in the dregs of coke at the bottom of a glass. What a dump, I thought.

I banged sharply on the desk with coins salvaged from the taxi-driver, and a fat little pig-tailed woman, wearing an old grey Army blanket as a shawl over her sari, popped like a conjurer's rabbit from behind a tatty curtain. She stared silently at me.

'Can you speak English?' I asked in a loud, clear, wogs-begin-at-Dover tone to cover my uncertainty. The fool of a taxi-driver must have dropped me at the wrong place.

She shook her head slowly, but I didn't know if this meant

No, or was just her way of registering amazement. I was pretty amazed myself at Rosie's choice of hotel.

'English,' I repeated, fortissimo. 'Speak English?'

No answer. I felt helpless. I picked up my suitcase – no eager bell-hops here – and was about to retreat when a rustle of silk and a billow of Blue Grass warned me that Rosie was nigh.

I spun round, and her enveloping kiss missed my ear by a hair's breadth.

'Charlotte, my dear! Oh, I'm so glad to see you! Where've you been? I've searched every hotel in town for you. I've been imagining the most *dreadful* things!'

Still wearing the wide-brimmed pink hat and pleated silk dress that I'd spotted at the Nishat Bagh, she looked cool and fragrant, straight out of a bandbox, in sharp contrast to my dusty stickiness after rushing about in the heat.

'How did you give that poor little doctor the slip so quickly?'

She laughed richly. 'I couldn't lie there another minute; I told you I was quite all right.'

She certainly looked a hundred per cent again. I said, conscious that my greeting had lacked warmth, 'Well done you. I thought you'd be there a week at least. So, where do we go from here?'

'Nowhere, dear. This is where we spend the night, then tomorrow we'll do a little shopping and buy you a few warm clothes; and the following day we're off!'

I said, 'You can't seriously mean to sleep in this dump?'

'Oh, it doesn't look much downstairs, but my room's lovely. Come and see. You look as if you could do with a wash and a cuppa.'

The dumpy little concierge waddled from behind the desk and carried my case upstairs. She nudged open a door with her behind and displayed the room I expected: narrow iron bedstead, showing its lack of springs, mattress rolled up at one end; dusty bare floorboards, full of splinters – no padding about in bare feet for me – and fly-blown window with half-drawn blinds. The only furniture apart from the bed was a wardrobe sketchily constructed from two packing-cases. Like so many things in India, it looked as if it had been begun with enthusiasm and abandoned half finished.

'Lovely,' I said heavily. 'Just lovely.'

Water off a duck's back, of course. 'I'm next door,' said Rosie gaily, 'we share the balcony.'

Taking a formidable jangle of keys from her handbag, she unlocked two locks on the adjoining door and ushered me in. Her room was twice the size of mine, and ten times more comfortable. Like Khurram's unexpectedly luxurious apartments, it had a magnificent thick carpet with swirls and whirls of red and blue, and an opulent, fringed border. There were silk curtains hanging in heavy, expensive folds, and a heap of cushions covered in the same material. The bed had that taut, well-upholstered appearance that means proper box-springs.

'Crikey! What a home from home!' I exclaimed.

She looked around with satisfaction, her small round chin sinking into a series of soft folds. 'I thought you'd be surprised. It's my little hidey-hole. Amina keeps it just how I like it, and I can pop in here any time and feel comfortable. I've never cared for tourist hotels.

'Sit down, dear – that chair's the best – unless you prefer a cushion on the floor? Do take your shoes off; they're so constricting when it's as hot as this. I'll soon have a kettle boiling.'

I was glad to obey. My feet felt enormous after tramping round the lake road, and my dress clung damply to my back. Worse, I could feel from the stinging soreness of my forehead and cheekbones that I'd had too much sun for what's laughingly known as a strawberry blonde, and would look more like a skinned tomato tomorrow.

Rosie bustled around, warming the teapot and measuring tea-leaves from a fat pink caddy. 'No milk,' she apologized, handing me my bone-china cuppa. 'I can't stand that powdered stuff.'

'How many homes from home d'you have, Rosie? This one's gorgeous.'

'It is nice,' she sighed contentedly. 'My poor husband used to say I had the knack of making any corner of a foreign field into an English meadow. Such a charming thought. When I sit here and watch the mountains I feel very close to him. He loved the mountains. We used to leave Rawalpindi, where he worked, for a month each year after the monsoon and come here. It made a wonderful change. I never envied those people who used to rush off to England. Eric always wanted to stay here. To him, this was home.'

I pricked my ears, curious now about this dead husband of hers. Nick had been right about his name; was he right about the manner of his death? I realized that she'd talked about him very little up till now, and I, fearful of having my withers wrung for sympathy, hadn't encouraged her to.

'Do tell me about him,' I said, fishing for an opening. 'He sounds such an interesting person.'

'He was, you're so right,' she said earnestly, bending to empty the dregs of her cup into a refined little slop-bowl. Was it my imagination, or had a smile flicked across her dumpling face before she averted it? I couldn't be sure.

'Did he, too, know India well?'

'Oh yes, indeed. He was an _active_ man. People, politics, agriculture – ' she laughed apologetically – 'all way above my poor head. He was mad about sport, too. We used to go on tiger hunts – that was before they were banned, of course – and up here in Kashmir he'd shoot duck and quail, literally hundreds of them.'

He was beginning to sound rather a bloodthirsty gentleman, I thought. I persevered, 'What fun! Did you go hunting and shooting with him?'

'Always. We did everything together.'

I tried to picture a younger, slimmer Rosie goat-footing about the Himalayas, heavy rifle in hand, but the image wouldn't real jell. She was off on another tack: I tuned in.

' – honestly, I was beginning to think I'd never find you. I called in to see if Khurram Mohammed had got my letter, and he told me he'd introduced you to Leila. Isn't she a sweet child? I'm so fond of her.' She added archly: 'You've made quite a hit with Khurram, my dear; quite a hit. Miss Granville, so pretty, so intelligent, such a good business woman . . . Your ears must have been burning.'

I could tell she was pulling my leg. 'I'm surprised he didn't mention that I was staying on the houseboat, then.'

'Oh, he did. But when I went across to it the boat-boy told me you'd gone to join a friend at the Shalimar. I couldn't imagine who that could be.'

Good old Ahmad. I hoped he'd say the same to Nick.

'I was so terribly afraid you'd deserted me –' Rosie laughed – 'for some more fascinating companion! Why didn't you stay with those nice young men?'

'They weren't all that nice,' I said shortly.

Her eyebrows arched into shocked golden half-hoops.

'Oh *dear*. You mean they tried – they – ?'

'No, no. Nothing like that. I can look after myself.' But I couldn't help thinking of my antics last night and how nearly I'd made a fool of myself.

'Then why weren't they nice?' she asked plaintively.

'Honestly, Rosie, you've got a mind like a sewer. There's more than one way of being not nice. It was just that we didn't . . . er . . . see eye to eye over – oh, various things.'

I could tell she still thought one of them had made an unsuccessful pass at me and been beaten off, but I hadn't the mental energy to tell her the full story. Later, perhaps. The passport pages were tucked into my zip-bag, still: I might see what Rosie thought I should do with them.

There was a knock at the door and Amina, the concierge, waddled in and started to clear the tea-cups. Rosie sighed and heaved to her feet.

'Make yourself comfortable here, dear,' she said. 'I've got to go out. I see my tonga's waiting outside.'

A patient pony, toast-rack thin, rested propped on one hip between the shafts of a brightly painted cart in the street below.

I watched from the balcony as Rosie whirled aboard in a cloud of scent and chiffon, and the driver woke his pony with a shrewd flick of the whip.

'See you at supper,' she called. 'I'll be back before dark.'

Feeling vaguely disconsolate and abandoned, I went back to my own room and lay on the hard, lumpy mattress, without bothering to unpack. I wondered what Nick was doing and whether he'd mind when he discovered I'd done a bunk. Then I wondered how long he'd wait for Leila's 'passage money' before he sent Sandy to look for it. When he did, I hoped I'd be far away in the hills. The thought of Nick finding out that I'd snitched his papers was not an attractive one.

I decided, in any case, to stick close to Rosie. Nobody would attack me while I was with her. It was clearly a good moment to take a trip into the mountains.

Chapter Nine

As our straggling cavalcade plodded up the stony path that wound into the hills, thirty-six hours later, my spirits rose like the bubbles on a glass of champagne. The morning was bright and cold and still; the ponies' coats stood on end, masking the animals' pitiful thinness. Hoar-frost glittered on the tip of each hair, and our breaths hung suspended at head-height like thoughts in a strip cartoon.

The ponies were scruffy-looking, with large heads and scraggy necks, prominent hip-bones and low-set tails. Anna and I used to ride a lot as teenagers, but I hadn't been on a horse since the day of her crashing fall. My Kashmiri saddle, I soon realized, was going to take a bit of getting used to. Roughly constructed of wood and secured with fiendishly knotted ropes instead of buckles and straps, it was poorly adapted to the English hunting seat.

I tried letting my legs hang straight: agony on the thighs. A jockey's crouch was, if anything, still more uncomfortable, and side-saddle meant putting more faith than I cared to in the stability of my harness. My mount ambled placidly behind his owner, taking no notice of my fidgetings. I eased my weight from one buttock to the other and thought about Nick.

I was glad to leave Srinagar. Dancing attendance on Rosie was no less tiresome here than it had been in Delhi, and a single day's shopping with her was a test of everyone's temper: hers, mine, and those of the patient, uninsultable, maddeningly humble merchants who bent over backwards and ate their own words in their efforts to clinch a sale.

First she shopped for presents. I could imagine the reluctant nieces and nephews and god-children sitting at their desks churning out thank-you letters for Rosie's extravagant and totally useless presents. 'You've got to get over the page,' their mothers would say. 'Spread it out a bit, darling. Another sentence will do it.' And the child would scowl, and chew the biro, and address the envelope, and wonder what on earth he could say about a papier-mâché begging-bowl, or a small brass tray, or a jug carved from a lump of teak.

Rosie fingered and fussed, and made a terrific palaver about getting her presents wrapped to her satisfaction, but she spent plenty, and there was a stir of excitement in the bazaar whenever she stopped at a shop or stall.

'See that lovely silk?' she'd say, stopping her queenly progress through the narrow streets. She usually chose a bale of material stacked high on the shelves beyond the merchant's reach. Out would come step-ladders, chair; a balancing act would begin.

'What d'you want to make with it?'

'I don't know . . . But let's have it down, anyway. No – ' she'd say, fingering it, 'poor stuff, really. Shoddy. But that one over there, behind that pile of boxes, that looks nice . . . '

So she'd go on, pointing, haggling, rejecting, till I was ready to scream.

'How will you get it all to England?'

She smiled. 'Khurram will arrange it for me.' She pointed to a shelf full of fat, papier-mâché ducks that lifted off their nests like Staffordshire china hens. 'Aren't they divine? I can never resist their faces. You ought to buy some – they make lovely presents.'

'I can't,' I said righteously. 'I'm spending Devereux money.'

'Spend it on these. Look how cheap they are – 10 rupees each. Ten one-and-sixes – a hundred and sixty pence, halve it for new pence – eighty – actually a bit less, because of that tiresome point four. What does that work out at? Fifteen bob.' Her maths amazed me. 'You could get twice as much for them at the General Trading,' she finished triumphantly.

I managed to steer her off the ducks, but there was worse to follow, for now she turned her attention to my clothes.

'The nights get very cold in the hills,' she said. 'What have you got in the way of woollies?'

'I'll wear my Husky jacket and trousers.'

'Quilted nylon? Heavens, that won't be enough. I can't have

79

you freezing to death. What you'll need is one of these hooded cloaks. I'll buy you one. No: I insist. And what about gloves?'

I hadn't thought of gloves, or heavy socks, or the fur-lined boots she forced me to buy. I let her pay for the cloak, because I simply hadn't enough money.

Two porters staggered back to the Excelsior under the weight of our purchases.

'Bring everything you've got,' said Rosie when I asked if I should leave my hot-weather equipment at the hotel.

'But if it's only for a week . . . '

'Much better keep everything together; you never know what you're going to need, or what the weather will be like. We've got a whole string of porters and ponies. They might as well have something to carry.'

I thought of the water-colourist ladies of the British Raj, whose bearers had to lug easels and paint-boxes up the hills, and the early photographers who used the same method of transporting their huge lenses and tripods. Rosie was carrying on a well-established tradition.

In many ways, I was beginning to realize, she was shrewder and tougher than she appeared, not at all the fat, rich feather-brain I'd first thought her. I looked ahead at her now, perched on her agonizing saddle with no sign of discomfort. Perhaps hers had special padding.

'How can you stand it, Rosie?' I called.

'Stand what?'

'These saddles. The original bloodless castrators.'

'That shouldn't worry you – or me.'

'I know; but it does.'

'You'll soon get used to it. Cheer up. Tiffin in half an hour.'

I've seen the same sort of change come over yachtsmen, quiet, unassuming chaps on land, who turn into tyrants once their hands grip the tiller. My discomfort seemed no more important to Rosie than seasickness would to such a sailor. The dove had become a hawk, and I wasn't sure that I liked the change.

Half an hour. I shifted my behind once more and went grimly on, remembering.

Nick had made no attempt to contact me yesterday. At first

80

I'd half-hoped he would. It was somehow unsatisfactory to slink away without seeing him again. Several times I was on the point of asking Rosie what to do about those beastly forged passport pages, and each time I hung back. Wastepaper baskets were a refinement one couldn't expect from the Excelsior, and I felt only the grossest of litter-louts would scatter paper on the smooth surface of Lake Dal, so there they had stayed, stuffed in my zip-bag, until last night when we drove with all our luggage to the mountain village of Gulmarg.

A dramatic road snaked up from the Srinagar valley, every bend a hairpin, and the gradients so steep that the rattly old Ambassador taxi Rosie had hired wheezed and groaned, changing gear constantly in search of more power. Tall pines cloaked the view most of the way, and the stuffy car made me feel sick, but when at last we reached the top, the oppressive shadow that had seemed to hover over me all the way from Delhi suddenly lifted into the mountain air and was gone.

Rosie must have felt some of the same freedom, for she stopped our driver on the final bend of the road, and together we walked to the stone parapet and gazed on the wide valley we had left.

It was evening, and the silver thread of the river showed only faintly through the mist which followed the waterline like a plume of smoke. Across the river, the massive Himalayan ramparts reared blackly towards the still-glowing sky. Here and there a peak caught the last rays of the sun, though the lower ranges stood in two-dimensional silhouettes, like cardboard cut-outs.

'Beautiful,' said Rosie. I'd heard her use the word a thousand times, but never before without gush. 'We'll sit here and watch the sunset.'

'The road's quite new, isn't it?' I perched on the parapet beside her.

'Yes. It was finished only a couple of years ago. Eric never saw it. He and I used to ride up from Tanmarg on ponies. It took all day. We'd sit here to rest at sunset.'

I felt vaguely uncomfortable and shifted uneasily on the cold stone. Perhaps she would rather be alone with her ghosts. Below us the cliff fell sheer for a couple of hundred feet – no place for

81

anyone who suffered from vertigo. Footsteps rang behind us on the rocky path. I stared into the gathering gloom and recognised Khurram. He stopped beside us.

'Join us, Khurram,' invited Rosie, without taking her eyes from the far hills. She knew who it was, all right. 'You remember this is my favourite view.'

'Because it is here that your power returns and mine ends,' he said, and I wondered vaguely what he meant.

'*You* don't need power to be happy, little man,' said Rosie in a gentle, teasing tone. 'Soon this will seem nothing but a dream to you.'

'What will?' I asked loudly, to remind them I was still there.

I felt their eyes on me, then Rosie gave her tinkling laugh. 'Nothing you need worry about, dear. You mustn't mind if we sometimes speak of things you don't understand. We share – so many, many memories.'

Did she mean Khurram was her gigolo? Was this a warning to steer clear? She needn't worry, I thought disgustedly; Khurram didn't attract me, rather the reverse. I found that smooth pale face and the flat black tilted eyes about as alluring as the face of a king cobra I'd admired in the Snake House: beautiful so long as half an inch of plate-glass separated the two of you.

I shivered.

'You're cold,' said Rosie at once. 'You should have worn your new cloak. Look! There goes the sun.'

The orange ball was disappearing behind the last pink-tipped peak. The mountain air bit through my clothes as Rosie stretched out a hand for Khurram to help her to her feet, and in silence we crossed the close-cropped mountain turf towards our hotel.

My room had a stove, a squat black furnace with a tin chimney that set off for the ceiling then panicked a few inches short and dived for the outside wall. Disposal problem solved, I thought with satisfaction. When Rosie had left me, after sharing a revolting supper of soggy rice and sloppy curry, instructing me to get an early night because we'd make an early start, I unearthed the sheaf of pale-blue forged pages and began to feed handfuls into the flames. The stove roared and smoked, greedy for more.

Someone knocked. 'Come in,' I called, stirring the ashes to make sure they were burned through. I expected the room-boy with more wood, but when I looked round I saw it was Nick.

My heart jumped, and I shoved the top of the stove back into place. I must have looked as guilty as hell.

'Look out!' he said sharply. 'That thing's red-hot.' He took the poker from me and laid it beside the stove. 'What are you doing – having a bonfire?'

I pulled myself together. 'The room was cold,' I explained. 'I couldn't get the fire to draw properly. But it's all right now.' I added hastily as he made a move towards the stove. He was carrying a small bundle which he now placed on the bed.

'Special delivery,' he said, and I saw with shame the river-sodden garments I had kicked into a corner of my bedroom on the houseboat and forgotten. Now they were clean and stiffly starched.

'Oh, you shouldn't have bothered. I'd forgotten all about them.'

'So I guessed when I saw them lying, unloved and unwanted, in your empty bedroom,' he said easily. 'Never mind. Mrs Songali's done her best with them, but I doubt if your linen jacket'll ever be quite the same again. She's got rather a heavy hand with the flat-iron. Still, it gave me an excuse to come in search of you. What made you run off like that?'

He seemed so open and friendly, standing there with his clear, light eyes looking a bit hurt at my stand-offishness. His brown, square face was typically English and open-air – not the face I'd associate with a dirty racket like forging passports for immigrants. I had to remind myself that the papers I'd just burned had been destined for him.

'I met up with Rosie,' I explained coolly. 'She was a bit lost on her own, you know; needs a bit of looking after. I thought I'd better take care of her.'

'Care?' He seemed amused. 'From what I've heard about your friend Rosie, I gathered she knows Srinagar like Brer Rabbit knew his briar patch.'

'Well, yes. But it seemed a bit mingy to leave her on her own.

She likes company, you know, and she's been awfully helpful . . .'

'You're sure you didn't leave the houseboat because of our silly row over those tapestries or whatever it was you wanted to buy?'

I said triumphantly, 'You admit it was silly?'

'Silly of me to assume you'd understood when I told you to steer clear of Khurram Mohammed Beg and all his works.'

Back to square one.

I asked carefully, 'D'you still think I oughtn't to buy from him?'

'Have you?'

'None of your business.'

'I said, 'Have you?'

'Yes,' I said defiantly. 'It's got nothing to do with you what I buy.'

He sighed. 'You're so wrong.'

'Why?'

'Because I'd hate to see you get hurt.'

'Hurt?' I stared at him. I thought I saw what he was getting at. 'Don't worry, I'm not poaching on your preserves. I prefer originals to forgeries. But I warn you, Nick, if you make any trouble at all for me I'm going to tell Khurram what you and Sandy are up to with his precious sister.'

'That would hardly be fair on Sandy.'

I shrugged. 'It's your choice. Take it or leave it.'

I felt I'd got the whip-hand at last. As a signal I'd had enough of his company, I started to walk about the room, folding and tidying.

Nick didn't go. He stood four-square in the dusty bedroom, watching me.

'Coming to help me choose a hotel site tomorrow?' he said at last.

'Sorry. We're leaving at dawn.'

'What?'

'Leaving. Going. Departing.'

'Where?'

I waved an airy hand. 'Up.'

84

'Not some hare-brained trek into the hills?'

'A sentimental journey. It's why Rosie asked me to come in the first place. Her annual pilgrimage; I told you all about it.'

'What d'you know about Rosie?'

'Enough,' I said flippantly. 'More than I know about you, for instance.'

'Fools step in,' he said quietly. 'Look, Charlotte, I don't know what I've done to get across you like this – I wish I did. But putting all that aside, I'm asking you – *begging you* – to give up this trek.'

'Why should I give up my holiday because you're scared?'

It must have been an effort for him to keep his cool. I noticed a nerve jumping in his temple, but his voice was rigidly controlled. 'I've got contacts in this country; business men, government officials, taxi-drivers: contacts at all levels. I've only been here a few days this year but that's enough to tell me that they're jumpy. They won't tell me straight out that there's trouble brewing, but from the odd hint here and there I get the picture. Sandy says the same. He's been in the bazaars and coffee-shops, chatting up the grass-roots. He's not greatly given to flights of fancy in matters affecting business, but he calls it the 'oosh before the storm.'

'They're pretty useless contacts if they won't tell you anything,' I said, unimpressed. One would never have guessed that Nick would be such a scaredy cat.

'They don't want to put the wind up a possible investor. Chaturvedi's doing all he can to reassure me that my money will be safe if Grand Mogul puts up the cost of a new hotel here. You can't blame him – the whole country's desperate to attract foreign money.'

I looked round the shabby room with its worm-eaten boards and dusty rough furniture. 'Yes, they'll need something better than this if they're going to serve the jet-set of the 'seventies.'

'Right. Their scenery's the best thing they've got to sell, and properly handled it could be a big money-spinner for them. Chaturvedi's quite on the ball, and he's careful not to discourage anyone who looks good for a few lakhs of rupees.'

Another penny dropped. 'Rosie, for instance?'

'Right,' he said again, in that Harvard-business-school, wake-up-you-dimwit way that irritated hell out of me. 'Your Rosie's a big spender. And talker. She cracks up Kashmir to the right kind of tourist; our kind of tourist. Obviously the powers that be aren't so keen on the way she's always disappearing into the hills with that oily Khurram Mohammed – '

'Then if the Ministry of Tourism approves, and the police don't mind,' I said, 'why are you so keen to spoil my fun?'

'I didn't say they approved. They don't. But they've nothing they can pin on her, apparently.'

Yawning, I sat on the bed. The wine I'd drunk at supper was sending heavy waves of sleep washing over me. I didn't want to flog over the same old ground again. I just wanted to lie back and let those waves wash. I *liked* Nick; why did he have to be so tiresome? Animal attraction was at work, and I shoved the passport pages to the back of my mind.

'Don't let's argue,' I said, trying to pitch my voice to a seductive coo, but sounding to my own ears merely sozzled-cum-sleepy. 'Come and advise me about this bed. It's like a sack of potatoes.'

He prodded the mattress experimentally. 'Hardish.'

'You get no idea until you lie on it.'

I demonstrated, stretching and wriggling as if to find a comfortable position. He watched me, deadpan except for a slight narrowing of the light eyes.

'Is this the advice you're after?' He took my hands quite gently, holding them apart behind my head and pressing me back against the pillow. I stared up at him, keeping his face in focus until the last moment as he bent and kissed me.

'More or less,' I agreed when I recovered my breath. 'But you can do better than that.'

'Can – yes. Should – no.' This time his weight was on me, crushing every knobble of my spine on to that plank-like bed. Blood drummed excitingly in my ears and I clung to him, locking my hands behind his head, stroking the soft feathers of hair on the nape of his neck.

'Why not, Nick?' I murmured.

'Because.' He was on his feet in one quick heave, detaching

86

himself from my clinging hands. 'Get up, sweetheart. Get up and grow up and don't play any more tricks like that. You might be – er – misunderstood.'

Hell hath no fury. I felt cold and sick with rage. 'I'm not playing tricks, damn you! What's the matter with you? Got a little wife at home?'

'You know I haven't.'

'Then why?'

'Come back to the houseboat and I'll tell you. Forget this trip into the hills. It's asking for trouble to go off into the blue with a slimy bastard like Khurram Mohammed.'

'I'm the best judge of that.'

'Believe me, you're not.'

It was his cool that maddened me. I jumped off the bed, my temper out of control.

'Shut up and get out,' I said furiously. 'Khurram's twice the man you are, and I'll go where I like with him. You can't stop me. And when you've finished rubbing your shekels in your greasy palms and squeezing the last drop out of your precious Minister of Tourism, you can go back to Leila and tell her the passage money has gone up in smoke. She'll know what I mean, and I expect she'll tell you. And now you can walk right out of here and out of my life. I'm sticking with Khurram and Rosie.'

For a moment he looked bewildered, then he flushed a dark, ugly crimson. I'd never seen a man change colour so dramatically.

He said quietly, 'You bitch. You stupid, pig-headed little bitch. You deserve everything that's coming to you, and by God, I hope you get it.'

He was gone. The door slammed and suddenly the room seemed very empty. I should have been pleased that at last I'd managed to stir him up, but instead from nowhere I seemed to overhear my mother saying, after one of our shouting-matches: 'What *can* we do about Charlotte? She's utterly unreasonable – not a bit like Anna.'

My father had replied jokingly, 'Find her a man with a worse temper than hers.'

'Worse than hers? Darling, it'd be like looking for the Holy

Grail. Tempers like Charlotte's don't grow on trees, you know,' I'd heard mother say gloomily . . .

I didn't see Nick next morning. Rosie woke me at dawn and after choking down some thin porridge and thick tea we joined Khurram and our caravan that was waiting on the path below the hotel. Rosie was hoisted with ceremony aboard the strongest pony; I sprang to the stirrup of another, and we clattered off uphill towards the rising sun.

Now the sun was high and my behind completely numb. I urged my pony alongside Rosie's and told her I wanted to walk for a bit.

'Goodness, no. That'd be most unwise,' she exclaimed. 'You'll exhaust yourself. You have to be very careful when you're not used to the height.'

'I'll take it slowly, don't worry.' To avoid an argument I slipped quickly down from my saddle.

'Charlotte! Get back on your horse this minute.'

'Oh Rosie, don't make such a fuss. I'm all right.'

Rosie called sharply to Khurram, and before I knew what was happening, he shouted an order to two of the porters who picked me up bodily and dumped me back on that agonizing saddle.

'Stop it!' I shouted in outrage. 'Rosie, stop them!'

'That's better,' she said calmly. 'Now, are you going to behave, or shall I have to tell them to hold you there?'

I was trembling with shock and the indignity of being manhandled like a sack of coal.

'Discipline is so important in these wild places,' Rosie went on earnestly. 'We all have to do as we're told. I'm sorry I didn't mention it before, but we never allow one person to put the rest of the caravan at risk. That's what you'd be doing, you know, if you insisted on walking.'

'I can't see why.'

'No? Well, for one thing, you're not accustomed to the altitude, so you might faint. Then you might slip and break some bone, which would make you an extra burden for the porters. As you can see, the horses are fully loaded already. Not least, there's the question of dignity. The men do like to feel they're serving someone important; if you scramble about on foot getting all hot and sweaty, they lose their respect for you, don't you know?'

'They weren't being exactly respectful just now,' I said sulkily.

'Don't let's talk of it any more,' said Rosie with finality. 'It's all my fault; I hadn't made the position clear.'

I said no more, but what was really clear to me was that Rosie on the mountains was a different kettle of fish to the easy-going ass of a woman I'd known up till now. Which was real? I wondered uneasily. I didn't much like the new model.

At lunch, or tiffin, as Rosie called it with a knowing smirk, I was kept very strictly to heel. She and Khurram and I ate slightly apart from the rest of the party, and the concentrated mountaineer's rations I was issued with – cheese, chocolate, Horlicks tablets and hard tack – seemed very dry and dull compared with the full-bodied aroma that wafted from the porters' black iron stewpot.

My request to explore and pick wild flowers was sharply turned down after lunch, on the grounds that my body needed an hour's rest. I started to say I knew what my body needed, thank you very much; then thought, What's the use? Never pick a quarrel on a submarine, my father used to say: you can't get away from the chap you insult. I guessed the same rule applied to mountaineers.

So I lay there in the sun beside Rosie, like a child with an inflexible nannie, wishing I'd found out a bit more about where we were going, and how long it was going to take, and hoping very much that Rosie would soon give up this safety-first attitude when she saw how good and sensible I was being. It was such a waste to be here in the scenery I'd longed for, but shackled to this fat old tyrant with her petty rules. The treacherous thought slid into my mind that the view would be ten times as splendid if Nick were lying at my side: I pushed it firmly out again.

'What was young Jameson doing in your room last night?' asked Rosie with apparent laziness, though I could see a slit of eye glinting keenly at me from beneath her half closed lids. 'Or shouldn't I ask?'

I ground my molars. Damn the old busybody!

'He brought some clothes I'd stupidly gone and left on his houseboat.'

'How kind of him. How did he know you'd be at Gulmarg last night?'

'Search me. Someone must have told him – one of your porters, I expect.'

She was silent a moment, then she said: 'I expect you told him where we were heading?'

'Well, I told him we were *going*, but not where, exactly. How could I? I don't even know myself. You and Khurram are surely the only ones who know just where your husband was killed.'

I spelt it out in words of one syllable because it seemed to me she'd rather lost sight of the original purpose of this expedition. No sign of the floral tributes and no mention of the dear departed for at least forty-eight hours. I'd expected the pack-ponies to be staggering under vast bouquets. They were heavily loaded, all right, but not with flowers. I couldn't imagine why we needed so many, either; it was impossible to believe we'd eat that amount of food on a week-long trek. Perhaps Rosie planned to leave just a single romantic rose on the grave; but if so, why the extra horses?

I gave up trying to work it out. I was here: that was all that mattered. I drew a deep, tingling breath of air from the roof of the world, and was annoyed to find a small, nagging headache start up behind my eyes.

'Ah, yes,' said Rosie. 'But did he seem – well – *interested* in where you were going?'

'Not a bit,' I lied, bored with this catechism.

'But I expect you arranged to see each other before you leave India, anyway?'

'Certainly not. I told you, ships that pass in the night.'

'So sensible. Such a practical attitude.' The glint of eye closed for a few seconds, then she heaved briskly to her feet. 'Well, perhaps we should be off. *En marche, en marche.*'

Khurram sprang to help her mount. She leaned heavily on his shoulder as she boarded the patient pony, and I saw her podgy white hand travel fleetingly over his hair in a quick caress, rather as one might stroke a well-behaved dog. He smiled, and I bent quickly to rub my ankle. I didn't want to see Rosie's expression, or let Khurram know I'd watched them.

My headache stabbed again as I moved and I groped in my saddle-bag for dark glasses, wondering if the expedition's first-aid kit ran to aspirin. Despising people who are always nibbling at patent medicines, I hadn't had the wit to bring so much as a bottle of TCP in my sponge-bag.

I spent more time that afternoon worrying about my own discomfort on that Iron Maiden of a saddle, and my headache, and the odd shortness of breath that would now and then give my lungs a painful squeeze, than admiring the scenery or pay-. ing much attention to where we were going. I know we crossed a ridge where the wind howled and the path was worn into glassy planes, sleek with ice.

The ponies bowed their heads so that their long manes fell forward to protect them, and shimmied sideways, trying to present their rumps to the icy blast. I pulled the hooded cloak Rosie had bought me tight over nose and mouth, and shut my eyes as we crossed the exposed summit.

Stealing a glance at Rosie, I saw she was sitting her beast imperturbably, like a lump of rock neither wind nor weather could affect. I marvelled at her endurance.

Then we began to descend, reaching thickets of rhododendrons whose flat, shiny leaves made a marvellous windbreak. It was off with cloaks and hoods, and on with sun-glasses again; I began to feel like a diver with the bends: surely we should halt for decompression?

Some hope. The ponies kept up the steady pace that looked so slow, like the uphill glide employed by *ski-lehrers* and stalkers. An easy gait to recognize, but difficult to imitate. We crossed the valley bottom, taking a long rickety bridge that spanned a wide, all-but-dry watercourse.

'In spring,' said Khurram, appearing at my stirrup, 'this trickle of water you see below becomes a torrent. A great river. Often it sweeps away the bridge.'

It was about all I could do to hoist my eyebrows. There was

really only one thing I wanted to know about the scenery, and that was where in it were we going to stop? And still more urgently, when? In a way, though, I was glad my pride prevented me from asking at that point, because if I'd known we were scheduled to travel for a further two hours, I think I'd have slid from my pony's back and refused to go another inch.

Those two hours ground by somehow, and when at last our cavalcade halted I was too stiff to get out of the saddle, and sat there like a dummy until Khurram ordered a porter to hoist me down. In a sort of trance, I remained where he dumped me, watching the porters water and picket the ponies, dolling out measures of corn and tying on nosebags.

I hardly registered at the time that this was unusual, though it occurred to me later. Indian animals very rarely get a sniff of corn.

Tents were pitched: squat black ridge-pole affairs for the porters, and at a seemly distance of twenty yards from them, a pumpkin-shaped horror in that vicious orange that French outdoor fiends favour for *le camping*. Two porters unpacked this monstrosity with great care, pegging its ropes into the stony ground. They held it in position while a third man – a massive, black-bearded figure addressed as Ram Das – tucked up his pyjamas, spat on his hands, and began to blow it up with a stirrup-pump.

When it looked as tight as a tick, Rosie hove in sight from where she had been conferring with Khurram, and was courteously invited to enter. I watched, fascinated, as she dropped to all fours and eased herself into the little round hole a third of the way up the pumpkin's side, just as a brontosaurus must have looked from behind as it eased into its lair.

Nobody laughed, however. The sides of the pumpkin shook and bulged as Rosie made herself at home; then, as I was wondering what arrangements had been made for me or if I'd be sleeping under the stars, Rosie's head reappeared in the aperture.

'Come on in,' she called.

'There can't be room.'

'Bags of room.' She sounded rather offended.

'No, really. I'll be OK. I'll sleep outside.'

'You certainly won't. You'd freeze. D'you know how high we are?'

I'd no idea. We'd been up and down so often that I'd lost track.

'Fourteen thousand feet, or thereabouts.'

I got up stiffly and creaked over to the tent. It was an effort to bend in the middle and crawl through that hole, but once inside I realized she was right: there was plenty of room for two.

'My igloo,' said Rosie contentedly. 'I've tried all shapes of tent and these really are the best, as long as you don't get a puncture, of course. You have to train the porters to handle them carefully.'

I found difficulty in keeping my eyes open. Warmth from our bodies and the relief of being out of the wind made me long for sleep. My head ached and the skin round my eyes felt tight. I took the sleeping-bag Rosie handed me, and crawled inside, feeling the day had gone on quite long enough.

'Wait a bit. They'll bring us supper in a few minutes,' said Rosie. 'You'll feel better for some food.'

'Not hungry,' I muttered. The thought of food made my gorge rise.

I felt her bending over me, peering at my face, but I kept my eyes shut and snuggled deeper into the sleeping-bag.

'Aren't you even going to wash?'

'Later.' It was surprising: I didn't even want to go to the loo. My whole body felt as if it had shut up shop. The bungy, blown-up floor of the tent was the softest bed I'd ever lain on.

Just before sleep overcame me, I heard her say, 'Oh dear, I hope you're not going to be ill. That would be the final straw.'

I wondered what the earlier straws had been and why, if I was such a worry and nuisance, they had bothered to bring me in the first place.

Chapter Ten

I went on wondering all next day – and the next. This may sound as if I'm ultra-sensitive to atmosphere, but nothing could be further from the truth.

When Anna and I used to stay in debby house-parties up and down the country, I looked forward keenly to the Sunday-night drive back to London when, if we were on our own, I'd hear what had been going on during our weekend. While I observed what you might call the bone structure – dance on Friday, point-to-point on Saturday, dinner and cards at another house, tennis on Sunday – Anna would have clothed this dry skeleton with flesh, blood and vitality.

She'd have noticed who said what to whom, how everyone reacted; why X danced with Y all Friday night and refused to speak to him at the races. By observing, remembering, and deducing she could turn the dreariest company of old stodgers into suitable characters for a whodunit; partly, I think, because one's instinct to amuse and entertain someone condemned to a wheelchair leads people to say more than they mean to, and Anna is a marvellous listener; partly because, if you're obliged to live your life through other people, you take a passionate rather than a lukewarm interest in their affairs. Anna was never much of a reader, preferring her company live, and I always relied on her to unravel situations for me.

However, unobservant as I am, I couldn't help noticing that Rosie's attitude towards me was odd, to say the least. Odd and – though I'd have laughed at this a week ago – somehow menacing. It was difficult to pin down exactly why, but all the cosiness had disappeared from her manner. At the same time she made far more fuss than was necessary over my bout of mountain sickness.

She took my pulse and temperature in a thoroughly professional manner, fed me glucose tablets and revolting messes of herbs which she ordered the porters to prepare, and generally carried on until, in sheer self-defence, I was forced to say I felt all right, although I didn't.

That didn't stop her moving on, though. They fixed me up in a sort of litter slung between two ponies – they called it a 'palki' – and on we slogged for a good eight hours next day. I dozed in my swaying conveyance, sick and wretched but nonetheless thankful to be out of that abominable saddle.

They told me I'd soon be feeling better; that it took time to get used to the altitude; I mustn't worry; but I couldn't stop myself. In fact I lost count of how many days I travelled with my worry growing bigger all the time. I was astounded by Rosie's stamina, which seemed equal to the longest hours and roughest terrain. There was an air of purpose about her, an air of barely suppressed excitement.

What were she and Khurram up to? I lay awake at night in the stuffy igloo tent, listening to the low murmur of their voices by the camp fire. I was beginning to wish I'd paid more attention to Nick, and scrapped the expedition when he asked me to. I tried to remember everything I'd seen and heard: the hurry and secrecy of our departure; the embarrassed policeman, Ram Sirdar; Nick's warnings; the heavy-laden corn-fed ponies . . . Suddenly the answer struck me in a blinding flash: they must be on a smuggling raid.

Where had Nick told me the border was? At the Ceasefire line, a mere forty miles from Srinagar. I would have betted my shirt that we were headed for some point on that dotted line. I had no map, but in this maze of mountains and valleys that was probably no great loss: I shouldn't have been able to read it in any case.

This simple explanation of all that had puzzled me worked like a tonic. I relaxed and slipped into a dreamless sleep, to wake next morning with my headache gone, and only a slight breathlessness to warn me how high we still were.

Rosie was pulling on layer after layer of thin sweaters, like the skins of an onion.

'I feel better,' I announced. 'I'll be able to ride today.'

'That's good news, dear; excellent news. We're crossing a very high pass today, and the palki would have been awkward to handle on such a narrow path. You'd better have this to wear – here.' She handed me a clammy little bundle. 'We can't have you spoiling your complexion.'

'What on earth . . . ?'

'A face mask. Skiers sometimes wear them; no, not that way,' she said impatiently as I tried it on skullcap-style, 'it goes like this.'

After a brief and violent struggle she forced it on over her own features. It looked horrible. The pallid chamois leather stretched tight over her nose, flattening it as a bandit's stocking would do, and making mere obscene bumps of her mouth and chin. Two cavernous eye-holes and a couple of rudimentary nose-slits made her look utterly sub-human.

'How's that?' Her voice was muffled.

'Revolting. You look like the Lord of the Flies.'

'Take it, anyway. You'll be glad of it later on. And now hurry up and get dressed, can't you? There's a long way to go today.'

At sunset that afternoon we stood in the most beautiful valley I've ever seen, its steep sides clothed with clumps of yellow berberis and wild pink roses, carpeted with tiny wild geraniums whose sharp, distinctive pungency filled my nostrils as I thankfully peeled off the wet leather face-mask, humid with my own huff, while we waited for the baggage anaimals to follow us over the pass.

Khurram, Rosie and I had ridden ahead, desperate to get out of the knife-edged wind that screamed and whistled like a lost soul between the rocks of the high pass. Suddenly, as we rounded a corner, the sound of the wind was cut off as if a solid door had slammed in its face, and there before us stretched the valley, green and peaceful as the Promised Land.

We let our reins hang loose as the ponies scrambled the few hundred feet to the valley floor. The contrast with the screaming ice-edged desolation above us was almost unbelievable. Birds sang in the soft, warm stillness, flowers were thick underfoot, and a majestic river, lazily curling like a whiplash across the valley bottom, lapped its banks with the gurgles of a contented baby. Rosie slid from her saddle and I followed her. The rocks we sat on felt warm to the touch.

'What a heavenly place!'

She smiled. 'Well, we made it. I was a bit worried about you up there.'

'You hid your anxiety very well,' I said rather acidly. I'd thought my toes and fingers were going to drop off, but all Rosie had done was to grab my bridle and drag my pony along even faster.

'It was no good stopping to argue up there. The only thing was to get it over; don't you think it was worth it?'

'This is it, then?'

'Where my husband was killed, yes. And where I promised – '

'Promised what?'

'Never mind that,' said Rosie briskly, as if recollecting herself. 'Come and see the grave.'

She led me to a mound of velvety green turf a little way from the river. Khurram followed. There was no cross or cairn of any kind; just the green mound above the water.

We stood for a moment or two in silence, with Rosie staring at the grave in a kind of trance and me shifting uncomfortably from foot to foot, feeling thoroughly *de trop*. Birds sang in the soft golden evening, grasshoppers creaked, the river sucked and gurgled.

Then, without warning, Rosie lifted her voice and began to speak. Not in English, and not in the light, artificial, gushing tones I knew. Now her voice had a deep, powerful resonance that seemed to fill the narrow valley, bouncing from rock to rock and crag to crag, and the tongue she spoke bore no resemblance to any language I knew.

Like a full-throated Brunehilde swooping over the battlefield or Boadicea goading on her troops, the oration was unmistakably a battle-cry, and in each lull as she paused for breath, Khurram – standing beside and a little behind her – his hands stiffly outstretched, palm downward, towards the grave, made a low humming sound in his throat.

Up to that moment, I think, I'd still clung to the idea that Rosie was a silly old trout, fussy and tiresome at times, but essentially harmless. Now, in this remote valley, surrounded by the porters who came, one by one, to add their voices to the humming chorus, she was suddenly formidable. Fanaticism always scares me silly – it's so unreasonable – and the moment Rosie raised her voice in that wild incantation, dedicating herself or promising who knew what, I recognized her as a fanatic, and dangerous.

She stopped as suddenly as she had begun, and turned away from the grave. The porters filed past her and to each she handed a small, clinking leather bag; after collecting his bag, each man moved to his pack animal and began to unload it. I kept an eye on my bag, and saw it unloaded with Rosie's and placed in a separate heap, but the men made no attempt to pitch our tent or build a fire.

Rosie came over to where I was sitting. 'So we come to the parting of the ways.'

'Rosie,' I said, 'please tell me – are we in India now, or Pakistan?'

She looked sly. 'Aha, that's the question, isn't it? Kashmir's sort of got a foot in each, hasn't it?'

'I want to know if we've crossed the Ceasefire Line.'

'My dear girl, how could we have? It's a military zone. You can't just stroll across – you might be shot at.'

'Was your husband shot?' I asked, watching her carefully. 'Shot while – smuggling?'

Was it my imagination, or had that soft face hardened? The light was going fast, and in the shadows it was difficult to see her expression.

'The ponies are ready to go,' she said without answering my question. 'I must say good-bye to the porters.'

'Good-bye? How can we get home without them?'

Ponies and porters were indeed beginning to file away upstream.

'Rosie! Stop them! They've taken our tent.'

'We won't be needing it.' Rosie was definitely smiling now, enjoying my agitation.

'What d'you mean?'

'We're going home, dear, and you're coming with us.'

Fear overcame me. That incantation had been the prelude to something horrible, like a human sacrifice. I felt it in my bones. Was I cast as the victim? I ran frantically after the retreating porters, calling them to stop, but they took no notice.

'After her!' Rosie hissed like a snake, and I heard the patter of Khurram's feet behind me. I put on a spurt, hoping to dodge behind a rock in the gathering dark, but in a few bounds he was level with me.

'Don't,' I gasped, as he caught my arm and spun me round to face him. His eyes glittered in the half dark, and I expected to see the flash of a knife aimed at my throat. Instead, he flung a heavily-scented cloth over my head, and it was only when I'd taken in my next lungful that I realized it reeked of some throat-catching drug. I struggled feebly to throw it off, holding my breath, but Rosie must have come up behind. Iron hands clamped the hood over my head, and I passed out cold.

The worst thing – or one of the worst things, about coming round from an anaesthetic is not knowing how long you've been unconscious. Days might have passed, hours or just seconds: there's no way of telling.

I'd been dreaming of a river, lying in a punt on the Isis. Alec's punt, and Alec was beside me. We had poled beneath a thick curtain of willow overhanging the bank and there in the green gloom, concealed from other river-craft, we were exploring each other's bodies, pressed together on the damp, wobbly floor-boards. Alec's weight was squashing me against a thwart; my face was buried in his jersey and I could hardly breath. I put my hands to my face, trying to free nose and mouth, and found it wasn't a dream. I was in a boat, but it wasn't Alec's, and the soft, suffocating wool around my head wasn't his jersey. I lay very still. This was what Nick had warned me about. If only I had listened!

It was very dark: not a pinprick of a star or glimmer of moonlight. How long had I been out cold? Surely no ordinary night was as black as this? I could feel people near me, hear the gurgle and plop of water, but even this didn't sound quite right, more like water in a pipe than the open rush of a river.

I tried with small movements to free my mouth from the hood. It wasn't exactly a gag, just a scarf giving off fumes. Gently I pushed it aside, but with the first gulp of clean air I took, disaster struck.

'Help!' I said urgently. 'Look out, I'm going to be sick.'

'You would,' said Rosie's voice from close at hand. 'Get on with it, then.' She heaved my head and shoulders over the edge of the boat, and I hung there miserably, feeling like death and hating the soft chuckle I identified as Khurram's.

Rosie dumped me back in the bottom of the boat where I lay limply. A torch-beam flashed in my face and before it snapped off again I saw that the river was running through a tunnel of rock; the curved roof no more than four foot above the boat. That explained the drainpipe noise of the water, and the queer way my voice had echoed and boomed. Alph, the sacred river, I thought, and deep shudders went through me. I hate being shut in.

'I'll gag her again,' said Rosie. 'We don't want her rocking the boat.' I felt her hands groping for the scarf and squirmed away.

'Keep still, can't you?' she snarled, slapping me across the cheek. I jack-knifed into a kneeling position, catching her in the tummy by the feel of it. She gasped, and the boat rocked beautifully. I felt better.

'Be still,' warned Khurram. 'The boat is not strong . . . '

I'd make damn sure they went down with me. I butted my elbow into the yielding mass of Rosie's stomach again, delighted to hear her wheeze painfully. Then I crouched up the far end of the boat, as far away from her as I could get.

'You little fool, stop thrashing about. I'm only trying to cover your head. I don't want you stung to death the moment we land. Here, put on this *chaudra* yourself if you won't let me help you.'

I was puzzled, though I recognized the word *chaudra*. It was the silky, all-enveloping cloak Moslem women hid behind, black, usually, with a little grille of drawn threadwork across the eyes so that you could see out. I'd tried one on while shopping in New Delhi, thinking it would make an unusual evening coat, but rejected it on the grounds that it would ruin any hair-do.

'OK, I'll put it on,' I said quickly, to forestall any more knock-down-drag-outs with Rosie.

'Hurry. We'll be there any minute.'

She tossed the soft bundle across to me and I quickly shook it out and fitted it over my head.

The dark was becoming less intense. I could see the shape of the boat, an elongated cockleshell, and the cottage-loaf silhouette of Rosie at one end. The subterranean river was not so wide here, no more than forty foot from bank to bank, I reckoned, but there was no knowing how deep it might be, rushing headlong through the tunnel it had carved for itself, smoothing the rock walls that glistened in the dim light.

Far ahead a point of brightness showed me the end of the tunnel, and this grew bigger as we shot towards it. The boat gave a last swerve in the full flood of the current, and we popped out into the star-bright night.

The boat swung out of the mainstream and glided towards the shore, and a great hum rose and swelled from the ranks of women lining the bank. Splashing into the water, they seized the boat and pulled it up a slipway, nearly lifting the craft from the water in their enthusiasm to get us ashore.

I crouched in the bottom on the floorboards, glad of the anonymity of the *chaudra*, wondering what Rosie meant about getting stung. The bank swarmed with women, and only when Rosie stood up to step ashore did I realize how small they all were. Majestic in her stature, she towered over the reception committee; even Khurram, who was about my own height, a slimly built five foot three, looked tall among these people.

I had no time to wonder who they were and why there were no men in the crowd, before Rosie pointed to me and dozens of skinny brown hands reached out to pull me from the boat. They weren't rough – on the contrary I've never been pushed around so respectfully – but I just don't like being pushed at all. Short of slapping these hands aside, which seemed undiplomatic since every woman there was armed with a long, thin rapier, there

101

was precious little I could do to stop them, and at least the merciful *chaudra* hid my expression.

I was guided to a curtained litter and gently pushed inside on to cushions of the rarest silk, lavishly fringed in the Chinese manner and obviously old. I tried to free my hand from the *chaudra* in order to finger the material, but the litter gave a sudden lurch as it was hoisted from the ground and I collapsed in a heap.

Khurram's smooth pale face peered in through my curtains. 'The way is steep.'

I was too bewildered to do more than nod.

'Don't be afraid. Sleep now.' He bobbed out of sight.

Sleep, I thought. Some hope. I squirmed from side to side as we jolted along, sorry for myself, sorry for any baby being lugged about in a carry-cot, and sorry for whoever was carrying Rosie just ahead of me.

Either we went very slowly or the path was, indeed, extremely steep, but the journey seemed to take hours. My watch isn't self-winding and had stopped at nine o'clock; while I was still out cold. I now judged the time to be near sunrise, and twitched the curtains slightly apart to get a glimpse of where we were. What I got, though, was a nasty shock and lurch of the stomach, for I looked straight into an abyss; my bearers were clambering along the very edge. Switching my attention quickly to the other side, I saw a sheer rock face a few inches from my nose. No wonder the bearers were climbing so silently, with none of that merry chatter and jovial horse-play you hear in Indian bazaars. Going home was a serious business to these ladies; one slip meant curtains.

Once I knew about the drop beneath us, I couldn't not look. Somehow it seemed worse to go blind to one's death, and I continued to peer through the draperies.

So it was, at the end of a jolting, lurching eternity, that I saw the cluster of women who buzzed round Rosie's litter reach the end of the rock path, where the thin trail polished by bare feet until it looked like a snail's glassy track ended abruptly in front of a granite face. But like the children who followed the Pied Piper, they didn't check; they walked straight into a crack in the

102

rock and disappeared.

Rosie's bearers, glistening with sweat, followed, and mine brought up the rear. I twisted round quickly as an ominously solid *clunk* told me the rock door had swung shut behind us.

There was something terribly final about that sound; up till then I'd felt a faint hope that sooner or later I'd find my way out of this mountain nightmare and back to sanity. Now, with the shutting of that rock door, I began to despair. I lost interest in my curtain peephole, and lying back on the beautiful silk cushion, I dozed and woke and groaned, and dozed again.

Chapter Eleven

'*Cora lami meglum begum*,' intoned Rosie.

There was an assenting buzz from the assembled black-robed women in the long, low-ceilinged hall.

'They say: "Hail to the Queen Bee!" ' interpreted Vashti in a whisper.

'*Cora lami magalainika niz begum.*'

' " Hail to the new Queen!" '

'Me?'

'Yes, you. Keep still and quiet, please. This is danger moment, when workers look if they like new queen.'

Her advice was superfluous: I was far too scared to move a muscle. Hordes of the tiny women were crowding round the grille of the large cage in which I sat enthroned on an ornate, fan-backed, golden chair. They pushed and jostled one another, poked thin fingers through the bars as they tried to touch me, emitting all the time a droning hum that swelled and died again as the front-rankers were shoved aside by those behind, and they in turn by more and yet more little women. I couldn't tell if the noise they made signified pleasure or annoyance, and their expressions were equally hard to read: a mixture of possessiveness, curiosity, and indeterminate menace. I sat still and prayed that the bars wouldn't give under the pressure of all those tiny, questing fingers.

Vashti was whispering again, clinging like a leech to the outside of the cage to prevent herself being swept away in the tide of bodies.

'Three time – no, four time – workers kill new queen.'

'*Kill?*'

'Cover her round so she can't breathe, if they not like.'

Claustrophobia threatened, but I dared not give way to it.

We were in this long low hall with a domed roof, in which hundreds of candles and the combined body-heat of all the swarming women had raised the atmosphere to Turkish bath temperature. I sweated, even in the ludicrous gauzy robes they had swathed round me, partly from fear but mainly from heat. At the far end of the hall, resplendent in gold brocade, golden hair woven into a high bee-hive and crowned with glittering stones, the Queen Bee herself sat watching her subjects as they crowded round my cage, silently waiting to see if they'd smother me or accept me.

In my terror, it was difficult to remember that this golden figure had ever been Rosie – a soft touch, a figure of fun as far as I was concerned, a silly old trout. She'd used that masquerade to lure me here, but now I was in her kingdom she'd sloughed off the gushing voice, the frilly clothes, the fussy, feminine manner as completely as a snake casts its skin.

When I'd woken yesterday from the deep sleep of despair and exhaustion, a platoon of little women in black-and-yellow striped suits had hustled me along narrow passages, through small doors and domed cells, up steps and through trap-doors until we reached this hall, deserted then except for the massive golden figure on the throne.

'Rosie!' I'd exclaimed in relief, starting towards her. 'What's happened? Where are we? I've been so – '

'You are addressing the Queen Bee,' came a high, diamond-hard voice from the throne. 'There is no more Rosie. I am the Queen. Keep back from the Queen. *Keep back*!'

I went on walking forward. 'Don't be so silly. I know you're Rosie, so please explain just what – '

There was a sudden angry buzz from the women who'd brought me in, and I cried out as a red-hot needle of pain lanced my thigh. Clapping my hand to the wound, I stared round at my escort, horrified to see that thin black rapiers had sprung somehow into their hands, and one of these stuck quivering in my leg. It was needle-sharp, about eighteen inches long, and armed with a barb half-way up the blade. Only the tip had pricked me, but the pain was acute, and if the barb had engaged there would have been no way of withdrawing it. I raised my hands to go for the woman who had stuck this dart into me, then lowered them slowly as hostile eyes and thin blades menaced me on every side. Unarmed, I hadn't a chance.

'Bees have stings to defend their Queen, and in the hive all must obey her commands. Kneel to the Queen.'

There was nothing for it; I knelt, and silently the rapiers were returned to wherever they'd been hidden in the women's voluminous black clothes.

'The Queen speaks,' went on the golden voice. 'Akbar's Hive must hatch a new Queen, and you have been chosen to carry on the line of Akbar. Now the colony is weak and too many drones have hatched to eat our stores, it is time to re-queen with a different breed. But first the workers must accept the queen of my choice and approve the nuptial flight with the Drone. If the bees refuse to accept you, I cannot help you, but I give you Vashti, who speaks your language, to tell you what you must do.'

I knelt silently throughout this mumbo-jumbo, not liking the general drift of her meaning any more than I'd liked her sudden translation into Queen, mad woman and fanatic. Oh lord, I thought. This is planned. She hasn't suddenly gone off her rocker: she's been off it all the time, and I never noticed.

'But why me?' I croaked into the silence.

'The Queen has spoken.'

'But why – ?'

A tall, slender girl with a mass of dark-brown hair and narrow, tilted cat-eyes uncoiled herself from the steps of the Queen's throne and raised me to my feet. The guard closed round us both and she hustled me out of the hall.

'Not talk with Queen Bee,' she murmured. 'I Vashti. I tell you.'

Over the next twenty-four hours, in my domed cell with its gilded walls and floor scattered with big silken cushions, she did her best, and pulled out all the stops in her painfully limited mission-school vocabulary to make me understand the situation. I won't attempt to reproduce her fractured answers to my increasingly frenzied questions, but this is the gist of it.

I had stepped back four centuries – into a nightmare.

According to Vashti, we were in a high, hidden, almost freakishly fertile valley close to the border with Sinkiang – a valley isolated since the sixteenth century when the great Mogul Emperor Akbar, stumbling on the place during a hunting party, decided to use the controlled conditions it offered for one of the experiments he was fond of making.

I knew, from my researches into Oriental history in pursuit of the job with *Junk*, a certain amount about the Great Moguls, and could pick up the story-line when Vashti explained that Akbar had 'much trouble with boys'. His sons had been a great nuisance to their enlightened, unbigoted, rather attractive and modern-minded father, and were constantly quarrelling and rebelling. No wonder, said Vashti, that the Emperor Akbar preferred the company of his daughters, and favourite among these was little Hsien-Kwan, his daughter by a Tibetan princess.

It was Hsien-Kwan who suggested to the Emperor one day that if his empire were ruled by women, he wouldn't be troubled by quarrelsome sons, and Akbar, amused by the idea, asked if she'd like to have a go.

Evidently Hsien-Kwan had been as keen as mustard, and stretched out her hot little hand for the orb and sceptre.

'Hold your horses,' Akbar had said, or words to that effect. 'I'm not sure that I ought to hand the whole caboodle over to you. It stretches all the way from Kabul to Bengal these days, remember. I think you'd better cut your teeth on something smaller. Now, when I was hunting in Kashmir the other day, I saw a dear little valley which would just do you nicely. You shall have it, my child, and rule it with women, and keep men for your pleasure and as slaves. We'll call it the *Taratid Akbar* – Akbar's Hive – because it'll be like a beehive which, I understand, is entirely run by females.'

Hsien-Kwan had been overjoyed, and readily acquiesced to her father's request that, no matter how far afield she went for a Queen to succeed her, she'd always keep at least one male of Akbar's family in the valley, and thus continue the family line.

So for the next two summers, the peaceful valley had echoed with the shouts of thousands of workmen; builders, carpenters, goldsmiths and silversmiths, gardeners and plumbers, the ring of their hammers and clatter of their tools as they carved Akbar's Hive from the hillside. The river was dammed to create a lake, well stocked with fish ; fruit, vegetables, and crops were planted in terraced fields whose irrigation system reached up to the coniferous tree-line; animals were driven by the thousand over the high passes, and although only dozens survived the journey, the valley was furnished with a respectable breeding stock of cows, pigs, goats, sheep, chickens, horses, and donkeys. Hunting dogs were brought from the royal kennels, for the valley already harboured an abundance of game – deer, wild pig, pheasant and guinea fowl, besides the natural predators, the wolf, bear and snow tiger.

By the end of the third summer, work on the Hive was nearly complete, and Akbar in a fever of impatience to start the experiment. He issued a proclamation asking for volunteers to people the valley, and most of the big families subscribed a daughter – or a son they wanted out of the way. It was a quick and easy way of currying favour with the boss. By that time it was clear that the crops and fruit-trees they'd planted in the first summer had done exceptionally well, and the wine from the valley's own vines was of rare quality.

It was time for Akbar to leave, and he planted a plane tree with his own hands to commemorate the founding of his model valley. Then he presented Hsien-Kwan with a farewell present: a full size bee-skep made entirely of beaten gold, perfect in every detail. The combs inside were woven of filigree gold, and each tiny cell held a precious stone.

'Good-bye, little Queen Bee,' said the Emperor. 'I'm giving you these as honey for your first year, but after that you must make your own. The first snows will soon fall, so I'm going to shut up your hive. Good luck to you all.' Then he ordered his engineers to blow up the pass leading out of the valley. Gunpowder was a new toy in those days, and whether intentionally or by mistake no one knows, the explosion blocked the pass so thoroughly that it completely sealed the valley.

Vashti sighed and lapsed into silence when she saw I'd followed her explanation thus far.

'*No* way out?' I prompted.

'Only for Queen. Queen fly out.'

'And Khurram?'

To my surprise, a slow blush spread up Vashti's neck until it reached her forehead. She was attractive in a sloe-eyed, doe-eyed, odalisque fashion, with a long neck and very sloping shoulders that accentuated the Burne-Jones effect.

'Queen carry Khurram out,' she said resentfully.

Was she jealous, then, of Rosie? Did she fancy her fancy-boy? I shoved this minor mystery to the back of my mind and concentrated on matters nearer home.

'Go on about the valley. Did Akbar's experiment work?'

It had, it appeared. Hsien-Kwan and her hive had prospered. They kept a few men within the castle walls as pets and for breeding purposes; the rest were simply eunuchs who provided the community's muscle-power. 'Not true men,' as Vashti delicately phrased it. When Hsien-Kwan grew old and felt she might be losing her grip, she had 're-queened' – appointed a successor and mated her with the current 'Drone', the sole male of Akbar's blood allowed to retain his manhood, as their founder had stipulated. Then, accompanied by a posse of favourite ladies, Hsien-Kwan had retired from the cares of administration, and ended her life in ease and luxury in a separate wing of the great hive.

Over the years, this practice had become *de rigueur*, with Queens starting to look around for a successor soon after they reached the menopause. Once the new Queen had been selected, it was necessary to ensure that she was fertile, and this, in Vashti's case, had proved the stumbling block. She came of a poor Punjabi family, and it sounded to me as if her parents had simply sold her to Rosie for a lump sum, without asking too many questions about why Rosie wanted her.

She, for her part, was glad enough to get away from the squalor of her home, charmed with the beauty and grandeur of her new surroundings, and delighted at the prospect of ruling this tiny kingdom. Her introduction to the worker bees had gone smoothly, and all seemed set fair until month after month went by and still she failed to conceive by the Drone.

'I must drink too much wine, smoke too much poppy,' she complained. 'They not good for making baby.'

After two unsatisfactory years, Rosie had evidently become impatient and given up Vashti as a bad job. She made more forays into the outside world, bringing back new white slaves: German, French, Nepalese, and Moroccan – on four successive trips, but then the trouble started. The workers, who had so readily accepted Vashti, were upset by this sudden influx of new blood, and savagely set upon each of the prospective new Queens, suffocating her before she could so much as meet the Drone.

Rosie had given her workers time to cool off before she made another attempt, and this time I was the fish she'd caught in her net.

'If workers see you like Vashti, they like you,' the girl explained disingenuously.

'I like Vashti *very* much.'

'Good; then they take you in hive, make you Queen, and Vashti will tell you what to do.'

Clearly she fancied herself as a sort of *eminence grise* behind me, and I had no objections. I didn't intend to stay long enough to learn how to rule such temperamental subjects.

'Why d'you keep talking about the *workers*?' I asked. 'Isn't everyone a worker?'

She shook her long glossy plaits. 'First child, then nurse, then mother. No work for these. No work for drones. Workers feed, make house clean, make pretty clothes, store food for winter months. Workers all old women, carry stings, guard hive, very fierce.'

It sounded like life on hire-purchase – fun first, work later. I knew all about the workers' secret weapons.

'One of them stung me.' I showed her the stab-mark in my thigh. She made little cooing noises of sympathy, and fetched a dressing which looked very much like a mat of cobwebs, which she placed tenderly over the wound.

'Queen Bee's guards have very special, very bad sting.'

I shivered. 'What if the workers don't like me?'

'Vashti look after you,' she said reassuringly. She wouldn't let them suffocate me. I hoped she knew what she was talking about.

By the next afternoon, though, I was so bored of my own company that I even welcomed the sight of Khurram, who sauntered into my chamber with a lordly air, as if he owned the place, followed by one of the ugliest old men I've ever set eyes on.

He must once have been strong, for his shoulders were so broad in proportion to his height that he appeared almost square, but a hollow square rather than a solid one, for he was extremely thin, and his long brown robe hung on him as if on a coat-hanger. Sinewy wrists protruded from his wide sleeves, and in his wrinkled, big-knuckled hands he carried a small ivory box, holding it in a rather ceremonious manner like a child miming 'We three kings of Orient are.' Apart from this, though, his appearance was anything but kingly; he had a long, sad face with eyes like dull brown pebbles, and his mouth hung slackly open so that a thin stream of dribble ran into his matted beard.

This scarecrow placed the ivory box on a low table, and bowed to me, touching his forehead with the backs of his joined hands. He stood behind Khurram, gazing at him in obvious admiration, and I was reminded of an old dog who has lost his looks trying to charm his master into some show of affection.

Khurram was indeed worth gazing at. My own eyes bugged as I took in the details of his attire. Gone were the seedy striped shirt and pyjama trousers I'd always seen him wearing; instead, he sported a huge, floppy turban shaped like an outsize Chelsea bun, but instead of having currants between the folds, it had jewels. The fringed end of his turban stuck skittishly out at the back of his head and dangled down his neck. Large pearls hung like blood-gorged ticks from the lobes of his ears, which drooped with the weight. His knee-length scarlet robe was loosely belted with an embroidered sash, this being pinned with another huge emerald, worn as casually as a safety-pin. Soft leather boots with curly toes and an extremely fancy sleeveless surcoat, glittering with gold thread, completed his odd but magnificent rig.

111

He laughed at my surprise, flashing white teeth beneath the thin little moustache. 'Good-day, new Queen,' he said politely. 'You like my fine clothes, eh? Men have finer clothes than ladies in Akbar's Hive.'

'I'm not the new Queen yet. I don't think I want to be. Oh, Khurram, I'm so frightened. Why did you bring me to this terrible place? Why didn't you warn me?'

He shook his head. 'Would you have listened to me, a poor shopkeeper, when you wouldn't listen to the warnings of Mr Nicholas Jameson? No, Charl Begum; I told my mother it was madness to try to capture an English girl for her hive, because the English have a nose for danger and tell too many people where they are going. But she said you were foolish and would suspect nothing, so I dared not meddle with her plans.'

'*Your mother*? Rosie's your *mother*?'

'Yes, I am son of Queen Bee. That surprised you, eh?'

'But – but how . . . ?'

He subsided gracefully cross-legged on one of the large silk cushions with which my room was well provided, and waved to me to do the same. 'Listen to my story, Charl Begum, and you will understand. My father was Hakim Shah, second son of the old Queen Bee who ruled this kingdom before I was born. When more than one boy of Akbar's family grows to be a man, who might fight his brother, the Drone, the Queen gives him much poppy to drink, then she flies with him out of the valley and leaves him in the snow. But my father Hakim Shah was a strong man, and did not die as all others have done. When his senses returned he had wandered far from the valley. Everything was strange to him. The men he met were strange, and he suffered much.'

No wonder, I thought, listening fascinated to this recital. Pitchforked out of the sixteenth century into the twentieth, no wonder he felt lost.

'Hakim Shah joined with a band of men in the mountains. Wild men, who had robbed or killed and lost their homes. Hakim Shah became their leader. When there was fighting at the time of Partition, they came down from the hills to the valley of Srinagar. They seized food and gold, cattle and women. In this way, they took my mother – '

'Ah. Tell me about her. What was she doing in Kashmir?'

He sighed at the interruption, but back-tracked patiently enough.

'My mother was then nurse and teacher – '

'Governess?'

'Yes; to the children of a rajah at the court of Hari Singh, ruler of Kashmir. Her master told her that after Partition she must go to England; there would be no more work for an English lady, and his servants would not wait on her. She was not pleased by having to go to the cold, hard work of England, with no money, no servants, no jewels or pretty clothes. She was happy when Hakim Shah carried her away and set fire to her master's compound. She married Hakim Shah at his camp, and there was much feasting. But while they were feasting, came the soldiers from India.'

He spat disgustingly on the thick rug in front of me, and I drew back my feet like lightning. He went on: 'For many months, while Indian soldiers hunted him, my father roamed the mountains. For when he was put outside the valley, Hakim Shah remembered a little, and now he was chased by soldiers with guns, he wished to hide in the valley where they could not find him. But he did not know the way in.'

Now I found that the picture of a younger, slimmer Rosie goat-footing around the mountains with her brigand chief sprang to mind quite readily.

'At last, in the month of June, they came over the high pass and into the Valley of Flowers. My father could feel that his home was near, and he built a little boat to sail down the river. The valley was pulling him to come. But when he floated through the tunnel under the mountains and saw his home, the Queen Bee – his own mother – trapped him and stung him to death.'

'Why didn't she – er – sting you and your mother too?'

'I was not yet born,' he said reprovingly, 'and in my mother the old Queen saw a chance to re-Queen her hive without leaving the valley. She gave her the rubies which now my mother sends to you.'

With a theatrical wave, he commanded the old man, whom he addressed as Gul Beg, to place the ivory box he was still clutching into my hands, and with a mixture of reluctance and curiosity I lifted the carved lid. I didn't want presents from that deceitful old cow, but all the same, rubies . . .

I blinked and the box slipped from my nerveless hand as I saw the flashing red fire inside it. I couldn't believe such rubies were real. It was a collar – too short and too heavy to be called a necklace – of the red stones, graded from jewels the size of a little finger-nail at the back to ones as big as a robin's egg in front near the heavy gold clasp.

My heart began to thump heavily. I forgot where I was, and my precarious situation. Jewel fever hit me like the blast of hot air from an oven door and I felt the blood rush to my face as, with trembling fingers, I lifted the priceless handful of stones from its box and held them up to the light.

I'm one of those people who turn weak with helpless cupidity at the sight of the Crown Jewels; I ache and shake with longing outside Cartiers, and if someone thrust a pickaxe into my hand as I stood there, I couldn't trust myself not to put it through the plate-glass.

I can't explain this magnetism jewels have for me. I'm not particularly vain – heavens knows I've nothing to be vain about – and I don't imagine that wearing jewels adds much to feminine charms; just look at the revolting rich old toads who own most of the world's best rocks. Wearing them isn't really the point. It's the *having*, the possession, the getting out and gloating over, the look and feel of precious stones that sends me into a frenzy. I knew without a doubt that this ruby collar was real, was priceless, and I wanted it more than anything on earth, more even than my freedom.

Khurram's voice seemed to reach me from a great distance. 'When you take this jewel, you agree to become the new Queen. It is the – ' he paused, searching for a word – 'the symbol of hatching a new Queen. When you are mated with the Drone and start your work, you will be given the bracelet which matches this, and which now the Queen, my mother, wears.'

It is at this point that my instinct is to shy away from the

114

truth, to pretend that what followed was forced upon me because I was a prisoner, and so absolve myself of responsibility. But the truth was that that was the moment when I stopped fighting and began to cooperate, because I wanted that collar and the bracelet that went with it.

'I understand,' I said. The effort of keeping my voice cool and steady was considerable. I put out my hand and took the jewels.

He rose in a smooth, graceful movement, and snapped his fingers for old Gul Beg to follow him. 'Good,' he said. 'Then tonight the Queen's Guards will fetch you to the ceremony of meeting the workers. After that, you will sleep with the Drone.'

'Wh – what's he like?' I asked nervously. Vashti had made him sound drunk and incapable; only by keeping my mind firmly on the rubies could I face the thought of the evening's revelry.

Khurram laughed, showing pointed teeth like fangs. 'You will see in a few hours.'

'No, *please* tell me.'

For an answer he merely tapped his forehead and sauntered out, leaving me cold with fright, clutching the ruby collar whose stones trickled through my fingers like drops of blood, still half convinced that this was a nightmare from which I should soon wake.

Chapter Twelve

'It is good that you are peaceful,' said Vashti, tugging an ivory comb through my still-damp hair, but in the mirror I saw her smile as I winced.

'If you mean calm, you could hardly be more wrong. I'm simply terrified and I wish you'd stop messing about with these ridiculous clothes.'

I looked with disgust at what the well-dressed bride was wearing in Kashmir this year. I'd submitted to the bath, the hair-wash, the oils and lotions that made me feel like a heavily-dressed lettuce, but the clothes that Vashti had chosen from a chest borne totteringly into the chamber by old Gul Beg were really the outside of enough. A *choli*, or short-sleeved blouse cut off at rib-cage level, of embroidered muslin, left my nipples clearly visible, and so, by virtue of being uncovered, was my navel. I twitched the long shawl of crunchy gold lace which hid most of my hair forward over my shoulders, but the result was disappointing. From the waist down, yards and yards of shimmering orange silk hid most of my feminine charms, but a single tug or, indeed, a misplaced foot on the hem would spell disaster.

'It feels so insecure,' I complained. 'Chilly and insecure.'

Actually the chill came from inside me, because I'd already noticed that the whole castle was amazingly warm, with fires and candles in every room, including the long-drop lavatory cell. The thick walls and windows covered with a kind of semi-transparent vellum which were opened only at midday to catch the noon heat and rigorously closed an hour later, kept the temperature high, and one could have promenaded in a bikini without discomfort.

Vashti paused in her labours. 'Workers must look well at new Queen,' she said seriously. 'All her life they keep her safe, fed, happy, for from her the hive is continued. They must see her hatch before they will work for her.'

It was evening, and I'd been walled up in that small room without a break since Khurram's visit. I'd dozed a bit, watched the sun creep across the slit of window, tried not to think, but longed for a book, pencil and paper, needle and thread, cards – anything to take my mind off the grisly prospect ahead. At first I'd felt claustrophobic and panicky; this had faded into resignation, and then, as the hours passed, into ever-increasing boredom.

Meals were placed in front of me by silent, soft-footed little women clad in bright quilted pyjama suits. I'd taken these to be workers, but Vashti told me they were just young nursemaids and servants, who waited on the ladies of the brood chamber and attended solely to their comfort. In time they would graduate to the status of brood chamber ladies, and ultimately become workers with the freedom to go in and out of the hive until they died of overwork. It was an inflexible hierarchy.

The food they brought me was plain but rather delicious; fish, rice, little buttery wheat-cakes shaped like thin rissoles, luscious ripe mulberries and, brightest spot of all, a silver goblet of really excellent red wine, heavy and fruity.

'When workers come round you, do not scream or fight,' advised Vashti. 'Be quiet and peaceful or they will smell your fear and attack you.'

'*Smell*?' I said in alarm. 'But I can't possibly prevent myself smelling frightened if I *am* frightened. I tell you, I'm scared stiff.'

Vashti thought deeply for a few moments, then conferred with Gul Beg. He went away and returned with a flagon from which he poured me a beaker of the rich red wine. I downed it gratefully.

'Now you will not be afraid,' said Vashti. For some reason, I was glad to observe, she was anxious that the ceremony should go smoothly. I guessed that Rosie had offered her some bribe to ensure that the new Queen was accepted, and this, I later discovered, was the case; the bribe being simply that of Vashti's own life. The hive could not afford to support useless mouths, and it would be ten years before Vashti could attain the status of a worker. Therefore my survival was quite literally a matter of life or death to her.

Then Gul Beg produced a small paper poke of silvery-grey powder, and Vashti, smiling her approval, added a couple of pinches to my second glass of wine. As I drank it, the door opened and in marched the Queen's black-robed Guard, their faces masked under Balaclava-type helmets, their stings waving menacingly in their hands.

'Oh, no!' I tried to protest, but my tongue felt thick, and I scraped it hard against my teeth without feeling any pain. A curious weakness was attacking my legs, and little prickles ran over my skin and out to my toes and fingers.

The guards gripped me by the elbows and surrounded me in close formation as we marched along a honeycomb of narrow passages, through doors and store-chambers, up flights of steps and down them, until I was completely bewildered as to my direction. At length we came to the long, low hall lit with many flaring torches where I'd last confronted the Queen Bee, and here my guard halted. I stumbled, and was quickly yanked upright again. My body felt so heavy and strange and my head so woolly and light that I couldn't take anything seriously, and only the sight of the waving rapiers stopped me dissolving into helpless giggles, as the women who were guiding me suddenly bundled me into a barred metal cage, and slammed the door.

'Sit on the throne. Get up. Sit on throne in middle,' hissed Vashti, outside the cage, and slowly the message got through to my dull brain. Cross-legged in the ornate chair, I was as far as possible from the bars of the cage. So long as I sat perfectly still, the stings of the workers couldn't reach me.

Apart from a pronounced cast in the left eye and a mouth that drooped vacantly open, displaying red-stained, uneven teeth, the young man seated on a small, fan-backed, turquoise throne beside Rosie at the far end of the hall, might fairly have been called a dish.

His clothes – from turban to jewel-studded boots – were

splendid enough to make Khurram look like a charity child. He was sturdily built, with a breadth of shoulder and length of leg unusual in this pigmy race, and his complexion was pale, almost European in tint. I saw him first in profile, and reflected muzzily that his heavily, handsome features might well have decorated a Hapsburg coin; then he turned full face, and his eyes gave the game away. They were flat and empty, totally without expression or curiosity, and as they followed the progress of my guard, pushing me in the wheeled cage twoards him, no flicker of intelligence showed in them.

The hall was swarming with the midget women, all dressed alike in rough-textured, almost furry suits banded in black, brown and yellow, their heads covered by black hoods with latticed eyeholes, like abbreviated versions of the *chaudra*; a moving sea of yellow and brown that surged forward to engulf my cage. The buzz of talk had risen to an excited whining hum, and I had the sensation of being trapped in a colony of enormous bees, an impression heightened by the claustrophobically low ceiling, only a few inches above my head as I sat, stiff with fright, in the raised cage.

The noise was almost unbearable; like a power-saw it rose and fell on peculiarly irritating notes, and dinned at my drug-thickened hearing until I thought my head would burst.

Far worse than the noise, though, were the small hands that strained at the bars, the thin black stings which probed towards me. I prayed that whoever built this cage had made a strong job of it. It looked solid enough, but who knew what the relentless pressure of thousands of bodies would do to it?

I could see no order or pattern in the movement of the bee-women as they swarmed against the bars, but Vashti told me later that they were, in fact, taking turns to view me in a thoroughly well-disciplined manner; when each worker had looked, tried her damnedest to touch me, and failed, she would move aside to let someone else try her luck.

Rosie, swathed in yellow silk on her fan-backed throne, looked enormous among these swarming midgets and so, for about the first time in my life, did I. When at last the crowd thinned from in front of my cage and I could look across at her and the young man planted like a puppet beside her, she began to harangue her subjects, using a sibilant speech I was sure I could never learn, her voice rising and falling in a buzz that was somehow soothing, while the tiny women crouched round her, listening quietly apart from an occasional hum of agreement.

'They like you; we are safe,' whispered Vashti jubilantly.

I've heard that extreme anger or extreme fear can last no more than seven minutes; try to keep it up longer than that, and you pass out from emotional strain. I don't know how long I sat in that cage before my extreme fear receded, but it was probably less than ten minutes.

Then I began to notice the discomfort and boredom of my lonely perch. I shifted from one buttock to the other, eased my back, and leaned my head against a knobbly throne, wondering impatiently what was going to happen next and whether a yawn would be interpreted as contempt of court. I'd had enough of Stage One.

Contemplating Stage Two, I gazed assessingly at the Drone, who sat staring straight ahead, his hands hanging loosely from the wrist, so that his heavy gold bracelet looked in danger of slipping off. I wondered if he were a half-wit, a drunkard, as Vashti had implied, or simply high on hash. Perhaps higher than me, or at a different stage. I'd never taken the stuff before, and didn't know how I reacted to it, but in any case it looked as if Miss World herself would be unable to stimulate him into creative activity in bed. Maybe sight-seeing and speeches were all that was scheduled for tonight.

As usual, I was wrong. When at last Rosie stopped her oration, the workers clustered round my cage again, and propelled it out of the assembly hall. There the Queen's Guard took over once more, chasing the other women away with drawn swords. They opened the cage and helped me stagger out on numb legs, my draperies dragging behind me as I was frog-marched into a smaller room hung with tapestries and furnished with an enormous canopied four-poster. My last hope that this was all a bad dream vanished; and I balked in the doorway like a steer reluctant to enter the slaughter-house.

'Be good or we shall both suffer,' muttered Vashti grimly,

yanking me forward as the guards slammed the heavy door.

'Please . . .' I tried to brace my legs, but they wouldn't obey me. Vashti and the guards dragged me across the room and dumped me on the bed, bundling covers over me and pulling the curtains so that I was hemmed in by four walls of rustling silk.

In my mind, I gave an eel-like twist and slipped away into the firelit shadows, back down the passage, through the hall, out of the hive, down the mountain . . . but only in my mind. My body was as heavy and helpless as a lump of lead.

Light glimmered through the curtains as hands pulled them back a little: the Drone, naked except for a variety of necklaces, appeared in the aperture with a suddenness that suggested a strong shove from behind. The curtains flapped shut again.

Back there in the hall, I'd doubted if he'd be up to it; I needn't have worried. His wide black eyes glittered above me in the dim light, then focused so that I could see the message getting through to the dull brain: there's a girl in my bed. He gave a loud grunt that sounded like a mixture of pleasure and surprise, and grabbing hold of me he waded in.

He was as single-minded and violent as an animal, and I remember thinking, at least this can't last long. Then the terror and hash combined to black out my mind, and all I seemed to hear was a faraway echo of Nick's voice saying: 'You stupid, pig-headed little bitch, you deserve everything that's coming to you.'

I wondered, if he knew where I was, if he'd be pleased.

Chapter Thirteen

When I was in my earnest teens, hot with religious fervour (it lasted all of two terms), I used to worry, as I recited the Lord's Prayer, because no one ever seemed to trespass against me enough to be worth forgiving, while my trespasses against others were, I knew well, rather thick on the Recording Angel's slate. But when I woke next morning in the ornate four-poster I knew that this was a worry that need never bother me again: forgiving Rosie, Vashti, and the rest of them for this one mighty trespass against my person would last me through Matins for the rest of my natural.

I felt battered: raw on cheeks and chin where that randy sex-fiend's beard had scraped me, bruised in the breasts, sandpaper-dry in the mouth, and stiff in the crutch. There was very little left of the gauzy shift they'd put me to bed in: the last thing I wanted to do was get up.

The hive seemed quiet as I lay and brooded on my wrongs, but when Vashti pattered in, all soft-soap and sympathy, with an armful of fresh clothes, the buzz of activity that followed her through the open door made me realize it was simply the room's efficient sound-proofing that had made everything seem so still.

'All good? Very good? Nice sleep?'

'All very bad,' I said emphatically. 'Very, very bad. I feel very ill. I'm staying in bed.'

She shook her head warningly and pointed to the ceiling. Puzzled, I followed her glance. 'Queen Bee watching; say no good new Queen. Better get up now, look happy.' She hurried out of the room.

'Watching? You mean . . . ?' Then I saw only too clearly what she meant. The canopy that roofed the four-poster had a panel missing, and the sunlight now flooding the room as Vashti pulled back the curtains showed a matching skylight in the ceiling directly above it. Anyone looking down through the skylight could see me in the great bed, had probably watched the whole candle-lit performance last night . . .

It was like finding yourself the fall-guy in a Candid Camera show. I sprang out of bed in a hurry and began pulling on the clothes Vashti had laid out for me.

She'd chosen a Chinese-looking outfit – tunic and pants of quilted yellow silk, fur boots, and a sleeveless leather surcoat with the fur on the inside and gay borders of flowers tangling up the front edges to take the chill off the morning air. Heavy silk bloomers, hardly chic but smelling divinely of cedarwood, were the ultimate luxury to slide over a sore behind.

I dressed, and was looking for a mirror to admire the effect when Vashti returned, and hissed her disapproval.

'Wrong way for trousers; they turn round.'

'I've tried the other way, but it leaves a great bulge of loose material.'

'No, no, that where baby grow.' She rearranged my clothes with little pats and snatches, like a groom checking a hunter's tack. Satisfied at last, she led me out of the room and up a steep flight of steps.

'You meet ladies and babies, then eat,' she promised, and my stomach remembered suddenly that it hadn't eaten since the previous morning, and growled in protest. We entered a room flooded with sunlight and full of noise and movement.

No one who hasn't seen twenty children between nought and five sitting on the floor eating rice and curry with their fingers can make even a rough guess at the amount of nutritional debris they'll cause, or the truly revolting sound they'll make. I've heard sickened fathers declare that no child under six should be allowed to eat a soft-boiled egg for breakfast; any one of this opinion would certainly extend the ban to include bare-handed tots with curry.

A sibilant slurping and grunting filled the air, like the sound of swill-fed pigs at the trough, punctuated by sudden sharp squeals and commotions as one child after another finished its own bowl of slop and turned to lay claim to its neighbour's, or to scoop handfuls of nourishing fall-out from the no-man's land of the floor.

A group of husky, dusky wenches dressed in brilliant silks were chattering softly on a window-seat well stacked with cushions, but as the children finished eating, they were called by their mothers. It was like a flock of ewes bleating to their lambs.

'Jai Khan!'

'Azim, Azim!'

'Nadira!'

An army of little maids, girls between ten and fifteen dressed in quilted cotton trouser-suits, hurried in to sweep up the mess, and Vashti and I moved out of their way to stand by another window. By my side was a high-barred, old-fashioned cot where a solitary small girl sat sucking her thumb. A mop of silky black hair hung forward, hiding most of her face, but it couldn't conceal the ivory pallor of her skin. She was very thin, with the vertebrae of her spine showing knobbles through the turquoise cotton shift she wore. I guessed she was two or three years old. Knees drawn up to chin, elbows on knees, she sat motionless, like a small, emaciated Buddha, staring fixedly at the panorama beneath the window.

I followed her gaze. The castle, hive, stronghold – whatever it was – perched on a jutting ledge of rock. Behind it, as I'd seen from my own cell on the first day, a sheer wall of cliff rose to the sky. But here the view gave no hint of the frowning claustrophobic rock behind.

Instead, a smiling valley unrolled like a patchwork quilt before me. It was appendix-shaped, steep-sided, with a wide, flat bottom. Snow-capped peaks formed a jagged fence all round it. Below these peaks, trees and shrubby vegetation made an irregular but distinct band of blackish-green, and below this tree-line, the slopes flattened into a broad sweep of evidently fertile cultivated plain. Here at the bottom lay the heart of the valley: multi-coloured tiny fields, each bordered with a white thread of irrigation channel.

Cutting a silver swathe, like a snail's trail across the patchwork, a river meandered in lazy curves towards the distant hills.

The thin air and bright, unshadowed sun gave the scene a definition I'd never experienced before – every outline sharp, with practically no blurring of distance. I really could see for miles.

My fingers itched for pen and ink. Landscape is my first love, or was before I had to start grinding away at design for my bread and butter, and here was what I'd always dreamed of finding – a man-made landscape untouched by the ugly contrivances of the twentieth century. No wire, telegraph poles, pylons, road daubed with yellow paint. No cars, buses, bicycles, tractors . . .

I turned to Vashti in sudden excitement. 'I must paint this view. I simply must. Can you get me pencils, paint, ink, paper, canvas – any of them would do. There must be something of the sort in this castle. What do they use to write with?'

She looked rather taken aback. 'I ask the Queen. There is a painter, yes, who makes pictures of all the ladies when they ask, but not of this.' She waved vaguely at the view. 'You like to paint?'

I thought furiously. I couldn't explain to her the excitement I felt bubbling up inside me; the agonizing fear that it was too much for me, that I'd never capture it. I had a small sketch-book and an absolutely miniscule L'Escherte-Barbe paintbox, last birthday's present from Anna. I used these as other people use a camera, but I knew I was more than half-way through the sketch-book already.

'Yes, but I've got practically nothing to paint with, and I'll be miserable until I've found something.'

An expression of alarm flitted over her pointed, cat-like face. 'Queen say you must be happy.'

Good: a lever. 'Then find me some paints,' I commanded. 'And I'd like to meet this portrait painter you spoke of.'

'I ask the Queen.'

Behind us the sucking and slobbering noises were dying out. Most of the children dozed, sprawled on their mothers' laps. I glanced back at the little girl in the cot, so twig-like and unchildishly still.

'Who's she? Doesn't she get any food?'

With a vicious glee, Vashti leaned over the back of the cot and tweaked a lock of the child's black hair. In a flash the little creature sprang up and round, clawing at Vashti through the bars, but her tormentor, giggling, had jumped out of reach. I was appalled, as much by the expression of naked hate on the child's face as by the deliberate cruelty.

'Stop it!' I said sharply. 'Leave her alone.'

Reluctantly Vashti abandoned the face-pulling with which she was goading the child into a frenzy of rage. 'That Jahanara,' she said sulkily, 'She no good; can't hear, won't eat, fight other children. Queen say she make her Queen Bee one day, but I think she die soon.'

Her tone was contemptuous, and I felt like slapping her and then taking the poor little girl in my own arms to hug until she smiled – two most uncharacteristic impulses. I stuffed my hands in the pockets of my suit, obscurely shocked by the strength of my feelings.

'Can't hear?' I said. 'How d'you know she can't hear?'

For answer, Vashti ducked behind the solid side of the cot, crept round until she was once more behind the child, and clapped her hands loudly over her head. The noise was enough to produce a sudden hush among the other children, but Jahanara didn't even turn towards the sound. Clearly something was very wrong with her hearing.

'But who is she?' I asked again. 'Who's her mother?'

Jahanara was, it appeared, of royal blood, daughter of the Drone by a Chinese mother who had died at her birth. She was three years old, unable or unwilling to speak, wild as an animal and alternately teased and ignored by the rest of the nursery party. The Queen had decreed that she should be cleaned and dressed and fed as befitted her station, so she was confined to her cot and treated very much as a dangerous beast, with food handed to her at arm's length. When it became necessary to clean her cot, she was prodded into a sort of playpen that Vashti showed me, and looking more closely at her blue shift, I saw that that, too, was badly in need of a wash.

Revolted by such human misery, I was determined to have a stab at helping poor Jahanara, but when I said as much to

Vashti, she covered her mouth with her hand and burst into helpless giggles. My new dislike of her grew.

We left the lonely, pathetic figure in the cot, and made the rounds of the other children, whose rosy-brown faces and shiny eyes were as alike as those of a litter of puppies.

Their shyly-smiling mothers, beautifully dressed and dripping with jewels, greeted me with friendly little bobs of the head and gestures from their soft, boneless hands, so different from the horny claws of the workers that had tried to reach me last night. It was hard to believe that these gentle, feminine creatures would turn into the restless, ever-active older women once their child-bearing and rearing stint was over. But the mothers were at least prepared to be friendly to the new girl, I saw with relief; though because of the language barrier we couldn't exchange a word.

I didn't see Jahanara again that day.

After a guided tour of the brood chamber, whose cosy little rooms, concealed doors behind tapestry curtains, twisty passages and unexpected flights of stairs appealed to the child in me who was still perpetually on the look-out for a good place to play hide-and-seek, I joined the other ladies for an al fresco lunch in a walled garden. We ate roast mutton and wheat-cakes, goat's cheese and tiny, sweet grapes, washing them down with more of the sweet, strong wine that had contributed to my downfall last night.

When I reminded Vashti about my paints, she took me to meet Zaid Khalifa, a bird-like old man with a skull-cap and neatly forked white beard, who worked in a cluttered studio at the very top of the castle. The resinous smell of glue and turpentine told me we had come to the right place before Vashti even opened the door, and to my delight the gentle, courtly miniaturist proved as helpful as he was well-equipped. Three little maids had to be summoned to carry the swag pressed on me by Zaid Khalifa, and I spread it all out in my cell and gloated over the rolls of vellum and pots of paint, bottles of ink and sheaves of fine brushes, sticks of charcoal and little jars containing varnish, fixative, gold leaf, and other painting aids of Zaid's own manufacture.

'Now you are happy,' said Vashti proprietorially, and I couldn't bring myself to deny it. The peace and beauty of the valley seemed to be spreading right through me; I couldn't remember when I'd last felt so relaxed and contented as here with the sun streaming through the window, flowers and fountains outside, warm and comfortable and well-fed, the terror of the night behind me and all I needed to paint with besides all the time to paint in. Obviously this mood was showing in my face, but I felt obscurely that I mustn't give in. How easy it would be to accept this fate, to eat lotus for ever in this remote corner of Paradise. Forget my job, and dirty, noisy, scarifying London; and Alan, who was never satisfied. Forget him, and the flat, and crippled Anna. Forget Nick . . . that, oddly enough, was what stuck in my throat. I disliked and distrusted him. More than that, I thought, screwing up my anger, I despised and, yes, hated him. But I couldn't, to my annoyance, forget him.

Chapter Fourteen

It's extraordinary how quickly one establishes and accepts a routine, no matter how peculiar the circumstances. When I'd spent a month in 'Akbar's Hive', I felt it had no secrets from me. I was beginning to think and behave like the valley people, to adopt their ways as protective colouring. It was as if I'd lived there half my life.

Some things took a bit of getting used to, of course. Chief among these was the misery of the men, the drones, who were segregated from the girls at the age of ten, and confined for the rest of their breeding life in a compound very much smaller than the quarters allotted to the brood-chamber ladies, surrounded by a high wall. Any boy who didn't measure up to the Queen Bee's exacting standards of physique was ruthlessly castrated; he, at least, was thereafter free to be apprenticed as a craftsman or to work in the woods or fields. On the broad shoulders of these eunuchs rested most of the agricultural work of the valley, supervised by the ever-active workers.

I've never liked seeing animals in cages – the brooding presence of Guy the Gorilla in solitary confinement used to spoil all the fun of the London Zoo monkey-house for me – so I avoided going past the gates of the drones' compound, from which sad brown eyes yearned after me and the rest of the bustling women, like kennelled spaniels pleading for walkies.

'They are not to be trusted,' explained the Queen to me, when I dared to ask why they weren't allowed more freedom. 'For centuries we have been trying to breed the aggressive instinct out of our men, and although we have achieved a measure of success, the drones are still unreliable. Perhaps in your reign you will feel justified in allowing them out more frequently, but they are not ready for it yet.'

I was now admitted to the Queen's presence once or twice a week, ostensibly so that I might learn her system of government, but actually because she wanted to keep a close eye on my health. I had passed the acceptance test; now I had to produce a baby to confirm my fitness to rule after her. I suspected that Vashti, for all her soft-soap and apparent friendliness, was eaten with jealousy in case I should succeed where she had failed, and only too ready to report any misdemeanour of mine to the Queen; I therefore trod with extreme caution on such delicate ground as the treatment of the drones.

However, today the Queen was in an expansive mood, and condescended to explain further.

'When you consider other male animals: bulls, for instance, or stallions, or boars, you realize that it's not surprising that men are dangerous. In a limited territory such as ours, we can't afford aggressive instincts. Everyone must work for the good of the hive, in peace, obedient to one Queen, and devote all energy to the common good. Women are not afraid of monotony – some might even call it drudgery – but my workers, who have lived a life of idleness until they attain the status of workers, know that it's the highest honour to be allowed to sacrifice themselves for the sake of the hive. They are dedicated to toil just as the drones are dedicated to frivolity . . . '

It sounded grim, but I was beginning to get a glimmer of what she was driving at. I was finding complete idleness a bit of a burden. That, and the need to escape from Vashti, who shadowed me everywhere I went indoors, but fortunately quailed at the idea of going outdoors like a soufflé exposed to a draught, drove me out to explore the length and breadth of the valley in the last of the golden autumn days. The Queen seemed perfectly confident that I wouldn't try to escape, and had it not been for my nagging worry about Anna, I'd have been far too contented to want to leave even if I'd seen a door labelled *Way Out*.

Sketch-book in hand, I wandered from breakfast to supper-time among the tidy patterns of fields and beside the broad shining river that flowed so smoothly into a banked and disciplined lake, carved from the hillside by myriad workmen in the far-off days of Akbar.

Beyond the lake, the river was again allowed to tumble with natural exuberance through a series of steep, rocky gorges that made me think of small salmon-rivers in Scotland, until it rushed through a real bottleneck just below the castle, where the mighty twin peaks called Gogoram and Makoram leaned their heads together over a narrow gorge, casting an icy shadow where the sun's rays could never penetrate.

This gorge divided the cultivated end of the valley from what Vashti referred to as 'wild-lands', territory which had once been farmed but which, with the shrinking population, had been given back to nature and formed a sort of game reserve, or meat-on-the-hoof store-cupboard.

Herds of deer, wolves, bear, mountain goats and snow tigers roamed and marauded in these wild-lands, undisturbed by humans except during once-yearly shoots, the only sporting entertainment permitted to the wretched drones, who had to amuse themselves during the rest of the year by gambling, squabbling, and dressing in fantastic finery for their interminable parties and feasts.

The Queen ordered old Gul Beg to escort me whenever I left the hive, and I soon grew used to having him at my heels, and even became fond of his unobtrusive companionship. If I sat down to sketch, he would produce a cushion for me, then lower himself to squat on his lean hunkers, patiently prepared to wait until I chose to move. He carried a carved sword and long-barrelled gun, no doubt with the idea of defending me from wild beasts in the rough country, though I doubted very much if the gun was capable of discharging a shot without blowing its own barrel apart.

Once we saw wolves, but they padded across the path like ghosts and vanished into the scrub without so much as a glance in our direction; when we returned to the gorge, Gul Beg ordered the slave in charge of the wolf-fire – a perpetually-burning bonfire that was supposed to deter wild beasts from raiding the cultivated lands – to build the blaze higher, and the man heaped on dry branches until flames leapt ten feet or more up the dark rock walls.

131

This gorge, which corresponded to the cross-over in a figure of eight, or the waist in a cottage loaf, was several hundred yards in length, and a wolf-fire burned at either end of it. It was cheerless and spooky because of the great inward-leaning peaks above it, but once out of their shadow, the sun struck warm again. The hive itself had been built of stone from Gogoram's slopes, and nestled against the mountain so closely that it must have been completely invisible from the air. The peaks themselves seemed to attract electric storms, and no pilot in his senses would have risked his plane near them.

When the first snows fell and I couldn't leave the hive, I turned my enegry to exploring the castle. I call it a castle, because that's the word generally used to describe a fortified dwelling, but really it was more like a whole town tightly huddled inside a red sandstone and white marble wall. It was built in the form of a double square, with a high central tower which was the Queen's residence, surrounded by the brood chamber, or nursery quarters, which was composed of kitchens, bedrooms, nurseries and formal gardens connected by cloisters between banks of flowers, where tame birds sang and fountains tinkled at mid-day in spite of the cold outside.

The central hall where I'd been shown to the workers was immediately below the Queen Bee's magnificent living quarters, and here she held daily audiences, seated on her silver and ivory throne with the restless, stringy old hags who were her senior workers clustered round her, buzzing assent to her orders.

A fretted marble screen between this hall and our brood chamber allowed me and the younger ladies to watch the Queen's councils without being seen, and although I could understand only scraps of what went on there, it amused me to watch Khurram, who would sometimes exercise his right to be present at council meetings, sitting at his mother's feet like a brilliantly plumaged bird. Inevitably after half an hour or so his interest would wane; he would start to fidget, scratch his moustache or trim his finger-nails, which would earn him a sharp reprimand from the Queen and expulsion from the council chamber. He would leave sulkily, lower lip stuck out like a moody child, utterly ignored by the buzzing, chattering women.

I say it amused me, but it was also rather pathetic to see the state his subservience to female domination had reduced him to mentally. His butterfly mind flitted from one subject to another, unable to concentrate, and while he obviously resented his lowly position in the hive, he was unable to improve it. He alone among the drones had travelled in the world outside, and knew that in other countries men tended to give orders rather than receive them from women. I could see his resentment smouldering, but the Queen either ignored or was oblivious of it.

Vashti encouraged Khurram to air his grievances to her, and since her night-cell adjoined mine, I often heard them murmuring together, Khurram's high-pitched giggle alternating with Vashti's soft, oily tones. At first I thought she brought him in as a sleeping partner, but when I made some joking reference to the frequency of his visits, she said snappishly: 'You are become like brood-chamber lady, Charl Begum; you think men are for nothing but to sleep.'

'Then why *do* you bring him in at night? Honestly, what with you nattering one side and babies squalling the other, I can hardly get to sleep.'

'We discuss,' said Vashti loftily.

'Discuss what?'

This she refused to answer, and though I noticed that the pillow talks were conducted more quietly thereafter, they continued to be just as frequent.

Among the women, I occupied rather the same invidious position as Khurram did among the men. By age and rank I belonged in the brood-chamber, among the young women doing their three-child, six-year stint to provide the hive with its next generation. Here in our comfortable rooms, thickly carpeted, the walls hung with gay, draught-excluding tapestries, latticed windows open to the morning sun and shrouded with fur-lined curtains against the icy nights, lived all the valley's females between the ages of seventeen and twenty-five.

Waited on hand and foot, fed with the best the valley could provide, these plump and idle young matrons had neither work nor worries. All they were expected to do was produce the

133

goods, and this they did with a single-mindedness that I found nothing less than terrifying.

I had nothing in common with them. It wasn't only the lack of a language – though I admit I could have tried harder to learn the rapid, sibilant speech that contrasted so oddly with their languorous movements – it was something more basic than that. I couldn't really believe that such beings were human.

I've never considered myself particularly energetic, but they really were bone idle. After three or four days of marvelling at their inertia – for apart from feeding themselves and their children they did nothing at all but talk and sleep – I decided that I must have a Project: a routine of work and exercise that would satisfy the long-buried Puritan in me who was fairly snorting disapproval at these beautiful ivory-skinned lotus-eaters.

Firstly, I would keep a sketch-book as one keeps a diary, I decided. Every day, without fail, I would draw something different and actually finish it. Alan always criticized me for working so slowly: I would gear myself to a higher rate of production.

Secondly, I would try to tame Jahanara, and prevent the children and nurses from teasing her for their amusement. Whether at that stage it was pity, or love, or some other emotion I couldn't identify that drew me to the tiny silent figure in the lonely cot, is no longer clear to me, if it ever was. The important thing was to have contact with a personality that hadn't yet been programmed and brain-washed into a cog in the Queen Bee's machine – a rebel, as I still liked to think myself. For this purpose Jahanara, with her wide, wild eyes and sudden tumults of temper appeared, for all her deafness, more human than anyone else in the hive.

So every day that golden autumn, after rolling out of my silk sheets and fur rugs, washing in rose-petal scented water from a silver bowl, dressing in a multitude of my brilliant tunics and surcoats which I could shed like onion skins as the day warmed up, and breakfasting on pancakes, soft white cheese, a chicken drumstick, lightly curried, sun-dried peaches or tiny sweet nectarines washed down with watered wine or, if I felt really strong, a bowl of goat's milk quickly followed by a couple of neat dollops of the thick, dark, almost smoky honey that was the valley's pride. I would sashay along, painting materials in hand, to the nursery.

The girls and old women who looked after the children would withdraw respectfully when the ladies – I couldn't help thinking of them as the brood-mares – swirled in, rustling their silks and tinkling their bangles. There'd be a moment or two of chaos: tiny children knocked flying as bigger ones rushed to their mothers: women scolding and fussing, babies shrieking, shrill, penetrating Oriental voices clamouring. Then as the dust settled and kith found kin again, I'd pick my way over and around the bodies to Jahanara's window.

Perched on the carved cedar chest beside the cot, I'd make rather a business of getting out my brushes and crayons, the violet ink which the miniaturist had pressed on me, and the two well-sharpened quills I'd acquired from the same source. Zaid Khalifa had generously allowed me a whole roll of dingy vellum. It smelled extremely nasty and had a line of illuminated text ending with a gold blot across the top. I had some idea of working the text into a border, as Leila had done with her pictures. I was keeping it for best.

Jahanara didn't even glance at my preparations the first few mornings, though I was in full view of her. She went on gazing blankly at the window.

I schooled myself to take no notice of her, either. 'Let them come to you: never chase after them,' my father used to say of his young horses. 'Young animals are curious, and soon or later curiosity will win.'

After a week of this routine, sure enough – when I was really ignoring Jahanara, not just pretending to, and busily blocking in the masses of my first sketch of the day – a thin hand reached through the cot-bars and made a grab at my pencil.

It was one of my two proper pencils, and instinctively I jumped and jerked it away. Cursing myself for this reaction, I put it back in position, holding it loosely, and next time the snatch connected. Jahanara gave a funny little crow of triumph, and started sweeping her prize back and forth across

135

the head of the cot, in imitation of me. It wasn't long before the soft 4 B point gave way under this treatment, but by then the cot was well scribbled-over, and Jahanara looked as pleased as if she'd finished the brush-work on the Mona Lisa.

Unfortunately, a small boy chose that moment to wander over and see what was going on. In a flash, Jahanara was on her feet, grabbing at him through the bars. He flinched away and, with a scream of rage, she flung the broken pencil at him, gibbering hate like a monkey and stamping her small feet on the floor of her cot.

He ran away as she continued to scream, and I found my concentration had gone. I put away my painting things and left the nursery.

It was the start of a long hard road, but slowly, very slowly, our relationship progressed.

As some lonely people talk to dogs or horses to relieve their sense of isolation, I exercised my voice on the withdrawn child, babbling a sort of idiotic running commentary while I drew. She seemed, in the end, to like it.

'How's that coming on?' I'd ask, putting down my pencil and holding the drawing at arm's length so that she could see, but not grab it. 'What d'you think? Perspective – rather proud of that. Those far hills a bit dark, would you say? What? Oh, no. I don't agree. That's being unfair. It may not be perfect – I don't say it's perfect . . . Jahanara, you sound like dear old 'Orrible Oliver at the Central Art. "Orrible rubbish, Miss Granville," was his war-cry. We all used to imitate him: Anna had him absolutely taped. You'd like Anna, my pet. I wonder how she is . . . I wonder if Alan went to see her like he said, or if he sent that old dragon with the blue rinse . . .'

When I thought of Anna, a tiresome, unswallowable lump would form in my throat, and I'd feel a terrible sense of helplessness and frustration. She must think I was dead. I'd concentrate my mind, trying to send her telepathic waves of aliveness. I learned from Vashti that our returning porters had been primed with stories of an accident in the hills. Rosie and I were alleged to have been killed; Khurram to be recovering in a remote monastery. The policeman, Ram Sirdar, had been well paid to make no further enquiry possible.

'Paid?' I asked. 'Whose money pays him?'

Vashti looked sly. 'Papers better than money for keeping secrets.'

'Papers? What sort of papers?'

'Many Indians wishing to travel in England. They pay much rupees for papers which Leila makes in Srinagar; make Ram Sirdar rich. He take the money from selling these papers for himself, and he stop other police from troubling the Nishat Treasure Palace. But Ram Sirdar is greedy policeman, and soon Khurram must go again in Srinagar to give him more of these – ' She hesitated, searching for the word.

'Passports.'

'Yes, passport papers. The Queen is angry because she say Ram Sirdar has taken already too much money, but she wishes to keep her valley secret. Khurram say kill Ram Sirdar, but to kill policeman makes bad trouble.'

I felt as if I'd been punched in the stomach as I took in this information. So Nick had nothing to do with the passports, I thought dazedly. He really had been puzzled as well as angry when I'd turned on him. Leila had given me that bunch of papers – yes, that must be it – because she'd had enough. She wanted to expose the racket. What had she said: 'Tell Sandy that I pay for my journey.' She wanted out. She'd been trying to escape with the only currency she possessed.

Vashti said, 'You feel bad, Charl Begum? You like to sit?'

I must have gone pale, for she was staring at me, and once again I sensed malice in her gaze. Pretend as she might, she didn't really like me.

'I'm all right,' I said shortly. 'It's a bit hot in here.' I went and leaned on the window-sill, thinking furiously. I remembered that unbecoming scene in the hotel bedroom, when Nick rejected my advances the night before he left for the hills. What had I said? Did I mention passports? He was fairly quick in the uptake: would he have put two and two together?

No, I decided miserably. I'd been so sure he knew what I meant, and so conscious of sharp-eared Rosie next door, that I'd confined myself to remarks as ambiguous as they were wounding. Oh, wah tah nah Siam! Not for the first time, I cursed myself for acting on impulse.

I straightened up too suddenly, and felt the waves of giddiness that had attacked me when I got out of bed that morning sweeping back in full force. I swayed and clutched at the window-sill behind me, and next moment Vashti had pulled me down on to a cushion, and was pushing my head between my knees.

'Leave me alone,' I muttered crossly. 'Don't make such a fuss. I'll be all right in a tick.' Cautiously I opened an eye and surprised a horribly knowing expression on her pointed cat-like face.

'I tell you, it's nothing,' I repeated, though she hadn't said a word. 'I expect that chicken I had for breakfast was a bit . . . '

'No, no, it is not food. It is starting of baby. I am counting days, Charl Begum, and I know this for sure.'

Counting days! I felt abused and spied on. 'What rubbish, Vashti,' I said briskly. 'That's because of the altitude. Look; I'm perfectly all right again now, so don't start – '

'It is baby coming,' she said stubbornly, and slowly I sat down again. The thought of anything resulting from that unspeakable night with the Drone revolted me; it also seemed utterly unreal. I felt, apart from this fleeting giddiness, a hundred per cent fit. Hungry, energetic, hair and skin in good order – how could she be right? But I dredged up a memory from long ago, when Anna and I had tried to make our fortunes by breeding mink, and the text-book had warned there'd be little discernible difference between a successful mating and a knock-down-drag-out battle. Perhaps it had been the same with me.

'I don't think so,' I said, but uncertainly now. 'Where are you off to?'

Vashti was tidying her hair at my mirror. 'I go tell Queen this good news.'

'I'll tell her myself,' I began, but with a tinkle of laughter she slipped out of the room before I could move.

Slowly I collected my painting gear and slung a heavy cloak round my shoulders. The atmosphere inside the hive seemed stifling, and I was glad to feel the sharp crisp cold air on my face as I came out into the courtyard and beckoned to Gul Beg to accompany me.

Chapter Fifteen

The Queen Bee was pleased all right, and I liked her courtly, old-fashioned way of showing it. No empty compliments or congratulations – you couldn't put those in your pocket. Instead, she sent Khurram to call on me, bearing gifts.

Khurram was a great favourite with the ladies of the brood-chamber and their children. He had a ready hand with the slap-and-tickle which they enjoyed, and was often followed by old Gul Beg, who carried a tray of bonbons of tooth-aching sweetness for Khurram to distribute. But it seemed to me that his frivolous, *jeunesse dorée* pose was carefully calculated; beneath it I suspected a streak of bitterness which would express itself viciously if it got the chance.

Glittering with jewels, chattering animatedly with the ladies or ordering servants around, he flitted about the hive as freely as a butterfly.

I wasn't the only one to treat him with reserve: Jahanara was definitely anti, and Khurram reciprocated her dislike. Apparently she'd once flung a sweetmeat back at him and marked a new brocade surcoat with syrup.

On the afternoon of the day I suffered my first attack of giddiness, just as the hive was beginning to rouse from its siesta-time torpor, he flung open the door of my cell, and posed elegantly, one hand on hip, the other grasping a jewelled lead attached to a large, boisterous, creme-brulee coloured puppy. I'd several times seen Khurram attired for the chase, sporting a hooded falcon on his wrist, but the dog was something new. Its silky coat just matched his turban and rajah-coat.

'Greetings, Charl Begum,' he said ceremoniously, sweeping a bow when he was sure I'd had plenty of time to admire his finery.

'Hallo, Khurram. What a lovely dog! He goes so well with the yellow silk.'

Khurram looked down at the puppy, which was trying to wind the lead round his legs.

'The dog is yours,' he said grandly. 'A gift from my mother, the Queen, who is expressing much pleasure at the news that you will have a child. The dog is of a famous breed; very special, very rare. But,' he added, shifting his elegant, curly-toed slippers as a pool spread from beneath the puppy, 'he is young and has not good manners.'

I laughed, and took the lead. 'That doesn't matter. I love dogs, I'll train him. Please tell your mother I'm delighted with her present.'

'The dog is not all.' Khurram snapped imperious fingers and Gul Beg shuffled forward to show me the contents of an ivory box. Ear-rings and finger-rings to match my rubies winked at me from a velvet nest.

'They're lovely,' I said. 'Really beautiful. Thank her very much for such a magnificent present.' But I was even more pleased with the dog.

'You must try the jewels,' said Khurram. 'This is a ring, see.' He lifted it from the box and offered it to me. Indian bones are unbelievably tiny: after a brief, abortive struggle that skinned the knuckle of my ring finger, we managed to wrestle it on to my little finger.

His embassy completed, Khurram drifted over to snoop at the sketch I was working on.

'It is Jahanara,' he said in surprise. 'Why do you draw Jahanara?'

'You see a likeness?'

'Very much like. You are a good painter, Charl Begum; I think more good even than Leila.'

'Oh lord, no. I wish I was half as good as her.' What I actually wished was that he'd leave me alone to make friends with the puppy. The jewel-studded collar was done up too tight, and I bent to loosen it, noting the clod-hopping Pluto paws and round, almost drooping tummy. Although it was already the size of a half-grown Labrador, I could see that it was a very young puppy, probably no more than six weeks old, and would be enormous when full-grown. He had a mastiff-shaped face with a black mask, and long smart black stockings reaching above his knees. His thick plumed tail wagged furiously as he bent in a half-hoop around my stroking hand, whining a little and quivering with pleasure.

'What breed of dog is he?'

'He hunts after wolves and bears when he is grown,' said Khurram absently. 'He is a special breed.'

He fidgeted with the drawing, turning it this way and that; glanced at me and away again, and finally came out with what was on his mind. 'I like you to paint me in royal clothes, Charl Begum.'

'Oh, Khurram,' I protested, 'I'm not much good at people, I'm afraid. I only do it for fun.'

'Fun, yes,' he said quickly. 'You will have fun to paint me. Babies and little children, that is boring, but a prince in royal clothes is very nice to paint.'

I could see he'd keep on at me until I gave in. 'All right,' I said reluctantly, 'but I warn you you'll have to sit very still.'

He laughed delightedly. 'Many, many hours I sit still.'

Of course, he did nothing of the kind. He was as restless and undisciplined as the puppy, whom I named Gandhi because, for the first few days, he frightened me by refusing to eat. I expect he missed his mother and the warm jostling of the other puppies. He was a very cuddly, affectionate dog, despite his size, and would squirm and stretch and wriggle himself into a comfortable position in any odd corner where I happened to be working.

The winter weeks passed with dream-like swiftness. Khurram drifted in to pose for me whenever he felt like it, and whether I did or not. He was a portrait-painter's nightmare as a sitter; always complaining, fidgeting, and criticizing.

'When d'you leave for Srinagar?' I asked in exasperation one day in February or March. It was difficult for me to be precise about dates since the days seemed to flow smoothly into one another, and the weeks became months before I realized it.

Khurram's hands stopped in their restless polishing of an

emerald turban-ornament he held. 'You know I go to Srinagar?'

'Vashti told me. Why? Is it a secret?'

'Ah, Vashti.' He held the jewel up to the light, then gave it a final polish. 'You think this pretty stone will please Vashti?'

'Of course,' I said noncommittally, working hard at his mouth. It wouldn't come right; I thought it would be easier if he didn't talk so much.

'Vashti loves jewels more than men.'

I nodded. I suspected as much, too. I'd caught her trying on my rubies, parading in front of the mirror, when I returned for a forgotten paintbrush after she thought I'd left the hive for the day. Unlike Henry V, I found it yearned me a good deal when men my garments wore, and since then I'd put them on every morning and only removed them to sleep.

'Vashti likes me to sell jewels in Srinagar.' He looked sideways to see how I would take this.

I thought it over before replying. On the one hand, if Khurram were caught trying to sell a huge emerald, it might lead to enquiries and eventually to my rescue. On the other, it would mean the opening up of the secret valley and its eventual destruction and that, I found, I didn't want at all. Also I disliked the implied theft, master-minded by Vashti, using Khurram as her stooge. Whoever got into trouble, it wouldn't be Vashti.

'If I tell this to the Queen, she won't let you go to Srinagar at all.'

He stuck out his lower lip. 'If you do not tell, I bring you what you ask for.'

'When are you going?'

He shrugged. 'In one week or two. Now the snow starts to melt in the passes. There is danger with downfalls.'

Spring already – where had the winter gone? It seemed impossible that I'd been in the valley half a year.

'Avalanches,' I said automatically.

'Yes,' he agreed. 'It is always a hard journey. I stay in Srinagar with Leila all summer, but when I return with many goods for the valley, the Queen will give a bear-hunt in my honour. You will come to watch.'

I licked my brush to a fine point. 'No, thanks; I rather like bears.'

'Yes, you must come. I order it. Also your dog must get the smell of bears.'

I looked at Gandhi, flopped bonelessly at my feet. He was so soft and cuddly I couldn't believe he'd ever hunt wolf or bear. He'd made a great difference to my relationship with Jahanara, and I'd never once seen her lose her temper when playing with the big puppy.

'I'll see,' I said for the sake of peace. 'When the time comes I'll see how I feel.'

He was silent for a moment and I worked hard, then he began on another tack.

'You are sad, Charl Begum. Why are you sad when everything is good for you? The Queen is pleased because you will have a child and rule this valley after her; you have jewels and fine clothes and no work to do. In this small, pretty kingdom it is only the drones who should be sad.'

I was surprised and rather touched by his interest in my emotional state, so I told him the truth. 'It's just that I'm worried about my sister. She must think I'm dead. If only you could take a letter to Srinagar and post it for me – just to tell her I'm alive and happy. That's all. I won't say anything else. Please, Khurram; say you'll do this for me?'

But he looked scared. 'The Queen would be angry.'

'She wouldn't know.'

'She knows everything. Gul Beg is a spy for her.'

'Oh, please,' I urged. 'Surely you're not afraid? You, a prince.'

He shrugged. 'A prince is nothing here. Women have the power, and the Queen with her workers orders everything in this kingdom. It was not always so. In the days of the great Akbar and Ho Tsien, his son, men ruled and fought while women stayed behind the harem screen. But with years of peace, the men grew slow and stupid. It was forbidden to leave the valley, and no one came to fight, so our weapons rusted on the wall. Men feasted and drank and became foolish, and women began to rule, as in the bee-hives. Only I, of all our men, have seen the world outside and know how men should live.'

'I thought Akbar gave this valley to his *daughter*.'

He smiled. 'The women's story is always a little different. There was a son and a daughter – it was many years ago. Who knows how it happened?'

He paused, then went on dreamily: 'For Azam and all the drones, this valley is the world. They know nothing more. But I am not so; I will rule not one small, pretty valley, but the kingdom of my fathers, the Moguls.'

Abruptly I stopped feeling sorry for him. I sensed the hand of Vashti in this disaffected talk; so this was what they burnt the midnight oil discussing!

'The Moguls were not always great,' I reminded him. 'They started in a very small way, as far as I remember.'

'And ended big,' he said triumphantly. 'The empire of Aurangzeb, son of Shah Jehan, son of Jehangir – son of Akbar, stretched from Pondicherry to Kabul. This I have read, although,' he added reflectively, 'such an empire is too big for me.'

'I'll say. And one valley is too little; how much is just right?' It was beginning to sound like a dialogue out of *Goldilocks and the Three Bears*, but Khurram saw nothing funny in it.

'The kingdom of Kashmir,' he declared, eye flashing. I looked at him closely. He had an oddly wild and woozy expression; I guessed he was high on poppy.

'Steady on,' I said soothingly. 'I don't imagine Mrs Gandhi will hand you that on a plate.'

Hearing his name, the puppy waved a languid tale from the prone position. He had spent the morning hunting butterflies and needed his rest.

'Then I fight for it!'

'Oh, Khurram – ' I couldn't help smiling – 'you're living in Cloud Cuckoo land. Fighting nowadays needs jets and megatons and SAMs and ICBMs, and all the rest of those ghastly initials, not to mention *soldiers*. How would you get those? Much better stay safe in your small pretty valley and just dream about conquering the world.'

He stuck out his lip mulishly. 'You laugh, Charl Begum, but

145

one day you and all the women will remember my words and tremble.' He rose from his cross-legged position on the green silk cushion. 'I am tired of being still,' he announced, although he hadn't been exactly motionless for more than two minutes on end throughout the sitting. 'With so much talk, my throat is dry. I think, Charl Begum, you are the most slow painter in the world. I go to refresh myself with tea.'

He swept out of the room, and I cleaned my brushes and put them away, wondering if hive security demanded that I report our conversation to the Queen. But it was all so vague; I felt strongly inclined to let sleeping dogs lie. My own sleeping dog yawned and stretched, curling back his lips to show needle-sharp fangs of solid ivory. Lines floated into my mind:

> Those that sharpen the tooth of the dog
> > Meaning death;
> Those that glitter with the glory
> of the humming-bird,
> > Meaning death;
> Those that sit in the sty of contentment,
> > Meaning death . . .

Was Vashti sharpening the tooth of the dog? I wondered, while Khurram glittered like a humming-bird? Should I bestir myself from the sty of contentment?

But there was nothing Khurram could do, I reassured myself. His pipe-dreams were just that – poppy-pipe dreams: castles in the air. The result of frustration and inactivity upon a fertile imagination.

I beat the gong for my afternoon drink of lime-juice and honey, deliberately trying to quash the worm of unease that was poisoning my tranquillity.

Spring in the valley was an artist's dream come true; wild flowers carpeted the mountain slopes, baby animals frisked and gambolled beside their dams, grass sprang emerald-green from beneath the receding snowline. In spite of the barbarisms

146

of sixteenth-century living which made the place something less than Shangri-La; in spite of my anxiety about Anna; in spite of my unwanted pregnancy – which I could now no longer doubt since the baby had developed a nasty trick of booting me below the belt whenever I lay at my ease – I was idyllically happy.

Khurram left for Srinagar, accompanied only by Gul Beg, as soon as the passes were clear. He'd be away several months, and I was glad of it.

Vashti's constant shadowing of my movements within the hive had become no more than a minor nuisance; she was scared of both Jahanara and Gandhi, and kept her distance when either or both of them were with me. I was also developing a better relationship with the Queen, who would summon me once or twice a week to wait on her and learn the lore of the hive.

The first warm day of spring, when the air felt soft, without the crisp bite that was noticeable on even the sunniest winter days, I was bidden to accompany the Queen on her first visit to the hill-side beehives which produced the valley's supply of honey. Deeply apprehensive when I learned the purpose of our mission, I put on all my thickest padded clothes, and sweltered in my litter as the Queen's bodyguard carried it up the rocky path behind the castle. At noon we reached a sheer face pock-marked with the entrances to caves, and here the litters were placed on the ground and the bodyguard withdrew a few hundred yards. A deep hum rose from the nearest cave, and bees flew in and out in a steady stream through a slit-shaped opening about head-height in the wall.

I tried to follow the guards, but the Queen grasped my shoulder and held me back. 'Stay by me,' she commanded. 'This is the ceremony of the Spring Awakening, which only the Queen may perform. First, we tell each colony how the valley has fared during the winter months, while they slept. Stay by me and listen, for one day you must do the same; I will speak in English, since all tongues are the same to the bees.'

Reluctantly I followed her out of the sunlight, into a huge cave in which were ranged row upon row of wooden beehives, like cars in a municipal car park. There must have been at least a hundred, I saw as my eyes adjusted to the dim light, filtering in through holes high up the cliff-face, each with its flight-board crawling with bees, and the noise was almost deafening. Right in the centre of the cave, and slightly apart from the other hives, was one that gleamed with a soft yellow light: the Golden Hive of Akbar, guarded by millions of tiny sentinels.

I kept as close as possible to the Queen, as she walked confidently between the rows of hives, ignoring the insects that buzzed in clouds round both our heads. 'Do not be afraid,' she said, 'the bees will not hurt their Queen. This is the power handed down from one queen to the next, and when my turn comes to swarm and leave the hive with my chosen followers, I will give this power to you. But, until you receive it, never venture in this cave without me, or the guardians of Akbar's treasure will sting you to death as soon as you cross the threshold.'

As she spoke, she was inspecting each hive, removing the lid and glancing quickly inside before replacing it. 'All is well here, and here, and here,' she murmured. 'But here we have trouble. The colony has died for lack of a Queen.' Suddenly she was angry. 'This should never have happened. Buldeo! Buldeo!'

At her call an aged troglodyte, so muffled in cloaks that it was impossible to determine its sex, materialized out of the dark shadows. It gave a moan of dismay on being shown the empty hive, but launched immediately into an explanation which seemed to satisfy the Queen, for she passed on to the next hive after only a moment's pause.

'Buldeo knows the ways of the bees, and he alone can collect their honey,' she said, working her way up the lines of hives. 'In spring the colonies are weak after the winter sleep, and he feeds them until they can gather nectar for themselves. All summer they work, building up supplies to carry their workers through the winter, and it takes a brave and skilful hand to rob them of their stores. You see the big, round cells here? That is a bad queen, she lays too many drones: too many idle mouths for the workers to feed. And here – this is an old Queen whose egg-laying days are nearing their end. She must be replaced.'

I couldn't see much difference in the interior of each hive, but dutifully peered down at the ever-moving insects as she ordered me to, praying that they'd keep their stings to themselves. At length the Queen completed her inspection and halted by the golden hive.

'Now we will tell you the news of the world, Oh bees,' she announced. 'The deaths in the valley have been few: Rohanara and Mumtaz Nur from a fever; Jela Begum died in childbirth, but the baby – a girl – survived. Two children – boys – drowned in the river; Hamid Khan was crushed to death beneath a falling rock. Apart from these few casualties, the population of the valley remains the same, with the addition of the following babies: eight girls, and eleven boys, and your new Queen, Charl Begum, whom you see here. Khurram Mohammed, my son, has travelled to Srinagar once more, and with him his bodyguard, Gul Beg.'

Consulting a list from time to time, she rattled on about the valley people's doings with the practised nonchalance of a priest bucketing through early Communion for fear his breakfast egg would hard-boil.

'Greetings from your Queen,' she ended at length. 'We wish you a good season of work. Sun and snow, disease and famine will not trouble you while you are under our protection, but beware of the hornet which Lord Akbar foretold would destroy your hives. Be on your guard, and if you see him, bring me word.'

'Hornet?' I asked.

'It is the earliest of our prophecies relating to the bees, and you must learn the precise words. Now I will show you Akbar's treasure before we leave. No one but the Queen may open the golden hive.'

She pressed a catch, and the front of the model hive swung open, like a doll's house, revealing perfectly modelled honeycombs made of gold filigree of amazing delicacy, on which golden bees with eyes of ruby and turquoise were thickly clustered. Just as in the real combs, some cells were hexagonal and some round, and in some the wink of red, blue, and green stones represented the baby bees hatching within.

'We will find the Queen and move her to another comb,' said the Queen, kneeling down to hunt through the sections of honeycomb, like a small girl playing with her dolls. 'Where did I put her last year? Ah, yes – here she is.'

The Queen Bee's body was made entirely of diamonds and twice the size of her workers and drones. She glittered in the dim light, and her large, faceted eyes seemed to wink at me with evil pleasure. Her abdomen drooped, heavy with eggs that would never be laid, and her wings were silver, beaten so fine that it was nearly transparent.

'She's magnificent,' I said, as Rosie placed her on the back of her hand and moved her to make her body flash. Then she replaced her in another part of the golden hive, rearranged a band of workers round her to represent her bodyguard, and posted four different sentinels on the model flightboard.

'Good,' she said at last, 'now she is ready to hatch a new Queen, just as we are doing. She will lay half a dozen, and the first one to hatch will kill all the others before they leave their cells. By that time, of course, the old Queen will have swarmed . . .'

Clicking shut the model, she moved purposefully towards the cave mouth, but I, still entranced with the golden hive and its jewelled occupants, was slow off the mark in following. By then, anyway, I was feeling quite debonair. We'd been inside the cave a good half-hour and not a single bee out of all those millions had attempted to sting me. Clever, gentle, industrious little insects, I mused, bumbling along in Rosie's wake, and turned at the doorway for a last look at the treasure-hive. But the instant that the Queen's shadow vanished through the cave-mouth, and I was alone in there, the contented buzzing deepened its note like a two-stroke engine changing gear, and before I realized the danger the bees were on me. I was a mere two strides from the door, and accelerated like a racehorse leaving the starting stalls, but in those two strides the bees settled like a muffler round my head and shoulders, clinging and stinging until I was nearly mad with the pain. I blundered screaming into the sunlight, slapping and shaking as I tried to scrape myself clear of the furry insects, and finally rolling on the grassy slope in my agony. Red-hot needles lanced me in so many places that I couldn't tell which hurt the most.

150

'Poor bees, poor bees,' mourned the Queen, picking them off me tenderly and laying each individual insect on the grass. 'Now they've used their stings they'll die. Why didn't you keep close to me as I commanded? You've murdered hundreds of bees by your disobedience, just at the time of year when the hives can least spare them.'

'They attacked me,' I mumbled through swollen lips. 'I didn't do anything to provoke them. I'm on fire. Can't you do anything to ease these stings?'

'I am the Queen, not a healer of wounds. The pain will soon pass, and until it does it will serve to remind you that my orders are not lightly disobeyed. Vashti, too, was stung when she lingered to covet the golden hive of Akbar; she may know of some salve to anoint your wounds.'

Vashti could hardly conceal her pleasure when she saw that I'd fallen into the same trap as she had two years ago. I was sure the Queen had deliberately hurried out of the cave, partly to demonstrate to me her power over the fierce little insects, and partly to ensure that I was too frightened to return to the home of the bees without her protection. The golden hive, I reflected, could hardly be lodged in a safer place.

The evil-smelling grease Vashti smeared on the stings soon stopped them hurting, but the whole episode made me more wary than ever of the Queen and all her works.

Khurram had set something of a fashion by posing for me, and now hardly a day went by without some lady of the brood-chamber begging me to immortalize her or her child. Far from resenting this encroachment on his territory, dear old Khalifa, the Court miniaturist, and his young assistant, Tarkhum Malik, went out of their way to help and admire and instruct. From them I learned how to scrape vellum, grind paints, and design intricate borders in the Persian style, though they shook their heads over my landscapes, which appealed not at all to their eyes.

As often as I could, I escaped to the valley floor with Gandhi and Jahanara frolicking ahead, and my new bodyguard, a shambling, black-bearded woodman named Hamid in loose attendance, to spend whole days sketching. The child and dog

151

were ideal companions for such expeditions, since neither could talk, and both seemed perfectly happy to play in silence while I worked.

Our favourite bolt-hole was a little glade beside the river, where a waterfall had carved an almost circular pool between two narrow necks of rock. In spring it was a shapeless white torrent, but now that the stream had digested the overflow of melting snow, it curved and twisted idly in the smoothly sculpted basin of rock, while little eddies flooded into shallow backwaters – ideal for paddling or, if you were Gandhi, simply for wallowing.

Jahanara soon became an enthusiastic paddler, quite unafraid of the water. Imitating me, she kicked off her curly-toed slippers and dipped an exploratory foot in the icy, light-green water, kicking the spray high and chuckling in her funny, throaty way. Gandhi despised such half measures, and would bound straight into the pool on hot days, sinking flat on his belly with legs stuck out fore and aft. When his yellow coat was water-logged, floating around him like Ophelia's hair, he'd raise and shake the shining drops all over us, a manoeuvre which was as amusing to Jahanara as it was maddening to me. Many's the promising sketch he spoiled in this way, but there was always time to start another.

To myself, I called this hidden pool 'Jajanara's Pleasaunce', for there we were always sure of privacy since Hamid would hunker down a hundred yards or so upstream of us, where the fishing was more promising, to try his luck with the great golden carp-like fish until such time as we tired of watching the sparkling cascade and turned for home.

Though the nights were still crisp and fresh, by day it was very hot, and even my freckled skin gave up peeling after shedding about a dozen layers, and assumed a more or less even tan. The ladies of the brood-chamber drooped about the flower-filled courtyards, with bare mid-riffs and gauzy long skirts, but they seldom ventured farther into the open than the walled garden.

As summer wore on, the fresh young green of the tiny terraced cornfields I painted turned to yellow and then red-gold. Lambs and kids changed their first fluffy coats for silky deep fleeces that

152

would withstand the icy blast of winter, and grew so big they looked ridiculous butting underneath – and nearly upending – their patient mothers.

First cherries and apricots, then litchis, strawberries, and plums, and finally rich dark mulberries enlivened our diet. The grapes ripened on their neat vines: they would be gathered after the bear-hunt, the last of the season's produce.

One hot day, word went round that Azam was ill. It would be serious if he died, because unless my baby happened to be a boy – no better than an evens chance, after all – it would leave Khurram the sole surviving scion of the male line of Akbar.

'Poison,' whispered the ladies and nurses in the brood-chamber. It was one of the few words I knew – one heard it whenever anyone retired unexpectedly to bed. But before alarm and despondency could reach a peak, though not before a messenger had been dispatched to fetch Khurram from the bright lights of Srinagar, the Drone was back on his feet. He looked a bad colour, I thought, peering at my husband-for-a-night through the carved screen as he sat lolling on his marble throne during the morning council, and his hands shook in the well-known way of dipsos, but he didn't yet look a candidate for Death's sickle.

The whispering women relaxed and gossiped about other things, but at the back of my mind, forced out of sight most of the time, lay a feeling that all this peace and beauty was a bit too good to last. The little kingdom was poised on a tightrope with dark forces pulling from either side. I didn't want it to lose its balance.

Chapter Sixteen

Khurram returned, in response to the messenger's summons, in late July, and if he was disappointed at finding his cousin still alive, he gave no outward sign of it. He brought with him news which rippled the calm surface of valley life: Leila had vanished from Srinagar.

She'd flitted only a few days after our party had left for the hills, much to the chagrin of Ram Sirdar, who'd called for his annual tribute of forged passport pages and found the bird flown, with only her bewildered household still living in the luxurious apartments behind the tatty shop-front. Until Khurram re-emerged from his mountain fastness, it had been impossible to tell him of this development, and it was Ram Sirdar's threats of police action unless the supply of hush-money was re-established as much as the Queen's summons that had brought Khurram home in a hurry.

Good for Leila! I cheered, when Vashti relayed this news to me. Nick and Sandy must have sprung her from the gilded cage she'd found so irksome. My spirits rose like rockets at this evidence of their handiwork, and then wavered as hard on the heels of this thought came another: what if they came to rescue me? Leila knew of the valley's existence: did she know where it was?

'Why did the Queen leave Leila alone in Srinagar?' I asked Vashti. 'Why not bring her back here too? She could have printed her forgeries far more safely in this hidden valley.'

Vashti put down the muslin *choli* she was altering, and jabbed the needle against her forearm, miming an injection. 'Every day Leila must have this or she will die. Too much sugar in blood. So she lives since she was a little girl in Srinagar where she can be near the doctor and also work for the Queen.'

So it was diabetes. I wondered how old Leila had been when she was taken from the valley; how much she remembered. She must certainly have told Sandy, and through him Nick, about the passport racket: would they take it one stage further and guess my whereabouts? It would be a long shot. And if they did, could I bear to leave this lovely place and go back to the rat-race? How could I explain to anyone not as brain-washed as I was, about this misbegotten baby? By now I looked as if I'd swallowed a football, and the thought of Nick seeing me in this state was sharply repugnant.

In an effort to regain my peace of mind, I threw myself into an orgy of painting with the new materials that the Queen had graciously ordered Khurram to bring me from Srinagar, but once woken, you can't recapture a dream. I moved ponderously about the castle, unable to settle to anything.

The bear-hunt seemed to offer a diversion, and despite my earlier opposition to it, I found myself keen to go. Gandhi had grown enormously in the last few months and the long days in the open with me had hardened his muscles and whittled away the last of his puppy fat. If hunting bear was to be his métier, I felt it was time he got a sniff of his quarry.

The Queen approved my decision to go, and provided me with a litter to travel in. The hunt was the high spot of the year for the drones, who did the shooting with their ancient weapons, and only a small detachment of workers, some thirty or forty women, accompanied them to keep order and supervise the skinning and cutting up of the meat.

'We have cut a big, big hole in the ice to keep the meat,' said Vashti. 'This way it tastes good all the year. While you go hunting, I go with the Queen to see the meat put away.' She seemed excited by the prospect, and I reflected that ever since Khurram's return she had been keyed up, on edge, ready to laugh or to shriek at the children, very different from her apathy of early summer. She had also adopted a strikingly plain style of dress, so that she looked like a governess among all the brilliant silks and brocades worn by her contemporaries.

'Have you gone off jewels or something?' I asked.

'Gone off?'

'Stopped wearing them. Or have you given them all to your best boy?'

'Jewels are for Queen,' she said primly, 'not for those who work.'

'You won't be a worker for years, Vashti.'

But she refused to give me any further explanation of her lack of adornment, and I was left to speculate on whether she'd managed to persuade Khurram to sell them for her, or if she'd simply decided they weren't her style. She was more forthcoming about the hunt, though, explaining how the trackers had already been sent out to the farthest hills at the rim of the valley, fanning out in a huge circle and slowly moving inwards, taking several days to drive all the game in the forests that cloaked the mountain slopes towards a certain narrow glen in the wildlands. When this gong-beating, rattle-carrying human net was drawn tight, they would funnel the quarry towards the guns waiting in ambush.

At daybreak a couple of mornings later, the hunting party began to assemble in the courtyard, with all the drones dressed up to the nines and in riotous spirits. For them this was the high spot of the year, and high was about the right word. The sweet smell of hash was everywhere; the hunters smoked with a slightly frenzied enjoyment which reminded me of a fox-hunting field downing its jumping powder.

Just before noon, the long ragged column began to straggle out of the hive's massive bronze gates and wind down the path to the river, making enough noise to scare into hiding every animal for miles.

At the head of the procession rode the Queen's young breeding studs on small but dashingly-dressed ponies. There were only about a dozen, but a fine-looking bunch they were, with dark flashing eyes and hawkish features, lean bodies all a-jangle with necklaces and bracelets. It was the first time I'd seen them allowed *en masse* out of their monastic quarters, and no wonder the excitement was going to their heads. They brandished long, barrelled guns which even to my eye looked dangerously antique. I hoped they weren't genuine survivals from Akbar's armoury.

Behind this élite came the open litter carried by four sturdy eunuchs on which poor Azam the Drone rocked and swayed. The Drone looked yellow as butter both in face and in the hands gripping the sides of his litter. Beside him, as befitted the man to whose honour the hunt was dedicated, rode Khurram Mohammed Beg, resplendent in purple brocade and turban, waving his gun in a manner far more debonair than safe. *He* wouldn't be popular on anyone's grouse-moor, I thought, observing his antics sourly.

The Queen's lieutenants were posted at strategic points in the column and it was they, I soon realized, who kept the straggling procession moving steadily, and were ready like sheep-dogs to herd either hunters or the servants laden with provisions back into line if they strayed too far. The sun was hot, but we kept up a good pace all afternoon, and when the shadows grew long, the servants pitched tents in a glade where mulberry trees had showered their fruit on the velvety grass.

We had travelled beside the river, and now there was a rush to fill cooking pots and light camp fires before the night's sharp chill struck us. Soon fat-tailed sheep carcases were spitting and hissing into the flames, and the thick black smoke from burning mutton-fat, which would have been nauseating indoors, was making my mouth water. The hunting-dogs thought the same, prowling from one circle of firelight to another, whining and snarling as they scavenged for unconsidered morsels.

Gandhi was on his best behaviour, somewhat bewildered by the noise and bustle, so that he stuck to me like a burr. I'd taught him the elementary commands in English: 'Heel', 'Sit', and 'Stay', spending far longer over each stage of training than was strictly necessary because he was a pleasure to teach and I'd plenty of time. He'd become more mastiff-like as he grew, with a thick silky coat, cream rather than yellow, set off by his black stockings and mask.

Vashti glided into my tent with a steaming bowl on a tray, but stopped short at Gandhi's menacing growl.

'Sit down, dog,' she said uncertainly, hovering in the doorway.

He took no notice and she flapped a helpless hand at me. 'He does not obey me, your dog. How can I speak with you when that great animal is showing me his teeth?'

'All right, Gandhi,' I said, and he lowered his nose to his paws again. 'What is it, Vashti?'

'I bring a message from the Queen. She wishes you to watch the hunt from far away, so that your dog does not spoil it with his excitement. In the morning early I must take you to a place above the shooting-ground where you may watch without danger. There you will stay until I bring your litter-bearers to carry you home when the killing is finished. It is the Queen's command.'

It sounded a sensible plan. I wasn't sure whether I could control Gandhi if the excitement went to his head; rather like taking a young horse hunting for the first time. I thought discretion was certainly the better part of valour.

'Where will you be during the hunt?'

'I go to make ready the meat store in the ice behind the castle, and when all is prepared the Queen will come to look if we have caught enough meat to feed the hive through the winter. Sleep now, Charl Begum, for I must wake you before sunrise.'

She was as good as her word. While the hunting party still lay in blanket-wrapped rolls shrouded by early-morning river mist, Vashti nudged me awake. I'm never at my best before breakfast, and blundered into layers of clothes, cursing all sporting activities from the bottom of my heart.

Vashti ignored my muttered grumblings, and set a cracking pace up the hill, following a narrow path between dense thickets of rhododendron whose frozen leaves rattled like castanets as they brushed against us.

'Steady on,' I gasped. My heart was pounding like a sledge-hammer. 'I'm carrying weight, remember?'

'It is not so far,' called back Vashti, gliding up as lightly as a panther.

'What's the rush?' But she was out of earshot already. I gritted my teeth and followed. Suddenly the mist thinned, and our heads were through to the sunlight. Another few paces and the vapour was below us, swirling and billowing along the line of the river. The ravine in which we'd camped had vanished from sight, but we were high enough to see the narrow neck through which the game would be driven, and beyond it the scrub-covered slopes which even now concealed the beaters.

Vashti halted at last. 'This is the place where you can watch.' She settled me with my back to a great rock and Gandhi, trailing yards of pink tongue, flopped beside me. 'Here is food, cakes and wine and grapes, and a big cloak to keep you warm. There, you are comfortable? I go now to meet the Queen, but you do not move away from here, eh? You wait for litter to fetch you. There is danger up the path; very steep, very dangerous. You and dog stay here.'

'All right.' I listened to the small stones rolling in her wake as she retraced her steps downhill. Silence settled all round me.

For a few minutes I felt like a deer calf, afraid to move from the hide its mother has placed it in. Slowly I recovered my breath and my bearings. I nibbled one of Vashti's wheat-cakes and took a swig of the cold red wine, better than coffee any day. I began to feel more adventurous but, after exploring up the hill a little way, I discovered an alarming drop sheer down into the mist. The path ended abruptly at a precipice. Vashti's orders to stay put began to have more point.

Below my eyrie, the mist was clearing. By degrees I could discern the spreading branches of the mulberry trees and then the tops of the tents. Ant-like figures around the camp site, and occasionally the faintest possible thread of sound, a shout or a bark, carried up to me.

With Gandhi snuggled in the crook of my knees, I snoozed in the early sunshine.

Some time later I became aware of noise over to my right, a rhythmic throbbing at the edge of my hearing. Drums, I thought. It must be the trackers beating out the end of the drive. Like a dripping tap, the beat thrummed at my brain.

I looked back to the river. The tents had been packed away, and the hunters were drawn up on both sides of the steep glen, gun-barrels winking in the sunlight as they pointed towards the narrow entrance. Straining my eyes, I could just make out the dark patch that must be the soberly dressed workers, drawn a little to one side of the brilliantly plumaged hunters. Khurram, in his virulent purple get-up, stuck out like a sore thumb. Serve him right if a wild boar chose him as a target, I thought.

A long time seemed to pass. I kept telling myself I wouldn't look down until something happened, but a mixture of boredom and curiosity always drew my eyes to the scene below. I finished the wine and wheat-cakes and dozed as the sun grew steadily hotter, and absolutely nothing happened. Even the drums had stopped.

A single, sharp report woke me. I scrambled to my feet, feeling dazed and seeing stars before my sun-struck eyes. A bunch of deer, thirty or forty at a guess, were cantering through the narrow neck of the gorge, strung out, perfect targets for the waiting guns. I saw one fall, then another, and then a bunch of them were down, with the survivors bounding over their crippled companions as they fled down-river. Seconds later I heard the shots.

Like Lord Raglan on the heights above Balaklava, I could see both sides of the battle. The trees on the far side of the killing corridor were pulsating with animals; I could see quick shapes darting in and out of cover, and every now and then some hapless beast would try to make a bolt for it down the gorge. Most of these singletons were shot dead, but when a bunch charged through together a fair proportion seemed to escape without damage. I guessed the marksmanship was none too hot; at least it wasn't the wholesale slaughter I'd imagined and dreaded.

For a time all was still down below, then I faintly heard the drums start up again to drive out the last of the quarry. I saw a moving, slinking mass that could only be wolves emerge from the mouth of the rock corridor. Difficult targets, surely, like foxes; all on the leg and moving faster than they appeared to be.

A ragged volley of shots wafted up to me, but it was hard to tell how many, if any, of the wolf-pack had copped it. Remembering those antique weapons, I thought any able-bodied wolf must stand more than a sporting chance of escape.

Now the drums sounded closer as they herded the remaining animals through the gap. Soon the trackers themselves would come into view at the edge of the trees.

At my side, Gandhi sat up, rumbling a warning, his hackles raised from his scruff to the base of his tail.

'Lie down, boy,' I reassured him. 'It's all miles away.' But he continued to growl.

The gunfire was dying out; single shots or small groups, instead of the volleys. Those ancient barrels must be practically red-hot. I saw the ragtag and bobtail of servants behind the hunters break ranks and swarm forward on the kill, hacking and stabbing. The floor of the ravine seethed with men and animals. Faint sounds reached me: the squeal of a pig, howling wolves and frantic yaps from the hunting dogs.

The defile was suddenly full of human figures. I hadn't seen them emerge from the woods, but these must be the trackers. They were running, crouching, and I was oddly reminded of old war films. They had the tense, purposeful look of soldiers moving in to attack. Like soldiers, too, they fanned out the minute they were clear of the corridor walls, and flung themselves into firing positions, some kneeling behind rocks, some flat in the classic tripod. How dangerous! I thought primly. They're pointing right at the hunters. Didn't they ever learn: *Never, never let your gun . . .?*

I looked for Azam and picked him out easily. His litter had been placed in the middle of the firing line, and he seemed to have been shooting from a semi-recumbent position. As I watched, I saw him hand his gun to Khurram beside him, then he swung his legs stiffly out of the litter and moved forward, presumably to count the bag.

He hadn't gone five paces before Khurram, with an extravagantly ceremonious gesture, raised the gun two-handed above his head, like a boxer's salute, and a split second later I saw the Drone pitch forward on his face, while the unmistakable staccato chatter of machine-gun-fire floated up the hill.

Flame spurted again from the gun-muzzle of the leader of the trackers, and cut a swathe through the line of women supervising the shoot.

'God!' I said. I couldn't believe it. 'They shot them.'

Khurram stepped forward, pointing again at the women, and

the guns rattled, mowing down the Queen's workers as they ran about, no doubt screaming, although I couldn't hear them.

My knees were shaking. I'd visualized trouble, but not this kind. Khurram had been back in the valley only a few days. Had this been planned before he went away? Who was directing him? It was impossible to believe that feather-brained Khurram, spoilt and arrogant as he was, could have planned a coup like this alone.

Where was Vashti? I peered into the ravine, but couldn't pick her out. Perhaps she was hurrying uphill to warn me. As if in extension to my imagination, I heard panting, and the sound of small stones rolling and bouncing downhill. Someone was coming.

Gandhi's growls were thunderous.

'Shut *up*!' I said. 'I'm trying to listen.'

The climber was making heavy weather of the steep path, slipping and stumbling. I twisted my hand into the thick fur round Gandhi's neck, gripping it as well as his jewelled collar, and hung on tight. He fought furiously to free himself, wriggling and jerking; he seemed to have forgotten all his training.

'Stop it!' I said. 'Behave yourself. What's the matter with you?'

The approaching footsteps were close now, just round the corner of the path. I could hear breath rasping harshly, and suddenly uneasy, I crouched back under my overhanging rock, wishing there was more cover. But the cliff fell sheer below the path to the rhododendron thicket some fifty feet below, and in my encumbered state I hadn't a chance of scrambling up the cliff above the path. A mountain goat might have managed it, but not an eight-months'-pregnant woman.

As I knew too well from my earlier exploration, the path itself didn't go much farther. It stopped abruptly twenty yards or so beyond the spot where I stood listening to the approaching footsteps.

My great fear was that it might be Khurram climbing the hill, but a glance down into the ravine reassured me. He was still there, vivid in his purple silk. He appeared to be standing on a rostrum, making a speech.

Suddenly I saw a short, stout lady in a fur coat hurry round the corner of the path and stop abruptly, silhouetted against the light. With a great plunge, Gandhi tore himself free from my grip, breaking half my nails as he did so. He hurled himself towards the stranger, baying in a deep, full-throated voice I'd never heard him use. Something seemed to click in my brain and I felt icy cold. I stood very still. My God! I thought, that's not a person at all. That's a bear.

Finding its way blocked, the animal rose up tall on its hind legs, pointing its mean snout at the sky, and weaving from side to side. It was only ten yards away. I saw the front of its fur coat was sodden and matted, and as it stood there a sticky red pool formed at its feet. The hunters must have wounded it, but it still looked capable of considerable damage. The short fore-arms hung apparently limply, but the stiff, raking claws were clearly visible and I knew that once in the grip of those arms I'd be done for.

I didn't know much about these bears. *When the Himalayan peasants meets the he-bear in his pride, He shouts to scare the monster who will often turn aside.* It seemed worth a try.

I shouted: 'Shoo!' at the top of my voice, but apart from pricking its ears forward, the bear didn't move. It must be female, dammit!

Gandhi was taking appalling risks, dodging about in front of his enemy and barking furiously. Occasionally he ran in close for a nip, but the bear fended him off easily, lunging at the dog with a serpentine twist of the head. All the time, though, its little reddish eyes were fixed on me. To get on up the hill, it had to pass me, and there was nowhere I could duck out of the way.

One thinks of idiotic things in moments of crisis. Hard on the heels of the Kipling came another, more sinister couplet:

> *Algy met a bear, the bear met Algy;*
> *The bear was bulgy; the bulge was Algy.*

Only it wasn't the bear that was bulgy, it was me; and if only I wasn't, I'd stand a better chance of escape. Slowly, feeling behind me with one hand on the rock wall, I backed away uphill, terribly conscious of the abyss where the path ended. As the gap between us widened, the bear dropped on all fours and snapped viciously at Gandhi, who was playing his luck too hard and getting careless.

'No!' I shouted.

There was a sickening crunch as the brute's jaws met over Gandhi's jewelled collar, and blood spurted out to stain his yellow coat, but the gems which I had sometimes thought a bit flash for the well-bred dog to wear now proved their solid worth. After a single shake that swung Gandhi limply to and fro, the bear's face took on the expression of someone whose teeth have hit a rock in a currant bun or a pellet in roast pheasant. As the shock shot through its favourite molar, the bear must have slackened its grip, and Gandhi twisted free leaving a tuft of yellow fur in the slavering muzzle.

The dog was yelping but still game. I hoped he'd have the sense now to keep his distance.

There wasn't a scrap of cover for me. As I edged away, my eyes glued to the bear's in a vain effort to dominate it, my groping hand reached the end of the rock wall. I could go no farther; dizzyingly far below, the valley tree-tops rustled and swayed – above rose a sheer wall of rock, smooth for a dozen feet.

As if seeing it had me trapped, the bear grunted and shambled forward, dripping blood from its wounds. Pinned against the rock, paralysed with fear, I watched it rise again to its full height, arms outstretched to hug me, teeth showing beneath the long, mean snout. Gandhi was taking fearful risks, nipping again and again at the bear's trousers, but it was after bigger game and ignored the dog's attacks.

Then, so close that I felt the scorch of the blast, a shot rang out and the side of the bear's head disintegrated in a pink shower. It fell forward on top of me, twenty-odd stone of heaving, struggling fur and blood stinking breath, and I collapsed under it, not sure whether I was alive or dead.

Not dead but dreaming, I decided, when I recovered from my

brief black-out. The bear's carcase had been rolled off me by some kind hand, and I was propped in a sitting position with the fur cloak bundled into a pillow between me and the rock wall. Looking round, dazed, I saw a stocky, black-bearded desperado bending over Gandhi, inspecting the wound in his neck.

'Good dog, you'll live,' he said, straightening up with a final pat. 'Now let's have a look at your missus'; I very nearly fainted all over again, because he spoke in English.

Chapter Seventeen

I tried to speak but no words came, just little squeaks and grunts like a piglet's.

The man turned to face me, and under the peasant's padded clothes and matted black beard I recognized the face I most wanted to see in all the world; filthy dirty and darkly sunburnt, but the give-away light blue eyes made nonsense of his disguise and I knew him at once.

'Nick!' I croaked, getting my breath at last.

He crouched beside me, his arm round me, patting and stroking as one would a scared animal. 'Take it easy,' he said, and with that phrase I knew for certain it was him, and not my imagination doing a spot of wishful thinking. 'It's all right; you're all right. The bear's dead. Don't be frightened, it's all over.'

'I can't believe it.' But even as I said so, I began to believe it, and a great wave of thankfulness rushed over me. It was all right. Nick said so. There was no need to struggle any more. My whole body began to shake, and I burst into childish sobs.

'Steady on, honey. Take it easy. Have a good cry.'

'It's because I'm so happy,' I wailed, snivelling dismally, the tears streaming down my cheeks. 'I don't want to cry but I can't stop.'

'It's just reaction, I expect. You'd better get it out of your system.' He kept up the pressure, hugging me against him rather as the bear would have done, and presently my sobs turned into sniffs, and my sniffs to small hiccoughs which finally died out altogether. I felt much better and even started to worry about what I looked like.

'I'm sorry,' I said at last, wiping my nose on the hem of Vashti's cloak. 'It's just that I'm so glad to see you.'

166

'Not half as glad as I am to see you,' he said, hugging me harder. 'We'd nearly given you up for dead. How did you get here? What happened?'

Bit by bit, in no kind of order, I told him the story of the past year, from our quarrel in the hotel bedroom at Gulmarg to my flight from the bear. There was a lot I wanted to skip, but prompted by his questions I managed a fair coverage of my activities, and the warmth of his arm round me steadied me over the tricky bits, like explaining about the baby.

'It's incredible,' he said, looking rather dazed, as I finally ran down and stopped. 'I can hardly believe it, but in a queer way everything you say fits in with what Leila told us.'

'Leila? Where's she? Did you take her to Delhi with you?'

'Yes. She slipped out one night when her brother was away, and we took her to Delhi and then to England. She and Sandy were married right away, and we've got her into the Slade – at least, when they saw what she could do, the Slade pounced on her – and she's doing fine and very happy. I believe she's expecting a baby too,' he said, grinning. 'Won't that make it a cousin of yours?'

'Crikey, I suppose it would. But what did she tell you about where I was?'

'It was all very vague, because she'd been only a small girl and ill as well when she arrived in Srinagar, but she had sort of dream memories of a secret castle high in the mountains where an old woman reigned – she thought the old Queen was her grandmother. She could remember a river, and ladies wearing great ropes of pearls and rubies . . . '

Wordlessly I pulled aside the neck of my fur jacket to show my rubies. His mouth literally fell open.

'You mean it's true?'

I nodded. 'But how did she guess *I'd* be here?'

'She didn't really. But she knew Khurram made these mysterious journeys into the hills and came back with jewels and old pictures. The trouble is, she's such a sensitive, imaginative kid that she honestly couldn't tell what she remembered and what she'd dreamed. She's a diabetic, you know, and used to go into a coma quite often before she got the proper treatment.'

'And you. How did you come to find me?'

'I was frantic after you disappeared,' he said simply. 'We'd had that row, you remember, and I thought I'd driven you away. So your brother-in-law and I took his plane . . .'

'*Brother-in-law*? I haven't got one.'

'You have now – Alan Devereux. He married Anna – oh, about six months ago. Just after Christmas.'

Anna married – to Alan! Things were crowding in too thick and fast; I couldn't take them in. I said weakly, 'I always thought he was as queer as a coot.'

'Then let this be a lesson to you not to judge by appearances. Never mind, I won't tell either of them. So that's the picture. Leila was convinced there was some monkey business going on in the hills. Yes, she explained all about the passport business. I see how you got the wrong end of the stick –'

'I'm sorry.'

'Forget it. Then we had Anna going all fey and extra-sensory and saying she knew you were alive and in trouble, though I'm sure she didn't realize how literally you were in trouble. What were Alan and I to do but start a hunt? The police and Interpol weren't much help, and you know what it's like trying to get some sense out of Indian officialdom – turns you white over-night. So Alan and I flew his little plane to Srinagar last March, and we've been looking for you off and on ever since.'

He spoke flippantly, but I could imagine the fears and delays and frustrations and expense he didn't mention.

'As I say, we were on the point of giving up, when we got our first real break. Khurram Beg reappeared in town, and was spotted by one of our spies. You remember old Mr Songali on the house-boat? Well, his grandson's sweet on the sister of one of the gardeners in the Nishat Bagh, and *his* sister works in the kitchen of that frightful tourist-trap of Khurram's. Between them they alerted me to the fact that he was back, and when he took to the hills again, we trailed him.'

'On foot, you mean?'

'By air. Some of the hairiest flying I've ever done, but Alan kept as cool as a cuke. We had to land the plane in the end about thirty or forty miles from here, and Alan's waiting for us there. I intercepted Khurram and his guide at one of those terrifying passes. There was such a blizzard, you couldn't tell if you were going uphill or down. He led me right down to the river. Whew! That tunnel! Quite a trip. It scared the living daylights out of poor old Sandy, I can tell you.'

'And you?'

'Scared out of my mind,' he admitted. 'Still, it was worth it to find you. Now all we've got to do is get back to join Alan and Bob's your uncle.'

A plane only forty miles away; the world suddenly seemed frighteningly near. The twentieth-century world where cars crashed and bombs dropped, where there were electricity and television, the male-dominated world . . . I didn't know if I was strong enough to face it.

I said, hesitating, 'I can't travel like this. My baby's due in less than a month. Snow must have fallen already in the high passes, and I doubt if I'd make it. Can't we wait till the baby's born?' He looked doubtful, and I hurried on: 'You see, it belongs here. I don't want it.'

'It'll be *yours*, my good girl,' said Nick with a touch of exasperation in his voice. 'You won't be able to abandon it here.'

'Not really mine,' I insisted. 'Or at least, I don't feel as if it will be. I've been brain-washed. I suppose. I feel I'm just the vehicle for producing it.'

'That's all very fine, lass, but you won't talk like that once it's born,' said Nick gloomily. 'But you're right; you're really in no shape to cross the passes.'

'Even if we could leave the valley.'

'There must be a way. How does Khurram come and go?'

'I've no idea. I've searched all over the place since I've been here without finding it. And after this freak-out of Khurram's, the whole place will be in chaos. Somehow he must have got the eunuchs – the ones they sent out as trackers – armed and trained to shoot, though heaven only knows where he got the guns. He can't have carried them back from Srinagar, surely. I knew he was in an extremely bolshy state of mind, but I never thought he'd actually rebel against his mother, and if he succeeds in overthrowing the women, it'll be the end of Akbar's

Hive, because he hasn't the least idea how to run it himself.'

'No bad thing, from what you've told me.'

'I don't know,' I said doubtfully. 'Rosie's utterly bonkers, of course, but if you strip away all her absurd mumbo-jumbo about bees and the hive, you find all she's really trying to do is run a community that's self-supporting.'

'Sounds to me as if she couldn't face the prospect of buckling down to her own housework when the British were chucked out of India,' said Nick sardonically. 'OK, then; say she's doing no real harm here – but why the hell does she go and involve you? Anything more calculated to let the cat out of the bag than to kidnap an English girl and imprison her in this valley . . . I suppose you've no idea of the diplomatic fuss your disappearance caused?'

I was absurdly pleased. 'I thought nobody would mind . . .'

'You nitwit, of course they did. There was the most almighty stink, stirred up by me and Alan, to a large extent. Notes from the Foreign Office, denials from Delhi, columns about you in the popular press, mediums gazing into their crystal balls. Questions in the House . . . Honestly, there's been nothing like it since Colonel Fawcett disappeared.'

I was silent, trying and failing to imagine all this activity while I basked in the sun and swelled slowly like a pumpkin, believing that the world had forgotten me.

'Why did she risk it?' he insisted.

'It's hard to say. I think perhaps it was a matter of pride, more than anything. *Folie de grandeur*, if you like. She was the magician, the Queen Bee who could produce anything her hive needed. I think she regretted bringing me pretty soon. You should have heard the string of complaints and curses when I collapsed on them on the way here. She wanted to dump me in the nearest crevasse – she told me so. Then by some extraordinary fluke I started this baby after only one –'

I was about to say 'mating' when I remembered that Nick might not find the idiom of the valley as easy to stomach as I now did, so I left the sentence in the air.

But Nick wasn't worried about figures of speech at the moment; instead he said slowly, 'They didn't look like eunuchs to me, those chaps shooting down there.'

'How could you possibly tell?'

'I thought they were Chinese.'

'Oh no!'

'We're very near the border with Sinkiang, you realise.'
My mind flashed back to that evening so long ago – was it
really less than a year? – on the good house-boat *Convolvulus*,
when Nick had tried to give me a lesson in Kashmir's history
and geography.

He said slowly, 'If Khurram's recruited a bunch of Chinese
bandits to help him . . .'

'And if Vashti's sold her jewels to pay them . . .'

'If they're after this treasure, or golden hive you told me
about . . .'

We looked at each other. A nasty selection of ifs.

'We ought to make a dash for it,' he said firmly. 'Now's the
moment. We may not get another chance.'

'But *how*?' I almost shouted at him. 'We're stuck here. You
don't seem to realize it's a one-way ticket. Anyway,' I said,
remembering with a sudden pang that I should have even
contemplated leaving her to her fate, 'I can't go without Jahanara.'

'For crying out loud, who's Jahanara? This great lump?' He
prodded the recumbent Gandhi with a toe.

I shook my head. I found it difficult to explain who Jahanara
was and what she meant to me. 'A little girl. She's – she's been a
sort of mascot for me. I can't possibly go without her.'

Nick rolled up his eyes to heaven but said nothing, and I
hurried on, 'We must go back to the castle at once. Khurram
will certainly want to kill her, because, apart from him, she's
now the last of Akbar's line. The only hope is that he won't
march on the castle tonight.'

I felt frenzied. So much time had been wasted as we talked.
I'd been lying at ease, secure in Nick's protection, while Jahanara was alone, facing heaven knew what.

Nick helped me to my feet. 'Are you sure you're all right?' he
said doubtfully. 'You're the size of a house.'

'It shows more because I'm naturally thin,' I told him curtly,

171

displeased by this description of my figure. 'Don't worry, I'm pretty fit. Heel, Gandhi.'

We hurried down the winding path, away from the flies that buzzed around the bear's carcase, at the best speed I could manage, but as we rounded the final bend I slowed and stopped, hardly able to believe this was the place we'd pitched camp last night. It seemed a lifetime ago.

The velvety grass was trampled and stained with great blotches of rusty red; flies rose in humming clouds from their feast on the severed heads of deer and beasts of all kinds, piled in a rough heap near the still-standing tents; there was a throat-catching smell of blood and death.

'Horrible,' said Nick, halting beside me.

Together we stared at the scene of desolation worked in half an hour by antique firearms and cold steel. Gandhi roamed forward, sniffing at the pathetic remains of the galloping, leaping animals I'd admired from the heights, and I ordered him sharply to heel. Apart from us, the flies, and a pair of vultures which flapped up reluctantly from the heap of carrion, there was no living creature in sight.

'Think you can make it back to the castle?'

'I can find the way all right,' I said doubtfully, 'but I don't think I could walk there. It must be six or seven miles at least.'

He thought for a moment. 'I'll see if I can find some transport. Wait here,' he said, and, hitching his dirty tunic higher to free his stride, loped off in the direction of the river.

I sank to the ground in the shade of the tent that had been mine last night, wondering vaguely what time it was and where everyone had gone. It was hot, and I felt very tired and disinclined to move. As I stretched myself flatter, the baby booted me under the breast-bone and I thought wearily, only a month to go. A month and I'd be as light and slim as I'd been when I left England. It didn't seem possible. I stared at the roof of the tent, embroidered with a hunting-scene: short-legged horses at full stretch while slit-eyed, turbaned princes used both hands to pull their bows. Deer galloping, staring back over their shoulders, dogs leaping to nip at their fat haunches. All those stitches . . . I drifted off to sleep.

I woke in panic, hearing the jingle of harness and hoof-beats thudding across the grass outside. They were coming back. I was trapped. Where – oh where, was Nick? The sun had shifted to blaze full on the tent-flap under which I lay; inside it was stifling. Cautiously I crawled to peer through the doorway and caught my breath on a sigh of relief. It was Nick himself, cantering easily on one pony and leading another. I stood up and waved and they pulled up stylishly in front of me.

'Look what I found,' said Nick, grinning, his black hair plastered with sweat and runnels of it ploughing dirty furrows down his cheeks. 'I nabbed the one with the widest back for you. Sorry I've been so long.'

'I've been asleep.'

'Good; best thing to do. But now let's get the hell out of here. This place stinketh one in three.'

He boosted me on to the wide, smooth back of the fatter pony, and we moved off sedately, threading through the heaps of carnage down to the river bank. Our outgoing tracks were still plainly marked, and I anticipated no difficulty in finding the way back. I blessed the wandering instincts that had taken me the length and breadth of the valley before the baby made walking such a burden.

'How did you get here?' asked Nick, echoing my thoughts. 'You didn't walk, surely?'

'I was carried in a litter, but it shouldn't take us nearly so long to get back. I'm worried about Jahanara, though. We must hurry.'

I dug in my heels and the pony broke obligingly into a trot. I balanced as well as I could, clutching a handful of the thick mane and found that by keeping the other hand clasped on my stomach, sitting well back with my feet almost straight out in front, I could minimize the joggling; but it would be an exaggeration to say that it was comfortable.

We walked and trotted, walked and trotted, following the path that wound first through the trees and rhododendron thickets, then between fields of tall maize and millet as we approached the great twin peaks of Gogoram and Makoram that hung like a double sword of Damocles in the narrow pass separating the wild from the cultivated end of the valley.

'Is that safe?' said Nick, drawing rein and staring at the threatening overhang.

'Yes, of course. The path goes underneath. I've been here dozens of times; the trick is not to look up.'

He still hesitated. 'Come on,' I urged. 'You can see the hive once you're round the corner. The rocks hang right over it.'

He was staring, not moving. 'That snow on top of the rocks –

'That's been there all summer,' I said impatiently. 'It never melts. Do come on; my pony won't budge without yours.'

The wolf-fire still glowed, although there was no one stoking it, and at the far end of the dark passage a pin-prick of red showed that its fellow, too, was down to embers. The Queen would have something to say when she knew the firemen had deserted their posts. Nick at last stirred up his pony and led mine along the passage, though I noticed he didn't speak again until we were well clear of the overhang. We emerged into sunlight again and, as I'd told him, the castle could be seen in the distance, crouched up against the sheer hillside like a limpet on a rock.

I heard Nick catch his breath. 'That's it?'

'That's it.'

'Fantastic.'

The rocky walls seemed to float above the valley, where a thin mist was rising from the winding river. 'It'll soon be dark,' I said in agitation. 'They shut the gates at sunset. We'll have to hurry – at least I will. You and Sandy better lie up while I see what's going on. If you keep Gandhi with you, I'll have an excuse to come out tomorrow to pretend to search for him. I'll bring Jahanara and we'll make a plan. What's that?'

A droning hum filled the narrow rock passage behind us, increasing in volume until it nearly burst our ear-drums, bouncing and reverberating off the steep sides.

'An aeroplane! Not Alan, surely? It's coming right in here – look out!'

The hum tuned up to a deafening roar and I had to put both hands over my ears, and the ponies cowered, hanging their heads low. But with his wing-tips nearly scraping the rock walls the pilot, whoever he was, thought better of chancing the width of the cleft and wheeled in a tight turn.

'Whew! He must be crazy!' I exclaimed.

'That wasn't Alan,' said Nick decidedly. 'My guess is that that's reinforcements for Khurram. One of the old Wang-tsu hedgehoppers, unless I'm very much mistaken – a real antique. Lucky he was too wide for the passage; a helicopter would have got through with feet to spare.'

'The Queen once told me that no plane could attack the castle because there's nothing small enough that's got the range to get here in the first place. I hate to leave you here, but I must go on alone now.'

Nick dismounted and took hold of Gandhi's collar. 'And I hate letting you go; I keep thinking you'll disappear again in a puff of smoke. Promise you'll meet us tomorrow?'

'Promise.' I buried my face briefly in his evil-smelling tunic, then tore myself away. Later I could relax and leave decisions to him. As soon as Jahanara was safe.

'Sandy and I'll camp down by the river by that pool where I saw you with a child yesterday.'

'*You* saw me by the river?'

'Sure. But you had your great ape of a bodyguard within shout all that afternoon and I didn't want to get stuck like a kebab on that snickersnee he carries. You might not have recognized me straight away.'

'Oh, Nick.' It's a curious feeling to be told you've been watched when you imagined yourself alone. I thought back to yesterday's paddling-party: had I done anything unbecoming, picked my nose or gone to the loo, thinking myself unobserved?

I said, 'It makes me nervous, knowing you're slipping like a ghost unseen from tree to tree. Hoot like an owl next time, to let me know you're about.'

'Come without your bodyguard and I'll appear in person,' he said gravely. 'Tomorrow, then?'

'As early as I can make it. Stay, Gandhi,' I said, taking the lead-rope of the second pony. The animals started enthusiastically towards home.

'Look after yourself,' he called. I turned to wave but the

gathering dusk had swallowed him up. I felt very alone, but only for a minute. Both ponies suddenly flattened their ears and humped their backs in alarm as a whitish shape bounded up behind them, and I heard a despairing yell of: 'Can't hold the brute!'

Then Gandhi was running ahead of the ponies, leaping towards the castle gates which he knew as home.

Chapter Eighteen

The Queen seemed to have aged ten years since I'd last seen her. Beneath her elaborate golden head-dress, her jowls drooped like a pair of pink balloons that have had a lucky escape from a children's party. Her own escape from Khurram's coup had indeed been narrow, because it appeared that a detachment of armed Chinese had tried to take possession of the ice-chamber where the meat was to be stored, and only the gallantry of the Queen's bodyguard had saved her from being captured. The Chinese had been cut to pieces, and though the bodyguard had been decimated, they had given the Queen time to regain her hive.

'And Vashti?' I asked.

Vashti had not distinguished herself for her bravery, I gathered, but neither had she damned herself in the Queen's eyes by declaring an allegiance to Khurram. Yet I was sure that was where her sympathies belonged; sure that she was the snake in the grass, the nigger in the woodpile, the instigator of all the trouble. I had no proof, but I felt it in my bones.

When I stumbled stiffly into the hall, cold and tired and saddle-sore, I could see at once that the hive had given me up for dead. The workers looked like several hundred Macbeths confronted with Banquo's ghost. Eyes rolled, jaws dropped, bundles cascaded to the floor, released by nerveless fingers. And then there was a sudden warmth of chatter and laughter, small hands patting and clapping my frozen fish fingers, leading me to the fire, easing off my boots from feet that looked as blue as over-ripe Gorgonzola. It was a heartwarming moment: I felt at last, fleetingly, that I belonged.

The emergency had broken down social barriers, I realized, looking around and noticing that the soberly-dressed workers were equalled or even outnumbered by my glamorous young frineds from the brood chamber. But far from threatening me, every worker there seemed eager to outdo the others in making me as comfortable as possible. I sat there and let them minister.

My stumbling questions were met with a spate of explanations which I couldn't understand, until the Queen spoke to me.

It was clear that, although puzzled and shaken by Khurram's treachery, she was rallying her forces to defend the hive.

'We should have foreseen this trouble if we had taken to heart the lessons of history,' she said slowly and clearly, and the workers replied with a long-drawn-out: 'Aaaah!'

'The hive that has too many drones becomes weak.'

'Aaaah.'

'Winter is coming; it is time to kill off the drones.'

'Kill them, kill the drones!' responded the workers, their voices rising in volume.

'Drag them from their hiding places; don't let them escape.'

'Kill! Kill the drones!'

Blood thirsty as the words were, the orders and responses acted on me very much like a party political broadcast on behalf of the Liberal Party; I simply could not keep my eyes open.

'Who will kill the drones?'

'We will, we will!'

'Rohana, then; yes, and Taidi. Choose twenty workers and come to my armoury for explosives. The drones and their mighty bird will be sleeping now. This is the time to kill.'

'Burn, destroy!' boomed the voices.

'The rest of you report to your section leaders. We must carry the treasures into safety. We must guard the golden hive of Akbar.'

'Guard, guard . . . ' I drifted off to sleep.

Vashti woke me long before I'd felt I'd slept enough, and urged me to dress quickly. Things had gone badly in the women's camp during the night, and the Queen wanted me to be present when she interviewed the returning scouts.

Stringy, vinegar-tongued Rohana, who was on the seamy side of sixty and therefore the only living worker who remembered a previous revolt of the drones some fifty years before, and her section's second-in-command, the plump, cheerful Taidi who often played her lute to lull the children to sleep on winter evenings, had not only failed in their mission to blow up the rebel's plane, but had themselves been captured and killed by the drones.

The rest of the scouting party had escaped by the skin of its teeth, and it was clear to me that the Queen had seriously under-estimated the strength and the resolution of Khurram's fighters.

When I entered the great hall and made my obeisance to her, she barely acknowledged it but waved to me to sit on one of the cushions below the throne. Then she continued with her cross-examination of young Hanatu, whose pale face still bore weals and scratches testifying to her frantic flight back to the castle in the dark.

The Queen spoke slowly, for my benefit. 'You say there are more than twenty strangers?'

'More than twenty unknown to me. They had made a great fire on either side of their mighty bird, and this sat silent between them. Seeing that the drones were merry and drinking wine freely, as in their feasts, and that the bird slumbered, Rohana and Taidi crept beneath its wings to fasten the bundles of sticks you gave us to its pinions.

'In the firelight, I saw Taidi signal to me to put a flame to the cord I held, but as I bent to strike my tinder-box, I heard a door slam, and Taidi's screams. Men jumped from the belly of the great bird and caught them before they could flee. In a moment, the feasters round the fire had flung down their goblets and surrounded the great bird, and I saw they were not warm and fuddled with drink as they pretended, but cold and sharp, with glittering eyes such as I have never seen on a drone.'

'Bad; that's very bad,' murmured the Queen, almost to herself.

'I heard Rohana calling, "Run for your lives," went on Hanatu. 'They were too many and too strong for us to fight. One chased me closely and I turned and stung him – '

'Dead?'

She shook her head. 'A wound only, my Queen. There was no

time to kill him for the others were chasing me hard . . . '

The Queen assured her that she was not angry; Hanatu had done the best she could. It wasn't her fault that the *sortie* had been such a failure. She sent the girl away to rest, and beckoned me to stand before her.

'If the drones have been taught to fight, to set guards and lay traps,' she said in English, 'it will not be as simple as usual to bring them to heel. How would the new Queen solve this problem? Would she close the hive, although it is a month too early to do so, and trust that the drones starve to death in the snows? Would she lead them into an ambush, or talk with their leaders as Vashti would like? Speak, new Queen, and tell me what you would do, for one day you will rule the hive and face its problems alone.'

This put me on the spot. I said, hesitantly, 'Perhaps it would be best to talk with them, find out what they want. I don't believe Khurram wants to rule here – '

'That is as well, since he is quite unfitted to do so.'

' – but I'm sure he wants to be free. After all, he's seen the world outside the valley. He knows that men are not always second-class citizens. He's read about the battles fought by his great ancestors, and I suppose he thinks he could do the same.'

'You have spoken much, then, with Khurram? You have discussed such matters as freedom, and fighting, and men born to command?'

'Well, a bit,' I said cautiously. I didn't want her getting the idea that I'd put him up to this rebellion. 'You see, it was while I was painting him that the – What's that?'

The drone of an engine, so alien a sound in that peaceful place, came to our ears, and with one accord the Queen and her guards hurried to the courtyard. I followed in time to see, through the narrow cleft between Gogoram and Makoram, Hanatu's mighty bird which appeared as a tiny speck growing rapidly larger as it flew for the gap.

There was a groan of dismay from the workers; many of whom flung themselves on to all fours in an attitude of prayer, banging their heads against the ground and wailing softly. I watched horrified as the plane loomed nearer, diving to less

180

than a hundred feet above the path I had taken last night as it sought the widest point of the gorge, and the snarling roar of the twin engines seemed to shake the valley, reverberating from one wall of the rock tunnel to the other.

When your ears haven't heard any kind of internal combustion engine for nearly a year, they get out of training for the noise and vibration which, at close quarters, comes as a physical shock, a real pain. I clapped my hands to my head, holding it tightly. 'It *can't*!' I shouted.

I was right: it couldn't, or it dared not. At the last second, when collision with the jagged walls seemed inevitable, the plane sheered off in a tight upward loop and roared back up the gorge. Blue trails of exhaust eddied gently towards the castle.

I breathed out hard, snorting the smell of the twentieth-century from my nostrils like a frightened horse. The workers were clustering round the Queen, rubbing her as if to draw reassurance from physical contact.

'Don't be afraid, my children,' she was saying in low, soothing tones. 'Gather round your Queen; defend your hive against the raiders.'

'The Wang-tsu,' I said thoughtfully. I could see what Nick had meant. The machine's upward-tilting wings and over-size wheel-guards made it look very much like a Lysander, a gigantic insect capable of great manoeuvrability. But if it had been a helicopter . . .

I became aware that a hush had fallen on the courtyard and that I was the focus of two hundred stares, ranging from the accusing to the plain scared. The Queen said in a voice charged with menace, 'How do you know that name?'

I didn't want to explain about my would-be rescuers, and improvised quickly. 'It's a well-known plane, the Chinese equivalent of our Lysander. My – my sister and I used to spend a lot of time plane-spotting when we were children. It's the sort of thing you don't forget.'

'Do you know what it means in our tongue?'

My efforts to learn the old language had been faint and spasmodic, since Vashti's English had been adequate for most communication. I knew a good many words connected with painting, thanks to Tarkhum Malik, and had a good grasp of the imperative case for short, sharp orders to the servants: 'Wash!' 'Go!' 'Come!' 'Carry!' and so on, but I still found it hard to string together a whole sentence.

'No,' I admitted.

The Queen turned me so that our backs were towards her subjects. 'It means Hornet. It is the name we most fear in this valley. I told you of the prophecy?'

I thought back to that sunny morning when we'd inspected the hives – the real hives – and the Queen's parting words to the bees before she showed me the golden hive. 'Beware of the hornet,' she said. 'The hornet which will destroy your hives.' A chill seemed to have settled over the courtyard, and I shivered.

'We will prepare to close the hive,' went on the Queen. 'From this moment no one must venture through the gorge that links my territory with the wild-lands. That is now forbidden ground, and if the mighty bird seeks to fly into our domains, the walls themselves will crush it between them. Come, to work.'

'What does she mean?' I whispered to Vashti, my shadow, as the Queen and her satellites swept away, leaving us alone in the high-walled courtyard.

'I think she make explosion.'

'Does she know how to?'

Vashti nodded. 'Since the time of Akbar, the Queen Bee always keep engineers for making holes in rock. But now I think the engineers are with Khurram; we will see if the Queen's workers can use their tools. I think not.' She moved closer to me, dropping her voice as if she feared to be overheard. 'When you are with Queen alone, did she speak of Vashti?'

'She said you'd advised her to arrange a meeting with the drones.'

'This she will do?'

'She hadn't decided.'

Anger flickered in Vashti's eyes. 'She must meet them. She wastes time with her councils, and talks of shutting the hive. The Queen is old and has forgotten how to rule. She should go out and meet the drones, only then will she have peace.'

'What's the hurry?' I asked. 'It seems to me that the longer she keeps the men hanging about, the stronger her position. The first snows will put paid to the drones' rebellion; they'll have to surrender or freeze to death. That's why they want to rush us.' I looked at her speculatively. 'You seem to know a lot about Khurram's plans. Whose side are you on, anyway?'

Vashti turned away, muttering impatiently, 'You know nothing, Charl Begum. You are nothing but foolish. I will tell the Queen how to drive away the drones, and this time she must listen to my plan.'

I watched her go, unconvinced either of her loyalty or wisdom. It seemed to me that the Queen's strategy was the only sensible one in the circumstances. Time was on our side. Apart from the danger from the air, which would be greatly diminished by blocking the Makoram gorge, our position was secure. Far the larger loop of the valley's figure-of-eight formation was under our control, and though the castle itself stood perilously near the cross-over, at least from within its walls we could keep an eye on the enemy's movements. Camping in winter among the wolves in the wild-lands wouldn't be my idea of fun, and apart from what they could shoot or fish for, Khurram's rebels were soon going to be very short of food, not to mention clothes and blankets.

Reassured that there was no immediate danger, I scooped Jahanara up from her nurse's charge, released a yelping, prancing Gandhi from durance vile in the courtyard kennels, and the three of us made our way unobtrusively in the direction of the river to keep my rendezvous with Nick.

Chapter Nineteen

'Makes your blood run cold, donnit?' said Sandy. His pale ferret-face with its ginger eyelashes and long, pink-tipped nose had a curiously Beatrix Potter-like effect as it peered out of an enveloping felt cloak, hooded in the manner of the mountain peasants.

He and Nick had camped the night in the cave at the back of Jahanara's pleasaunce, within a few feet of the river. They had seen no one.

'What does?' I asked.

'The thought of that old besom f... I mean, playing around with high explosive. This rock's none too stable, you know, and if she wants to blow that keyhole it's got to be just the right charge. Too much or too little and she's going to make a heap of trouble for herself. I was a sapper, so I should know.'

I'd told them of the Queen's preparations for a siege, and introduced them to Jahanara who, mercifully, hadn't thrown a screaming fit at her first sight of European men, but simply lapsed into a trance-like silence, her eyes enormous in her ivory face.

'Pretty little thing,' said Nick, 'though she's not exactly going to increase the mobility of our party. Nor's that great dog of yours. I suppose you wouldn't care to leave him behind? No? I thought not. You don't believe in travelling light, do you?'

'Wait till you see the rest of my luggage. Rubies and emeralds the size of pigeons' eggs,' I said, exaggerating a bit, but not all that much. 'Bales of silk, furs, embroidered linen and cheesmen in gold and ivory. Tortoiseshell boxes. Miniatures in solid gold frames. I've picked up a lot of stuff since I've been here. I'd hate to leave anything behind.'

'Give me strength,' sighed Nick, but Sandy, with a guttersnipe's saucy appraisal of my figure, said: 'I'll say you've picked up a lot,' which made me seethe with rage.

Nick suggested, with unusual tact, that we worried about the portage *after* finding the way out of the valley, rather than before, and I had to admit I hadn't discovered anything since I spoke to him last night about where the exit lay.

'Too bad,' said Nick, 'but if there's a way out of this valley, Sandy will find it. I didn't bring him along just for his pretty face.'

Sandy aimed a playful blow at his head, and Jahanara flinched and gave a muted yelp. As I comforted her, I realized how silly I'd been to imagine that Sandy resented Nick's teasing in Srinagar last year. They were a team who understood each other too well to be bothered with their opinions clashed, and on another, deep-buried level, I was exhilarated to be once again with men who were their unfettered selves, neither cowed into obedience nor fretting at enforced idleness, splitting hairs and picking quarrels because they had nothing else to do. True, the intricate carving and embroidery, the time-consuming mosaics and over-decorated gold and silver work, even the delicately designed miniatures I loved and tried so futilely to imitate, were all the products of men who found time hang heavy on their hands; but now I felt, as I hadn't felt for months, that to condemn a whole sex to idleness was as cruel as sprinkling a monkey with flea-destroying pesticide. Some of the valley's men might be, as Rosie claimed, aggressive and dangerous; no doubt most of them were shiftless and lazy, and probably quite a few were, as she said, perfectly happy to exercise their craftsman's skills in peace with no demands of decision, bread-winning, or government. But to lump the whole lot together and forbid any man to rise above the lowly station to which his sex condemned him was not only cruel, but futile. It had led to this rebellion at a time when the hive was least able to cope with one.

Nick was saying, as I had this deep and disturbing change of heart: 'It shouldn't be beyond Sandy's powers as an engineer and geologist to find a way out of this Godforsaken spot.'

It had seemed like Paradise to me for so long that I was

shocked; then reluctantly admitted to myself that the valley was losing its charm for me, too. The hive was falling apart, and the Queen had lost her power to hold it together. Even the thought of returning to the world of machines and strikes and bombs and politics didn't alarm me as much as it had yesterday. My curiosity about what had happened since I'd been out of circulation was beginning to revive, and with it a powerful longing to see England again, and Anna, and even Marble Arch on a rainy day.

'How's Leila?' I asked, suddenly ashamed of myself for not thinking of her before. 'How's she taken to life in England?'

'Like a duck to water,' said Sandy with his rare smile. 'Goes off to the Slade every day on the Tube, and comes home smiling. I never thought she'd find it so easy to fit in. And now she's expecting, as well.'

I knew this, but said, 'Oh, Sandy, how exciting! When?'

'Couple of months after you, by the looks of things. That's why we can't hang around here too long. *I* wasn't all that keen to come looking for you,' he explained candidly. 'Thought it was some wild goose chase of Nick's, and if you got yourself into a jam out here, well, you'd gone looking for it, hadn't you? But Leila, she wouldn't leave it alone. "Go, Sandy," she'd say. "I feel in my heart she is alive. She is a prisoner in that valley I told you of, where I was born. It's like a dream to me, but I can't sleep to think of Charlotte as a prisoner of that evil old woman." Then she told us what she could remember about the castle, and the men who weren't allowed to work or leave the castle, and the hives full of bees.'

'She remembered that?'

'Remembered it best of all. She was only a kid when they brought her to Srinagar, you see. She said she was frightened of the bees and cried when she was made to go into the cave where all the hives were.'

'I wonder why she had to do that?' I said thoughtfully. 'The bees are frightfully fierce: only the Queen can handle them. I know: I've been stung to blazes just because I didn't keep close enough to her for protection. Why on earth would anyone take a child into such a dangerous place?'

'Suppose it was one of her last impressions of the valley,' said Nick slowly. 'Perhaps that's why she remembers it so clearly.'

'You mean . . . ?'

'I mean, if you've searched the valley for the best part of a year without finding the way out, and if no one's stopped you going where you wanted – '

'The Queen *encouraged* me to go where I liked.'

'Is she frightened of the bees?'

I stared at him. 'Far from it; she's crazy about them. She's the Queen Bee, you see, and she is quite literally crazy about them. Bonkers. She talks to them; tells them all the news of the valley: who's died; who's had a baby; all that sort of guff. She says they're the reincarnation of all the valley people who've died – quite crackers, but she takes it completely seriously. She lets them crawl up her arms – ugh! She took me there once.' I shuddered, remembering that sunny Spring morning. 'But I got stung and swelled up like a pumpkin, and refused point-blank to go again.'

'And Khurram?'

'He's immune – or so she says. She sometimes takes him along to visit the cave. I suppose he's been stung so often, poor chap, that he's used to it.'

Sandy said decidedly, 'Then that's the way out.'

'Oh, no!'

'It's obvious.'

'If there is, you can leave alone,' I said. 'I'm not taking Jahanara anywhere near those caves. It's terribly dangerous. There are over a hundred hives, and the least disturbance brings the bees out in swarms. Honestly, I'd rather stay here for keeps than poke about in that cave.'

'Don't be so wet,' said Nick briskly. 'It'll be perfectly safe at night. We'll burn some paper in there, and that'll make the bees stay at home. I've seen our gardener do it, when he takes the honeycombs. As soon as they smell smoke, the bees gorge themselves on honey. It's a sort of reflex action, because way back they remember forest fires mean they'll have to move house, and it's better to move house on a full stomach. But tanking up makes them too sleepy to attack intruders, and that's

187

when you can muck about with the hive without getting stung. I must say that castle – citadel – whatever you call it – is a fantastic piece of building. Just like the old-fashioned bee-skep, that great golden dome. It reminds me of the tomb of Agamemnon at Mycenae.'

Sandy looked sceptical. 'That's a right lot of codswallop about the smoke keeping bees quiet.'

'Scientific fact, you ignorant towny. Any bee-keeper would tell you so.'

'I can't wait to introduce you to the Queen,' I said. 'You'd have such a lot to talk about.'

'Unfortunately I'll have to forego that pleasure. Well, I'm glad that's settled. I've been worried by not knowing how we were going to get out of here.'

'You, worried?' jeered Sandy, but I could see that he, like me, didn't share Nick's conviction that all our troubles were over.

'So now we know where and how, the only question is when. Any reason why we shouldn't make a bolt for it tonight?'

Tonight! All my fears rushed back. I said, hesitating, 'Couldn't we wait until after the – my baby is born? It's barely a month away, and I don't know if I'll be able to keep up with you.'

'Think it out, sweetheart,' said Nick patiently. 'The longer we wait, the more immobile you're going to become. In a month, the snow will have fallen for sure, and the drifts will be far too deep for us to have a snowball's hope in hell of moving until the spring thaw. How long do you expect poor old Alan to roost there wasting his expensive time? And how long could Sandy and I remain hidden from your Queen Bee in a place as small as this? As for keeping up – well, luckily you're blessed with two good men and true to carry you if you founder on us. The baby will be safer inside you than out, too. No; don't kid yourself that putting off the evil moment of our departure is going to help matters: the sooner we hit the trail, the healthier for all of us.'

He was right, of course, but still I felt unreasoning fear of leaving this secure little world for the dangerous outside. Nick must have sensed this, for he said gently, 'Cheer up. *Kale phe*, as they say in Tibet. Take it easy. We'll look after you.'

I managed a wobbly smile and drew my cloak round me. 'Where shall we meet?'

'We'll do a recce this afternoon and see which of the caves looks the most promising. You say there are two?'

I nodded. 'Do be careful.'

'Sure. Softlee, softlee. Then we'll come back to the citadel as soon as it's dark. Say half an hour after sunset. You know that big boulder on the main track, just before you get to the gorge – where you left me last night, in fact?'

'The rock shaped like a Sacco chair?'

'That's it. We'll wait there. Sorry we daren't come any closer, but you won't have far to go on your own.'

'OK.' I picked up Jahanara from her perch beside the river. 'Come on, darling; home, Gandhi. We're not going fishing today.'

'Don't that kid ever utter?' asked Sandy. 'I wouldn't mind one like that myself.'

'It's because she's deaf, I think. She hardly makes any noise except when she's in a rage, and then she can scream blue murder. But she's a sweetie, aren't you?' I gave her a hug, and was rewarded by seeing the solemn little face spread slowly sideways in its adorable smile. I hoisted her high on my shoulder to balance the goat's wool bag with my painting things which I carried on the other arm, waved to the men, and pushed through the bushes back on to the main track.

Despite the bright sun, there was a nip in the air; a memory of woodsmoke and promise that winter lurked just round the corner. Red-gold leaves fell from the chenar and poplar trees, yellow from the oaks, dry brown needles from the larch, and they all made a soft, rustling carpet underfoot as we trudged towards the hive. The icing-sugar peaks surrounding the valley seemed to have grown taller since I last looked; Nick was right: fresh snow had already fallen and would soon creep lower to cover the tree-line. There was no time to waste, but still I couldn't bring myself to hurry. This was my last afternoon here, then. Perhaps this was the last sight I'd ever have of this sweeping patchwork of colour framed by the jagged white peaks.

Sighing, I pulled out my sketch-book, plumped Jahanara down on the crisp red leaves with a packet of my worn old felt-tips to play with, and settled my back against a smooth grey trunk. Just one more sketch – half an hour wouldn't matter. Gandhi crouched beside me, nose on paws; he knew the signs.

A party of women with a small cart came round the corner of the track, but I didn't move. They would stop, look, admire, chatter, giggle, and move on. Their bright cloaks and silk robes proclaimed them to be brood-chamber ladies on an afternoon stroll, rather than the sober, industrious workers, of whom I was still slightly in awe.

Out of the corner of my eye, I saw them halt the cart and felt, rather than saw, them move behind me to look over my shoulder at the sketch. My crayon flew, blocking in the castle walls, but at the back of my mind a small uneasiness niggled – something to do with the cart. Why should brood-chamber ladies push their own cart when they had servants to do it? My audience rustled and nudged as they crowded round. 'Get a move on, blast you,' I abjured them silently. 'You've all had a butcher's by now, surely.'

Then Gandhi growled, and my skin suddenly prickled a warning. I slapped the sketch-book shut and started to heave to my feet. Too late.

A hood reeking of opium was slipped over my head, and as I struggled to tear it off, I heard a wail from Jahanara and the snap of Gandhi's teeth. Then there was a furious growling, worrying noise, the rending of cloth and two explosions close together. Gandhi howled, a horrible dying fall of sound, and I tore at the hood screaming 'Damn you! Let me go. What have you done?'

The fumes of dope seemed to fill my head to bursting; I tried to get away from it but there was no escape. My senses swam and I knew no more.

I woke sobbing, remembering everything. The sketch, the struggle, Jahanara, Gandhi . . . It was dark, with a point of light not far away. I put out a hand, and felt padded cotton beneath me – some kind of mattress – and beyond it a soft, sandy floor. There was a curious smell, slightly animal, slightly damp.

190

Stone, I thought. Rock. I'm in a cave. Feeling around cautiously, my hand encountered something soft and warm up against me. It moved and whimpered.

Jahanara, I thought, in mingled relief and indignation, sitting up so abruptly that my head swam. I might have rolled on her and smothered her. But at least she's alive.

The light, I now saw, came from a camp-fire in the making. In front of it a figure knelt, blowing, until the embers flickered into flame. As the fire mounted with a roar and light blossomed into the farthest corners of the cave, I saw Khurram leaning against a wall, propped comfortably on one elbow, watching me with his flat black snake's eyes.

I had to swallow twice before my voice would work, and it emerged all cracked with rage and sorrow. 'Where's my dog? Why did you shoot him, you swine? Why've you brought me here?'

'Questions, questions,' he said mockingly. 'Why should I answer questions? The Queen never answers mine. And you are like her – much too like her. But I, Khurram Mohammed Beg, will break her power and yours. The time has come.'

I didn't like the sound of this at all. 'I'm not involved in your wretched politics,' I said. 'I was kidnapped. I didn't want to come here. Don't you remember? I don't care who rules Akbar's Hive – Queen or Drone – it's all the same to me.'

It wasn't, but my skin had never felt so precious to me as it did when I took a look at the slit-eyed, fur-hatted bandits with seamed faces the colour of well-soaped saddlery who lounged around the cave fingering wicked-looking knives. Having seen the way they'd bumped off Azam, I thought it prudent to assert my neutrality.

'Drone!' Khurram said scornfully. 'The Drone has no power. I shall not become the Drone.'

'Same old pipe-dream?' I heaved myself into a more comfortable position, hoping he'd be lured into one of the long monologues which always left him in a good temper. I knew practically every line of his 'If I ruled the world' spiel, thanks to our sittings.

'Dream that will soon be truth.'

191

I said, temptingly, 'I don't give much for your chances of bringing all Kashmir under your sway if you can't even conquer this small pretty valley. Your men are soft, Khurram Beg. They've been forbidden to fight so long that they've forgotten how to.'

Sure enough, it set him off. 'You lie, Charl Begum,' he flared back. 'Two nights now my men have suffered the hardships of winter in this cave, and not one has wished to return to the hive.'

'That's because you daren't go back. You're stuck here, now.'

'So you will be our messenger, Charl Begum. No one but you and this – this child is valued enough by the Queen to make her give up Akbar's honey.'

'*Honey*?' It seemed an odd swap for me and Jahanara.

'The golden hive,' he hissed impatiently, and suddenly I understood. The Chinese had come here on a treasure-hunt, pure and simple, and Khurram, poor deluded frustrated Khurram, was leading them to it.

'Good lord, Khurram, she wouldn't give that up for *anyone*. Certainly not for me.'

'She must,' he said flatly. 'It is the law of the valley. Akbar's line must continue, or the bees will swarm and leave their Queen to starve. With the death of Azam, only the unborn child within you, and Jahanara herself carry the blood of the Timurids, and this the Queen must preserve. It is the law.'

Game, set, and match, I thought admiringly. This boy's got brains after all. Then I thought of Gandhi again, and my anger hardened.

'If I bear this message to your mother,' I said coldly, 'there must be no harm done to Jahanara. Hurt a single hair of her head, and you can whistle for your treasure.'

He leaned back, eyelids drooping, mouth curled up under that nasty little bootlace moustache. 'No harm will be done to the child. When the treasure is mind I will raise an army of men and sweep the Hindus from the face of Kashmir. Then I will come as a ruler to visit 'Akbar's Hive', and tell the Queen Bee how affairs are arranged in a kingdom of men.'

It was as futile as trying to reason with General Amin. Like all men who had deliberately and artificially been deprived of initiative and responsibility, Khurram was mentally aged about eight, completely unaware both of his own limitations and how the world worked. All his life he had been under the thumb of the women. No wonder that the first taste he had of freedom went straight to his head.

I glanced round the cave. The dozen or so men that I recognized from the drones' quarters were looking distinctly unhappy, shivering in their thin, unsuitable silks, and edging ever closer to the fire. The Chinese bandits, in contrast, seemed aggressively at home. They wore long felt boots with enormous clod-hopping soles, and padded clothes with an extra layer of sheepskin worn wool-side-in; guns of a newer vintage than the Mogul blunderbusses were slung negligently on backs and shoulders. I made a quick head-count: thirty including Khurram; more if they'd left guards with the aeroplane.

'You've hardly enough soldiers here to make Mrs Gandhi tremble,' I taunted.

'When the honey is mine I will have many more. Hwan Lo Li, who gave me these soldiers, will come to my aid with all his people when we sweep down from the hills to slaughter the fat *banias* by the shores of Lake Dal.'

'You mean that's a Red Army plane?'

His thin smile widened. 'Hwan Lo Li is a war-lord whom even the Red Army cannot capture. He is old and cunning, and he loves jewels, gold and jewels. The golden hive will buy me many more soldiers and guns; enough to fight battles like my fathers, the Moguls.'

'Suppose the Queen refuses?' I objected again. 'Suppose she makes you wait until the snows have fallen and shut the passes. How long can you keep your men cooped up in a cave like this when winter begins?'

'Cooped?' He smiled wolfishly. 'When the snows come, the guardians of the golden hive sleep.'

'So the treasure is taken inside the castle.'

It didn't seem to bother him, and I guessed why. As soon as the golden hive was removed from the safe-keeping of the bees, he would risk an attack. It was the insects he feared. Once the treasure was in the castle, Vashti would let him in to steal it.

193

'The queen has summoned Vashti to her council,' I hazarded, watching him carefully. 'Vashti is clever, and the Queen rewards her with many jewels. I hope you're not counting on *her* to open the castle gates to you.'

His face darkened; I saw that the shot had gone home. He, too, knew that Vashti would always fight with the big battalions.

'So said Gul Beg,' he admitted reluctantly. 'It is for this that we must first try to barter the jewels for Jahanara's life.'

The moon was full, like a shiny gold coin in the sky as I left the cave under escort and crunched over hard frost with a powdering of fresh snow towards the Gogoram Pass. Any day now we could expect the first heavy snowfall which would seal the valley until spring. I wondered how long Nick and Sandy would wait for me by the rock, and for the first time I regretted not having my watch, which I'd stopped wearing when I stopped thinking about hours and minutes, days and weeks.

After the timeless peace of the last few months, too much had happened in the forty-eight hour period since the drones went hunting for these days to seem to belong to the same time-scale. I realized with some surprise, though, that instead of flopping about feeling exhausted as I would have expected after such a burst of unaccustomed activity, I felt keyed up and ready for anything.

My escort of ruffians stopped by the black circle that marked the embers of the wolf-fire, now completely extinct, and as I halted too, stirring the ashes with the toe of my elegant felt boot, the men motioned me forward.

'Aren't you coming?' I asked in my halting Turki.

They shook icicle-encrusted beards, their black eyes gleaming in the moonlight like slivers of coal. 'You – go – ' They made shooing gestures as if to herd me into the long tunnel.

I looked up. Only a slit of starlit sky showed between the two great peaks as they leaned inward like two old men eternally whispering filthy stories to one another. No wonder the Chinese pilot had lost his nerve when he tried to fly through that gap. I shivered, then braced myself and stepped forward into the darkness, trying hard not to think about the explosives that might or might not be waiting for a light, or the peril in which I'd had to leave Jahanara. I longed for the reassuring pad of Gandhi at my heels; poor, gallant Gandhi. There seemed to be more rubble than usual lying on the path, possibly shaken from the walls by the vibration of the aeroplane's engine. Stepping as fast and delicately as my bulk would allow, I hurried towards the end of the tunnel, fighting off a panic of claustrophobia. Like Nick last night, I'd made the mistake of looking up at those twin grim sentinels of rock, and felt a rising tide of fear.

Another hundred paces – fifty – twenty – then at last I was clear of the pass, and slowing down to ease my aching back and legs in the moonlight, which seemed twice as bright and beautiful after that narrow dark hell-hole.

It was tempting to sit and rest, but I resisted. Soon, surely, if they hadn't already done so, Sandy and Nick would give up their cold vigil and go back to their camp, and I hadn't time or energy to slog all the way down to the river to tell them the danger Jahanara was in. The two men were my only hope of rescuing the poor child because, whatever Khurram believed, I couldn't imagine that the Queen would trade her precious golden hive for the life of one small girl. She valued Jahanara because she carried the blood of Akbar in her veins, and for no other reason: I was sure that if it came to the crunch, she would sacrifice the child.

I stumbled on, occupied with these gloomy thoughts, and increasingly aware of the ache in my back which seemed to have spread to the pit of my stomach. Then, on the clear cold air, I caught a scent which transported me straight back a year – back to the sunlit Nishat Bagh with its poppies and peonies and marigolds, and Sandy rolling himself an evil black cigarette.

'Nick!' I called softly. Hardly had the word left my mouth before a light-coloured shape hurtled knee-high at me through the darkness. I flung out my hands instinctively, and my fingers locked in a texture I'd thought I'd never feel again. The silky thick ruff round the neck of my dog Gandhi. I hugged him, and he huffed and slobbered and bent himself in a circle, as pleased as punch at his cleverness in finding me.

'We thought you were never coming,' said Nick, appearing like a dark shadow in the dog's wake. 'What happened? We've been sitting here since dark, watching the castle. They've got lights all over the place, and twice we've seen parties of women go past . . . ' He sounded thoroughly aggrieved and I explained quickly where I'd been.

Nick whistled softly. 'That's why your dog came bolting back to us, the great booby. Half an hour or so after you'd left us, that animal came crashing through the bushes, tail between his legs, as if all the hounds of hell were after him. We tried to shoo him off, but then we noticed his fur all scorched along his back, and there's a deep graze, too. So we let him stay.'

'Khurram's men shot at him. I thought he was dead.'

'God, no. He's tough, this customer,' said Nick, rubbing Gandhi's chest while the dog squirmed with pleasure. 'It'd take more than a pot shot with a rusty flintlock to kill him off. The little girl, though; that's a different matter. I don't fancy her chances, I'm bound to say.'

'There's a terrific tradition of chivalry to children,' I said doubtfully.

'That'll wear pretty thin if she becomes a nuisance. No; Sandy and I will have to winkle her out of their clutches. If the men are all as weedy as you say, it shouldn't be too difficult to stick them up à la Bonnie and Clyde.' He turned to the shivering Sandy. 'You can be Bonnie.'

I couldn't raise a smile. 'You've got a gun?'

'Sure. We're both armed to the teeth.'

'You see, they're not all weeds. The Chinese, in fact, look extremely tough.'

'Not as tough as us,' he reassured me. 'What's up?'

I must have flinched as a spasm of gripe clutched my stomach, but it passed in a few seconds, and I didn't feel this was quite the moment to reveal to Nick the disorders of the inner lady.

'Just cold,' I lied.

'Ruddy perishing,' agreed Sandy. 'C'mon, Nick, don't stanc

there gassing all night.'

'Wait a bit. What exactly did you arrange with Khurram – about the transfer?'

'If the Queen agrees to the deal,' I said through chattering teeth, 'we'll light the wolf-fire at our end of the Gogoram Gorge. I came past it just now, and it's out. You can quite easily see a light from one end to the other. Anyway, as soon as they see our signal, Khurram and his merry men will light *their* fire and send Jahanara into the gorge. Four of our workers, plus me, must carry the golden hive in from our side, and when they meet Jahanara with her escort, they swap burdens. Oh, it's so complicated!' I said in despair. 'I can imagine a hundred things going wrong. For a start, I don't think for a minute that the Queen will play ball. She doesn't care a damn about Jahanara. I should never have left her in that horrible cave, with that horrible man. She'll wake up and be terrified – '

'Steady on, don't get in a stew. Just leave it to us. You go on back to the castle and get yourself into a hot bath, and we'll meet you down by the river tomorrow – same sort of time – and I promise you we'll have that child with us. See? I promise. Stop worrying and go on home and we'll see you in the morning.'

'Oh, thank you!'

'Best save your thanks for later,' said Sandy lugubriously, peering like some wild shy thing from the recesses of his hood. 'I don't doubt we'll have our work cut out finding where the kid is, let alone rescue her. Like it wasn't that easy in the caves this afternoon.'

'I knew it wouldn't be. Did you get stung?'

'Only Sandy did,' said Nick with brutal cheerfulness. 'But it was worth it. We found the way out.'

'You *what*?'

'Found the way out. You have to go right between the bee-hives, just as I guessed. It was obvious, really. The oldest trick in the world.'

'You sent poor Sandy into that inferno . . . ' I began indignantly, but he cut me short.

'On the contrary, like a good officer, I led my troop into the fray. Was it my fault that said troop tripped over a rock and sent

197

a bee-hive flying? He deserved every sting he got.'

'They always sting me,' said Sandy mournfully. 'Dunno why, I'm sure. I had an aunt once used to swell up something chronic if – '

But we never heard what happened to his aunt, because Nick hissed: 'Quiet!' as a light appeared on the path behind us. At the same time, a mutter of low voices told me who they must be: the search party Rosie had sent to look for me.

'*Ciao, bimba,*' breathed Nick, and I felt the light touch of his hand on my hair, the only uncovered bit he could touch. Then he and Sandy were gone, melting into the dark night as silently as ghosts.

I sank to rest on the flat stones, immeasurably comforted by the thought that Jahanara's rescue had been taken out of my hands. I didn't doubt for a moment that Nick's incurable optimism and Sandy's equally persistent pessimism would combine to achieve whatever they aimed at. All I wanted to do was get home and lie down with a flannel-wrapped heated brick clutched to my tummy, which seemed to have gone berserk and was giving me merry hell.

'Hallo, there!' I called, as the group of women drew nearer. 'I'm here, beside the rock. Over here. Can you take me back to the hive?'

Chapter Twenty

The Queen's golden head-dress waved slowly up and down as she nodded. 'My treasure in exchange for the life of Jahanara?'

'Yes.' I added after a moment, 'I'm sorry.'

'How did they come to capture her?'

I explained as well as I could, and she listened, and nodded, and at last sat brooding silently for a painfully long five minutes, while behind her throne Vashti's cat-like amber eyes stared at me with a mixture of condescension and triumph because I had at last blotted my copy-book so thoroughly.

'The great Akbar gave the treasure to be as honey for his hive,' the Queen pronounced at last.

There was a buzz of assent. The workers knew all about this.

'Without honey, the workers will starve and the Queen perish.'

'Aaah!'

'Yet the great Akbar also commanded us to preserve his line. Khurram must die for his crime of attempting to overthrow the established order; he is too dangerous now for us to pardon. If Jahanara dies too, where is the line of Akbar? Nothing would remain of the royal blood but the unborn baby in the belly of our young queen. As we all know, babies are in peril from many causes during their first years of life, and often they are born dead. Have we the right to sacrifice Jahanara, knowing that with her death the royal blood may also die? My ladies, draw near and counsel me.'

I fidgeted on my cushion, wanting to hear the outcome of the discussion, but longing even more for a private session over the 'long-drop'. My tummy was registering a sharp protest against irregular hours and unaccustomed exertion, and I hoped the Queen would soon dismiss me. When you've never had a baby before, you can't believe that the end of all those months of waiting has come in the shape of an on-off-on-again sort of tummy-ache. I remember feeling the same about Christmas and birthdays as a child. Here it is, at last, yet it doesn't feel different enough to be what I've been waiting for. Half of me wanted to reveal the cause of my inner turmoil to the Queen; the other half would rather have died.

Before matters became too pressing, however, the Queen turned to me and said graciously, 'This matter does not concern you, my child, and the hour is late. You have my leave to go.'

'But if you don't . . . I mean, if Jahanara isn't – '

'Vashti will bring you news of our decision. You can do nothing to influence it one way or the other. Now go.'

I made acquiescent noises, since it seemed the only thing to do, and removed my bulk from the council chamber to keep my date with the 'long-drop', though with no spectacular results. Slightly comforted and half convinced that I'd been imagining the tummy-ache, I submitted to my maid's ministrations and retired to bed, but not to sleep.

After an eternity of listening to soft comings and goings as I waited for news from Vashti, I heard the distinctive clang of the courtyard gate and hastily rose again, wrapping myself in every fur I possessed. I had to be there when the wolf-fire was lighted. I had to persuade the Queen that I, and no substitute, must precede the treasure-hive through the narrow gorge, or any attempt to rescue Jahanara would be in vain.

The night was almost unbelievably cold. I'd never been out long after sunset before, though I knew the temperature must plummet the moment the sun sank. Fur round my face kept my cheeks from freezing, but my eyelashes felt stiff and only by directing my huff upwards as I breathed could I keep any feeling in the tip of my nose, which is of a fairly flat variety anyway.

All quiet on the tummy front; I hurried along behind the bobbing lanterns, my boots squeaking on the frosty ground. It seemed a long way: there was our rendezvous rock, there the rhododendron thicket where Jahanara and I had often played hide-and-seek. The leaves pointed stiffly at the ground, frozen out of their shiny smoothness and hard to recognize. Gandhi's breath was small two-stroke exhaust at knee-level. He shaded into the white-rimmed landscape so well that he'd be invisible at five paces.

At last the lanterns ahead halted. This was the moment I'd meant to reveal myself, but I hung back, grappling with another badly-timed attack of gripes.

Suddenly the wolf-fire flared, showering sparks high into the air. They must have poured oil or butter over the wood to start such a blaze, and I watched, fascinated, as the light spread up the glittering sides of the rocky defile, ever higher and narrower until even the reflection of the tallest flames was lost in the vaulted shadows.

Almost at once, an answering flame leapt for the sky at the far end of the passage: Khurram was ready for the exchange.

I found I simply had to sit down. Gandhi snuffled and licked my cold face as I twisted and turned on the ground, trying to bring my innards under control. 'Stop it,' I growled to the baby. 'You're meant to be a month away,' but I was beginning to realize it was no use kidding myself. This was D-day all right. Longingly I thought of private rooms in hospitals, with soft-voiced, softer-footed nurses plumping my pillows and offering different methods of painless childbirth; gleaming, sterile, chromium stethoscopes and oxygen equipment coiled snake-like on the bedside table, banks of flowers and glasses of bubbly for a good job well done . . .

The dream faded; it was back to the frosty ground with only Gandhi in attendance, and a pain in my back where it was jammed hard against the rock-face. But no other pain: it had vanished as mysteriously as it had struck, leaving me a bit limp, but otherwise all right. Quick, I thought. Before the next session sets in there's work to do. Stumbling in my haste, I slipped and skidded down the rough path towards the blazing wolf-fire.

I'd delayed too long. As I rounded the last corner of the winding path that snaked down to the pass itself, I saw a little procession below that stopped me in my tracks.

A bulky, fur-wrapped figure waddled in front like a woman in the last stages of pregnancy, and I had to admit that whoever was masquerading as me in this role had captured to a T the way I marched over the rough ground, so utterly ungraceful and European, so different from the gliding, bent-kneed shuffle of the Valley women. It could, I realized, be no one but Vashti.

Behind her, four more muffled figures advanced in pairs, each holding a flaring torch in one hand, while with the other she grasped one handle of a sort of stretcher on which was balanced the golden bee-hive. The torchlight danced on the gleaming dome, and I let out my breath in a long sigh. So the Queen was playing fair. She was going to hand over the treasure as Khurram had asked. Up till that moment I hadn't believed she'd do it. I'd been afraid she'd have some trick up her capacious sleeve to save her precious 'honey', something that would put Jahanara in danger.

But this was on the level. She was following Khurram's directions exactly, in order to rescue the child who meant so much to me, and in spite of the bitter cold I felt a glow of warmth in my heart as I looked down on that stout, indomitable figure now standing alone by the wolf-fire, watching her most precious possessions carried out of her sight for ever. It was for my sake she'd given it up; I felt certain she had neither affection nor any sense of responsibility for Jahanara herself, but she wanted me to be happy, and she knew Jahanara's life mattered to me.

I leaned limply against the rock-face, looking down at the small procession which moved slowly because of the weight of the hive, thinking affectionate, sentimental thoughts about the old tyrant I'd cursed so hard and so often. Heart of gold, really, I mused. A great old girl. Why did I never see it before?

Now lights were moving at the men's end of the gorge. Craning my neck down and straining my eyes, I could see that one of the fur-hatted figures was carrying Jahanara, her head lolling on his shoulder. Doped, I bet, I thought savagely, remembering the poppy-impregnated hood they'd flung over me. Guaranteed to make you sleep quicker than a cup of Horlicks. True to the exchange arrangements, Khurram's procession was five strong too – four men and the sleeping child.

The lights met; stopped. This was the tricky bit. The hive-bearers set down their burden. Vashti held out her arms for

Jahanara.

I don't know what instinct for danger made me glance back towards the Queen at that moment, and I saw what she was doing in a terrible flash that made a mockery of my maudlin, muzzy feeling of goodwill towards her. She hadn't changed. There wasn't going to be a happy ending after all.

Slowly, deliberately, as if she had all the time in the world to do it, she dipped a long taper in the fire and moved to bend over a crevice in the rock, first on one side of the passage then the other. Majestically she straightened; stood with head bowed as if to reassure herself that the fuse was well alight, then started to roll with that peculiar, tank-like gait up the path towards my vantage-point.

I watched in helpless terror. The procession of women had turned and begun their retreat, the leader carrying Jahanara, the others empty-handed, but now crowds of the drones – Khurram's party in full strength, were swarming into the pass, crazy to see and touch this legendary treasure which they'd never dreamed of possessing. I could hear the shrill jabber of their voices, shouting and exclaiming. I could even distinguish Khurram, shoving the others aside . . .

Then, like a thunderbolt, or more accurately like a pair of Rugger forwards breaking through at Twickenham, Nick and Sandy burst into view, crashing through the astonished drones, who parted like the Red Sea under the impact of flying knees and fists. Past the men's wolf-fire, past the planted hive round which the crowd was thickest, they caught up in a few leaping bounds with the slowly retreating women. I saw Jahanara snatched from the leader's grasp just as a rugger ball is twitched out of the scrum, and clutched close as they hurtled on.

'Run! Run!' I screamed, my heart thundering away so hard I thought it would choke me. 'Save her!'

They couldn't possibly have heard me, but they seemed to put on an extra spurt which carried them clear of the passage just as the whole place blew up.

On form, you'd have expected me to lose consciousness at this point.

I used to be a great little blacker-out in those days; whenever things got too much for me and/or weren't going my way, I used to faint to give matters time to settle down. I didn't exactly do it on purpose, but Mummy once asked a doctor why it happened and he waffled away about subconscious wishes for oblivion and inability to face reality. This reassured my mother that I wasn't foxing when I keeled over, but it didn't stop the keeling. I notice that so far in this saga I've admitted to three spontaneous blackouts. When I fell in the Lidder river; when Azam invaded my bed; and when attacked by the bear, and each time consciousness was something I was delighted to lose at that precise moment.

But now as the night split apart in a dazzle of orange flame, immediately followed by a deafening *ker-ump*! that blasted my legs from under me and hurled me as flat as my figure would allow, I waited in vain for the comforting, familiar blackness to envelop me.

It did nothing of the kind. Instead, I saw with horrid clarity in the orange light, figures like broken puppets tossed sky-high by the blast, arms and legs spread in the manner of free-fall parachutists, but going up instead of down – going up and up until they struck the roof of the narrowing cleft between Makoram and Gogoram and plummeted back to the path. Some were caught by their clothes on the jagged pinnacles of rock; some hurled into the river; some even lodged in cracks in the cliff-face. Rocks and sticks and chunks of debris showered down into the pass: it was like looking closely at a suspect joint of meat and suddenly realizing that it was swarming with maggots. Wherever I looked there were more bodies. All the drones must have died in that first explosion, together with the procession of women who'd gone to fetch Jahanara.

I raised my head as the earth stopped trembling beneath me, and strained my eyes towards where Nick and Sandy had vanished. Could they have got clear? They'd been running full tilt and disappeared seconds before the blast: they must have guessed it was coming. But how – where – why?

The Queen had deliberately led the drones into a terrible trap, and baited it with the honey they yearned for. She must have decided it was worth sacrificing a few of her women to achieve such a coup; and Jahanara. What she would have told me about the failure of the rescue attempt I'd never know, because by now that tank-like gait of hers would have carried her half-way back to the castle, and I had no hope of getting there before her.

As if to confirm this, another spasm of pain gripped me in the guts, and for a second or two I writhed helplessly on the ground before pulling myself, trembling, to a sitting position. I must move; I mustn't stay here. The baby was obviously on its way in a hurry.

I rose unsteadily and looked round for Gandhi. He was crouching rigidly, ears flat back, eyes showing too much white, and made no move when I spoke to him. Oh lord, I thought, that's the end! The rock-bottom, bitter-chocolate end! Now he's hurt or shocked or something and I can't possibly lug him back up the path.

'Come on, you lily-livered hound,' I said encouragingly, and started to shuffle back to the path I'd left.

Like a flash, Gandhi was after me, and seized the trailing cloak I wore. Two tugs with his eighty-odd solid pounds behind them, and he had me down, sprawled back in our little niche, gasping with shock and indignation.

'Gandhi, you undisciplined animal! What d'you mean by it? Down, sir. Leave it!'

Growling, he held me down, his lip lifted so that I had a close-up worm's-eye view of his gleaming ivory fangs. All sorts of horrid explanations for this behaviour raced through my brain. Hydrophobia? Epilepsy? Hunger?

I tried to push him off, but his growls became more and more menacing. They were shaking the rock ledge on which we lay, echoing off the rock walls; the earth itself was moving . . .

Then I understood, and lay very still. The explosion had started an avalanche on the snow-covered tops above us, and we were right in its path.

Another perfect opportunity to black out, and again I didn't. Instead, I edged back to the very furthest recess of the niche, where the overhang afforded us a little protection, hugged Gandhi and waited for the worst. Quickly the rumbling grew to a roar that hurt my ears, and I covered them with the cloak, pressing back hard against our refuge as lumps of rock began to rain down into the pass, blotting out the moonlight, covering the wolf-fire, the treasure-hives, and all those poor bodies under thousands of tons of rubble.

I don't know how long Gandhi and I lay there in an agony of fear as the avalanche thundered past us. I prayed non-stop, out loud, though I couldn't hear my own voice above the mountain's roar. Once Gandhi leapt convulsively as a rock struck him, and no doubt he yelped, but the sound didn't reach me. Poor dog, he pressed against me with desperate strength, and though his presence was a shield and comfort, his weight certainly wasn't, and I soon lost all feeling in my legs.

After a bit I grew more confident that the rock overhang wasn't going to collapse on top of us. It seemed to act as a spout, funnelling the falling debris clear of our tiny cave, which must have been one of the few safe places on the entire mountain at that moment. If I'd taken even a few more steps along the now non-existent path . . . If Gandhi's instinct hadn't got the better of his training . . .

Hours seemed to pass before the mountain spent its fury, and even when the worst was over, the odd rock the size of a bungalow fell frequently enough to stop me sticking my nose out from the protection of the little cave, which was now filled with a curious white light – curious because although it gave the impression of whiteness and lightness, I still couldn't see anything except the alternation of light and shade as the avalanche gradually slithered to a stop.

At last all was quiet, except for Gandhi whimpering as he pressed close to me.

'It's all right, boy; it's over,' I said with more confidence than I felt. 'We'll wait until daylight, then see if we can get out of here. Lie down, now.' Cuddling my head into his ripe-smelling thick pelt, I made myself as comfortable as possible, and the warmth of our two bodies soon built up a delicious fug under the fur-lined cloak. Occasional muffled thuds outside failed to disturb me as I fell into an exhausted sleep.

I woke with a yelp, feeling as if some ill-intentioned giant had seized my abdomen in a pair of vast pincers and was putting pressure on them.

'Yow! Crikey!' I gasped, and Gandhi cocked an eye reproachfully at this rude awakening. The pain was gone in an instant, but it had been far fiercer than anything that had gone before, and I knew with chill dread that the baby was getting down to business again.

Daylight filtered into the little cave, but it brought no comfort because it showed that instead of being in a cave, now we were in a pit. The avalanche had filled up the narrow pass and built a wall of jumbled rocks well above the level of our refuge. Gandhi would be able to get out all right, through a smallish hole at the top, and given strength, I could probably squeeze after him.

Chunks of dirty snow and mud mixed with the rocks were giving off that white light I'd noticed in the night, and a sprinkle of snow had even found its way into our cave. Luckily for us, the first rock to fall on our level had jammed between the path and the overhang, keeping back all subsequent débris. If a smaller boulder had been the first to penetrate our hide-out, it would have been certain chips for me and Gandhi.

'Action!' I said out loud, feeling as limp as a piece of wet cloth. It was so painful to move my cramped limbs that I nearly gave up after the first attempt, and then when the blood started to circulate in my feet I roared with pain. Gandhi watched me, waving his plumed tail in a vaguely agreeable manner.

'It's no good, old boy,' I said, between tears and laughter at my own helplessness. 'I can't make it. I think we're done for. I'll have one last try, then that's it.'

The now-familiar cramps were bigging to grip me again, and I knew that in a minute or two they'd paralyse my power of movement. In a feverish rush before they conquered me, I hurled myself anyhow up the wall of loose shale, clawing from hand-hold to hand-hold, breath rasping in my throat and Gandhi moving easily beside me, non-retractable claws not-withstanding. He had all the balance and spring I lacked, and yet by holding on grimly I managed to haul my heavy body foot by foot towards that tantalizing gap in the rocks through which daylight was beckoning.

207

Somehow I made it, and dragged myself through the gap just as the spasm of cramp became too intense for me to think of anything else. I relaxed, half in and half out of our refuge-cum-prison, and let the pain wash over me like a wave and, like a wave, sweep back to disintegrate in nasty little twinges and aches too small to be called pain, but just discomfort.

When these had died away and I felt normal again, I heaved to my feet and surveyed the white desolation left by the avalanche. *Façon de parler* white – in fact, there was a lot of greyish grit and shale mixed with the snow, but to my eyes, accustomed for the last ten hours to the dark hole in which we'd hidden, it seemed tremendously, blindingly light, trackless and featureless. It was about as alluring as an uncharted quicksand on the moon to step on to, and I hesitated, trying to get my bearings.

The river? Obviously it still ran somewhere between the changed shapes of Gogoram and Makoram, but where there'd been a steep valley with a thread of river at the bottom were now a couple of small hills of loosely-piled rock. The gap between the mountains seemed to have widened, and great gashes in their sides showed where the landslip had wrenched slabs out of them.

I saw now that the main force of the avalanche hadn't gone over my cave, for around the corner, towards the castle itself, the two peaks which had always reminded me of a pair of old men whispering in each other's ears now looked as if the older of the two had buckled at the knees, collapsing on to his companion and bringing him, in turn, to a crouch.

I stared at it in consternation. All my hopes had been pinned on a quick retreat to the castle, and now I saw it was odds against there being any castle left to retreat to.

At my side, Gandhi had been studying the changed topography with equal surprise. But he didn't share my doubts about the castle. With a happy bark he pushed past me and bounded off into the soft snow, flinging loose spatters of it from his legs and tail as he gambolled away, as carefree as any puppy released from a kennel.

'Gandhi!' I shrieked. 'Come back, you great ape. Don't leave me here. *G-a-a-andhi!*

He paused, one foot raised, bent at the knee, in a heraldic sort of pose; looked deliberately back at me and then bounded on his disobedient way, taking not a blind bit of notice of my frantic whistles and shouts.

'Treacherous animal,' I sobbed. It's always a slap in the face to discover how little your pets love you. The affront was purely psychological, of course, because a dog was no use to me except as a hot-water bottle in this predicament, but as soon as Gandhi deserted I gave up, slithered back down the heap of shale I'd just climbed, and flopped into the indentation in the dust that still seemed warm from our bodies.

There I lay, no longer bothering to fight the waves of pain that gripped and released my guts in ever more rapid rhythm until, as if pleased by my passivity, the giant hands that were squeezing me lightened their pressure from agonizing to bearable, and bearable to positively agreeable. Like a surf-rider, I went with the waves instead of fighting my way through them, letting my limbs flop, eyes closed, and body carry on with no interference from me. It was tiring, though, very tiring . . . I lost count of time.

Chapter Twenty-One

Vaguely I became aware that I was no longer alone. A voice I knew was urging me to make an effort – wake up and *shove* – harder now; and *again*. You're not trying, it nagged; come on, show what you're made of. And again now, *push*!

Shut up and leave me alone, muttered the remnants of my free will, but I hadn't the strength to resist. The voice bullied and pleaded, cajoled and insulted me until I obeyed. I tensed my tummy muscles and shoved, but nothing happened.

'Harder!' commanded my tormentor, invisible to me at the business end of the operation. 'Again.'

I tried again and again, while the unseen voice nagged at me like a pantomime comic who incites the audience to sing their heads off, then asks blandly when they're going to start singing? It was very tiring.

Soon I discovered I could fool the voice into thinking I was trying harder than I was if I expelled my breath with a cavernous groan at the conclusion of each shove.

'Well done! Splendid! Keep it up!' enthused the voice.

Pleased with this simple ruse, I groaned with a will until my throat was sore. Something was definitely on the move; the shoving was having an effect.

A hand gripped mine: advice and encouragement worked up to a full head of steam. 'Harder! Now! Again!' as insistent and remorseless as a boat-race cox.

I can't pretend that it hurt, exactly, but all the minor discomforts were building up to a fairly intolerable whole. My feet were freezing, my throat sore, and I felt giddy. The voice drummed at my ears and the shoving was hard, monotonous work. I yearned to stop, to sleep, anything to arrest this straining and churning inside me; so gathering all my strength for one last effort, I gave a mighty heave.

Anyone who's been incautious enough to stand admiring a dead stag at the end of a successful stalk, and has watched as the stalker whips out a knife and slits the beast's belly, will understand what I mean when I say that the next moment felt as if I was being gralloched.

With a couple of bumps and a slither, something so huge slid out of me that I couldn't believe it had been inside me any more than it seems possible that the multi-coloured mass of organs and intestines which the stalker hauls out on the heather could have fitted inside the stag's slim, elegant frame.

'Yow! Don't! That hurts,' I yelled in protest as my innards seemed to spill out in a warm, pulsing flood; then stopped in mid-yell, realizing that it wasn't true – nothing hurt any more. It was all over. The cave echoed with the persistent mewing squawks of a new-born baby.

'Is it all right?' I asked, trying to sit up but falling back weakly before I'd raised myself more than a couple of inches. 'What is it? Can I have a look?'

No answer.

'Where are you?' I said, louder. 'Who are you?'

The rustling, bustling, rubbing and splashing noises continued, and the voice murmured to the baby in the intervals between squawks, but ignored me completely.

'I want my baby!'

It was no good. By twisting my head round I could just see a large shape moving around in a deliberate, businesslike fashion, taking no notice of me.

I felt helpless, and frantic. Blood was draining out of me, and I knew I could no more hoist myself upright to grab the baby than I could fly.

Then the soft bulk of the Queen loomed over me, and all my pent-up terror and sorrow burst forth before I could think.

'Give me my baby,' I sobbed. 'It's mine; you can't have it. You killed Jahanara. You shan't take this away from me.'

'Killed Jahanara?' she said coldly. 'You must be delirious.'

'You did! I saw you.'

She began to chuckle, a rich, deep buzzing sound which

211

struck a chill through me. I knew she would stop at nothing to protect her hive. 'You saw me kill Jahanara, and that serpent Vashti? She thought she could steal my treasure. She laid her plans carefully, leading Khurram to rebel against me, but the old Queen managed to sting her in the end. And before she died, d'you know what she told me? You'll never believe it. She told me you were the one who was stirring up trouble, telling the drones they should be free while you painted your pretty pictures of them. What d'you say to that?'

'I didn't. I promise I didn't. Please give me my baby.'

'He belongs to the hive, but you – you shall be cast out to die. You disobeyed my orders when you crept out to follow us last night, and the punishment for disobedience is death. A reigning Queen may not use her mighty sting to chastise a subject, but the cold will do the work soon enough. As you look down from the pearly gates to see your little drone at play, remember that you had the chance to reign beside him, and threw it away.'

The chill spread through me as I got her meaning. She was going, leaving me in this icy morgue, taking my new-born son with her.

'Please don't leave me here,' I whimpered. 'I'll never disobey you again. Only please don't go.'

She seemed to brood on it for a moment, then I sensed rather than saw the characteristic flap of her jowls that meant thumbs down to my plea.

'Farewell, Charl Begum.'

She was gone. I heard a diminuendo of barks as Gandhi, who must have led her to me, bounded after her; then silence so complete that I wondered if I was already dead.

Lying there in the dim white light, hoarding my dwindling core of warmth as blood continued to drain from me and my legs went numb, I was too frightened to mourn the loss of my baby. This, then, was it. One more night without food and warmth would finish me off. It seemed such an anonymous way to die – no wills, confessions, explanations, goodbyes . . . Easy tears trickled from my eyes as I thought of Anna, cosy in London; she'd never know what had happened to me.

Time crept past. The chill in my body tightened its grip, and

I drifted in a limbo of semi-consciousness, uncertain whether I was awake or asleep. Light faded in the little cave.

I was roused from this torpor by a shower of grit and pebbles on my face, quickly followed by a dog's tongue, warm and wet as a soapy flannel.

'Gandhi!' I squeaked, and was immediately struck in the face by another, heavier shower of rubble.

'She's here! Quick, Sandy, bring your torch. Thank God we've found her alive!'

I'd been so sure I was going to freeze to death, and my mind had gone so far towards acceptance of dying that I had difficulty in hauling it back. But it was Nick all right, patting and praising Gandhi, gingerly propping me up, exclaiming at the mess.

'Whew, this place smells like an abattoir. Quick with that brandy, she's about ready to peg out. My God, what's happened? The floor's awash with blood. She must have been hit by the avalanche, and crept in here. Can you speak, darling? Tell me where it hurts?'

'All over,' I murmured, storing up that 'darling' to think over later.

It was no good trying to take part in the rescue, the patching up, the resuscitation of the body I'd been ready to abandon. Far better detach my spirit as far as possible from the gory details, the humiliation of being rolled to and fro like a piece of meat as Sandy made a quick, expert examination and reached the right conclusion.

'She's not hurt – not seriously, but she's lost the kid. Leave this to me. I'll tidy her up. You go on out for a bit; I'll call you if I need you, but just now I could do with a bit of elbow-room.'

'Sure you can manage?' Relief at being dismissed was plain in Nick's voice.

'All in the day's work. Go on, and take the dog with you. I don't want you fainting to add to my troubles.'

Surly, indomitable, blessedly capable Sandy . . . gratefully I abandoned myself to his care.

When next I woke, the cave looked very different. A fire threw

213

light and warmth into every corner, and sleeping bags, rugs and mattresses were heaped against the walls. A metal tripod with a double hook supported a kettle and neat little black cauldron over the fire, and an appetizing smell of onions rose from the latter as Sandy lifted the lid and stirred the contents.

I was warm, comfortable, and ferociously hungry.

'Sandy?'

'Mm?' He looked round. 'Oh, you're awake, are you? How d'you feel? Care for a bite?'

'Yes, please. I'm absolutely starving. Thank you for fixing me up,' I said in some embarrassment. 'I thought I was a goner.'

'Don't mention it.' He brought me a tin plate of stew. 'It's only the dehydrated stuff, but it's not bad if you're hungry. Nick's gone to see if that fall blocked the exit we found in the bee-cave; we'll be sunk if it has. He said he'd be back by six for sure, and it's ten past now, so he won't be long. Here, I'll give you a hand to sit up; but careful, mind. You'll have to sit sort of sideways, because of your stitches.'

'Stitches? You stitched me?' I was astonished.

'Sure. I used to drive an ambulance,' he explained, 'before I started driving for Grand Mogul. I've done a fair bit of nursing, one way and another – had to, with some of the poor old crocks we get on our tours. Can't say I've ever acted as midwife, before, though.' He looked away, embarrassed in his turn. 'Sorry about your kid, by the way.'

Spooning stew into another plate, he went to the pile of sleeping bags. 'Here, wake up, ducky. Grub's up.'

My heart leapt in delighted disbelief as Jahanara's tousled black head rose above the pile of bedclothes. So he hadn't meant he was sorry about her – he'd been referring to my own baby!

'She – she's all right?' I asked, still almost unable to believe my eyes.

'Right as rain. She's been tucked up asleep for hours, ever since we – here, steady on!'

For Jahanara had cast one look round at me, and sprang across the cave into my arms, sending her plate of stew flying and uttering little whimpering yelps I'd never heard her make before. She buried her face against me, and I gathered the thin

214

body into my arms, feeling tenderness I'd never experienced for anyone before. *This* was my baby.

I held her close, murmuring, 'Jahanara, darling. Don't cry; I'm here. You're safe with us, darling. Oh, Jahanara!' Then I got the shock of my life, for she raised her face, all wet with tears, and looking into my eyes she said: 'Jana'.

'It's a miracle,' I said for the umpteenth time.

'*Changez de disque*,' growled Nick. He'd slithered into the cave, cold and cross and severely stung by bees, a few seconds after Jahanara had launched into human speech for the first time, but he hadn't actually heard her, since she hadn't repeated the performance.

'You heard her, Sandy, didn't you?' I demanded. 'I'm not making it up, am I?'

'I heard her. C'mon, Nick, get this inside you.'

Nick gulped down stew and Jahanara watched him. When he called to Gandhi to lick the plate and threw it across the rock floor, I saw her start at the sudden clatter.

'She can hear,' I said triumphantly. 'I know she can. She's quite different. She's not watching your lips to see who's speaking. She can actually *hear*.'

'You mean to say,' said Nick slowly, 'she couldn't hear at all before?'

'That's what I keep telling you.'

'Crikey. No wonder you're excited. I know you said she was deaf, but I didn't realize you meant stone deaf. I thought you meant – well, hard-of-hearing.'

'Absolutely, totally stone deaf.'

At last he was impressed. 'Did you realize that, Sandy?'

'Can't say I did. But then there wasn't a lot of time to think about it,' said Sandy reasonably. 'Rushing about the mountains looking for her, then looking for you, and the avalanche and all.'

'*The avalanche*,' I said.

'What about it?'

'That must be what cured her. Shock waves or something. The noise was frightful where I was, and you must have been even

215

closer to it than me.'

'We couldn't have been much blinking closer without being *under* it,' said Sandy with feeling. 'Blimey, Nick and I were hunched up against the cliff with the kid between us. It was like sitting under a jet revving up for take-off. It hurt right through my head. Then what d'you call her – Jana? – began to cry, and we muffled her up as best we could – '

I've talked to half a dozen E.N.T. specialists since that day, and none of them can explain how Jahanara was cured. In fact they all say there's nothing wrong with the formation of her ears and look at me as if I'm a lunatic. It's pointless to argue with them, so I prefer to think of it as a good, old-fashioned miracle. And I'm sure the cultural transition from life in a sixteenth-century palace to life in twentieth-century suburbia was eased for her by the fact that her early years had been no more informative than a silent film, and as easily forgotten. Having never spoken her own language, she learned English with great speed, and her voice is as free from oriental sing-song as my own – from which, I suppose, it is largely copied.

I talked incessantly to her during those dark days in the cave while the men waited impatiently for me to regain enough strength to travel. No one from the castle came near us; the Queen had shut her hive for the winter.

At first I couldn't believe she could abandon me so completely, without even coming back to check that I really had died of cold and hunger; but as the days passed and we saw no one I realized that her behaviour was in character. She had finished with me; taken all she wanted from me as a bee robs a flower of its nectar and then loses interest.

(Nick would roar with laughter if he knew I was comparing myself to a depollinated flower, but in the Queen's eyes I'm sure that's just what I was: empty, finished, thrown away, of no further importance.)

So my fears of an execution squad sent to polish me off diminished as each day passed, and instead – you have to have something to worry about – I began to share the men's twin

216

anxieties about weather and food. With me and Jahanara, not to mention ravenous great Gandhi, to feed as well as themselves, the supply of dehydrated food they'd humped on their backs through the passes which lay between us and Alan's aeroplane, was vanishing at a frightening rate.

For forty-eight hours after the birth of my baby, Sandy kept me deliberately short of food, and although I suffered a small degree of puerperal fever, with aching, swollen breasts and a high temperature, both soon subsided as my body realized it was far too hungry itself to have any surplus.

After that, they nobly awarded me double rations to hasten my recovery, and guilty as I felt to eat while they fasted, I have to confess I had no difficulty in cramming it down.

One evening, Nick returned triumphant to the cave with a pretty little spotted deer across his shoulders; he had ambushed the animal at the far end of the valley, and risked a shot with his revolver.

'*Beastly* little guns,' he said. 'I tried for a heart shot, but I had to be quick, and there wasn't anything except my own arm to rest the barrel on. Anyway, I shot; and the deer gave an almighty leap and took off straight up the hill. The echoes seemed to go on for ever, and I was scared stiff of bringing down another avalanche, but I scrambled after it as fast as I could and found it lying on a ledge about a hundred feet above where I'd shot at it – stone dead. Then I had a ghastly time dragging it back to the path. It was practically sheer rock, and I knew if I let go the carcase would bounce all the way to the bottom and get so bashed up it'd been uneatable.'

'It's fabulous,' I said, sinking my teeth into red meat for the first time in a week. 'You're a hero.'

'It'll keep us going for a few days, anyway. D'you think you're fit to travel yet?'

All my reluctance to leave the valley had vanished. I was in a fever to be gone. 'I'll try,' I said. 'I've been doing exercises these last few days, and I'm getting stronger.'

'Give it a day or so yet,' said Sandy. 'We don't want her konking out on us the moment we move. I went down to that cave today, where the bees live, and they're still pretty busy flying in and out. I thought you said they hibernated during the winter!'

'It may not be cold enough quite yet,' I suggested. 'Apart from that one snowstorm, the weather's been much milder than I remember it this time last year. Don't worry; as soon as there's a cold snap, they'll stay inside the hive.'

'But we can't wait for that,' said Nick impatiently. 'Don't you see, this mild weather's our one chance of reaching the plane. No, Sandy; bees or no bees, we'll have to leave as soon as possible. Alan's giving us a month at the outside before he quits – and when he does, we'll be stranded.'

'You're the boss,' said Sandy, and slowly I nodded.

'I'm ready whenever you say.'

So next morning, we emerged like sleepy moles into a dazzling blue-white-and-gold landscape, and set off for home.

Chapter Twenty-Two

The trouble about writing your own story is that you can't work up much suspense in the final furlong. Obviously the I-character survives to tell the tale, or how would the tale get told? Now and again you come across some desperate device such as a diary written by the narrator just before he finally pegs out, which has been unearthed and given to a publisher by some other hand; but I've always found it difficult to believe that anyone at his (or her) last gasp, feeling the icy breath of the Grim Reaper huffing down his neck, would be in a mood to write down exactly how he happened to be in such a fix. Would a narrator in this situation remember *the exact words* of every character involved in his story? Unlikely.

I've written this for Jahanara – or Jana, as we call her – to tell her who she is and how she happens to be where she is now. Not because I'm afraid anyone will try to snatch her from me – she's my step-daughter, by any reckoning, since her late father was briefly my husband, and now she's my adopted daughter as well, thanks to the industry of Alan's legal department, who got weaving on the problem of regularizing her identity as soon as we landed in New Delhi. I don't want her to forget her real origin, though, just because she holds a British passport. I feel that a Mogul princess descended in direct line from the Great Mogul Akbar should know and be proud of the fact. Sandy agrees with me, and takes a rather touching delight in reminding Leila from time to time that she isn't just a little suburban housewife, but an oriental lady of royal blood.

So . . . I've given it all away. Not only did I survive that grisly journey back over the mountains, but the rest of the party did too.

There were times when I thought we were done for; plenty of

times when I loathed Nick and detested Sandy and longed with all my heart to be back in the busy security of Rosie's hive, humming away with the workers as they stored food or spun or wove or toiled at some other mindless, ceaseless activity; but these bouts of longing for the valley grew fainter with every mile we travelled.

Really the worst moment was when I saw how the men proposed to leave the valley. I was prepared for the cave swarming with bees: we muffled ourselves and Jahanara in the quilted sleeping-bags and Nick led the way through the honeycomb of rock passages with a smoky torch of damp tissue to keep the insects at bay. It was the last of our loo-paper, but no one complained, and no one was badly stung.

'Why aren't you little sods asleep?' I heard Sandy mutter stumbling behind me after the faint glow of the torch.

'Shush! You'll stir them up more if you talk. A man's voice is supposed to send this sort of bee into a frenzy.'

'Pitch your dulcet tones up here,' fluted Nick in a high falsetto, 'or better still, belt up. I'm crawling with the little stinkers, too, but we're nearly there.'

Sandy swore and slapped but said no more until the buzzing faded behind us. Another hundred yards by the light of Nick's torch, and then brightness showed in front of us; we were near the exit.

I knew there must be some barrier to stop people leaving the valley, but when I saw what it was, I stopped in my tracks. The flight-board.

'I'm not going down there.'

'Yes, you are,' said Nick and Sandy with one voice. Jana shrank against my side and together we stared in horror at the abyss yawning below us.

'You're crazy.'

'It's quite safe if you do exactly as we tell you,' said Nick kindly. 'Sandy's been down once already, so we know it's OK.'

So this was what they'd been doing, those long mornings while I talked to Jana in the dark safety of our cave. 'You never *told* me,' I accused. 'You never said a word about jumping off a precipice.'

220

'We guessed you'd make a fuss if you knew,' said Sandy. 'So we kept quiet about it on purpose.'

'I am *not* making a fuss.'

'Splendid!' said Nick heartily, and I ground my teeth. 'Then listen to what you have to do. I'm going down first, on this rope –'

'It looks frightfully thin.'

'Two thousand pounds breaking strain; don't tell me you weigh more than that. When I reach the bottom, I'll tie on the basket which is obviously what your Queen Bee uses to get down in, and if it'll hold her, it shouldn't have any difficulty in holding you lot.'

I clung to this comforting thought as he explained how Sandy and I were to haul up the basket, load me, Jahanara and Gandhi in it, and lower away. Lastly, Sandy would climb down the rope.

'OK, then, let's go.' Without giving me a chance to argue or object, he knotted the long, thin rope round a rock as casually as if he'd been hitching a horse to a rail or a boat to its mooring, gave the end and a cheerful thumbs-up to Sandy, and disappeared backwards over the drop.

The next few minutes were some of the nastiest I ever remember. I have a horror of heights: even standing on a high diving-board with no intention of launching myself off it, gives me the screaming heebyjeebies inside.

'Try not to look down,' advised Sandy: but I found that looking straight ahead at the ranks of unfriendly spiky peaks opposite was no more reassuring than letting my eyes stray down to the greeny-silvery thread of river miles below.

Jana clung to my trouser-legs. 'Mum-mum-mum,' she whined plaintively, but I was far too scared to be pleased at this linguistic progress. Gandhi, on the other hand, seemed thrilled to be up so high, and lay with his paws on the very lip of the precipice, wagging his plumed tail and craning down to watch Nick's descent.

I pressed back against the rock wall behind us, clinging to its rough surface until Sandy called brusquely for help in pulling up the basket, and I knew at last that Nick was safe down. Hand over hand we hauled, and I even welcomed the rope-burns on my palms. Anything to take my mind off the drop.

With a last lurch, the basket swung into view: something like the gondola that hangs under a hot-air balloon, rickety wicker-work with low sides.

'We'll never get Gandhi into that,' I said, objecting to the last.

'You get in first and he'll probably follow.'

'You can't possibly hold it on your own.'

'Course I can. Get in, girl, and stop arguing.'

Gingerly I stepped into the swaying basket, bending my knees and sitting down as quickly as I could. Sandy smartly boosted the crying child on to my lap, where she buried her face and clung like a baby monkey. Immediately, with a leap that rocked the frail container, Gandhi was on top of us both.

'Sit!' I shouted as he attempted to put his paws up on the edge of the basket, and with a reproachful look he obeyed.

'That's what I call *training*,' observed Sandy, and pushed us off into space.

The first few seconds were a nightmare, as the basket swung and dropped at the same time. I thought at any moment our combined weight would tear a hole in the bottom, and did feverish sums: Rosie was twelve stone minimum; luggage, say, another three. Well, I was seven and a half, or should be – approximately thirty pounds for Jahanara and another six stone for Gandhi. What did that add up to . . .?

Then the basket was descending smoothly as wiry Sandy paid out the rope, and at last I dared to look down. Far below the copper wedge of Nick's face was gazing upward; then I could see the black of his hair and beard on either end of the wedge. It developed eyes, mouth, and a nose; whites to the eyes . . .

I glued my gaze to those eyes, willing the frail basket to last just another fifty feet – twenty – ten – We hit the ground with a bump that threw us all into a heap, and Gandhi was first out, leaping at Nick like a mad thing, licking his face and whining delightedly.

'Get *down*, you crazy animal. Down!' he ordered, pulling me and Jahanara, still welded together, out of the basket. 'Are you both OK?'

'After that, nothing can ever frighten me again.'

'Bighead. Wait till you see the drop we've got to get down tomorrow.'

I shuddered. 'Oh, no, Nick. I couldn't. Really.'

'Only joking,' he reassured me. 'Actually we don't have any more hair-raising descents to do; just steady slogging from here on.'

'You are a beast . . . '

'For telling you that? She's pretty hard to please, isn't she, sweetheart?' he asked Jahanara, gently disengaging her clinging hands from me and placing them round his own neck, where they went on clinging as if she hadn't noticed the change of scene.

'Mum-mum-mum,' she murmured.

'No, honey-pie. Dad-dad-dad . . .'

'You'll confuse her,' I said weakly. My knees had buckled and I sank down on a handy rock. The sun-warmed stone was comfortingly solid, and I held it with both hands while the world swayed like the basket for a minute or two. I'm free, I thought. Really free. Free of Rosie and all her works; free of the burden I'd carried around so long; free from fear. I felt slightly intoxicated.

'That's what I'd like her to call me,' said Nick.

'What?'

'Daddy.'

'Oh, but that'd be . . .' Then I realized what he meant.

'Say I can,' he insisted, settling the child on the ground beside me and grasping me by both hands. 'Say you'll marry me.'

There they were, the words I'd longed to hear ever since he pulled me out of the river last year. In the cave, shaken and sore as I was after Sandy's rough surgery and the birth of that poor baby, even so I'd had to keep my pulse under very strict control as I lay next to Nick in my separate quilted sleeping-bag – so near and yet so far – because I was damned if I was going to make the running a second time. As for him, his casual, friendly, altogether too brotherly manner had never wavered.

But now, with no effort from me at all, here was the proposal

I'd been yearning for, on a plate, and with it came to me the irresistible desire to tease that had so often been my downfall.

I sat silent, fighting down this unsuitable reaction to an offer of marriage.

'Wake up,' urged Nick, impatience edging out the romantic sincerity that didn't suit him, anyway. 'I'm asking you to marry me, dammit. I meant to do it before, but you were so hedged about with encumbrances . . .' He gestured vaguely towards the dog and child, but I was remembering another encumbrance.

'Nick,' I said hesitantly, 'there's something you don't know. I must tell you what happened – '

'There's a million billion things I don't know,' he interrupted, 'but only one I care about at the moment. Will you or won't you marry me? Speak now, or else for ever after . . .' because I can see Sandy's over half-way down the cliff, and once he gets here all tender romantic scenes will have to be forgotten while he and I plan our next move. Yes or no?'

That did it. Better self lost the battle and worst self decided to make him sweat a little. I wasn't prepared to be proposed to between bites at a sandwich, as it were.

'Oh, Nick,' I quavered in maidenly confusion, 'it's so sudden. I can't take it in. I – I just don't know.'

'*Don't know!*' He looked ready to explode. I could see all sorts of terse imperatives: 'Be your age, girl!' 'Use your loaf;' 'Get a move on your wits,' etc. etc. seething to burst from him, but at the expense of his blood pressure he managed to suppress them. Instead, he stole a quick look upward at the rapidly descending figure of Sandy, a mere fifty feet above us and going strong, and said, so humbly that it took the wind right out of my sails: 'I'm sorry, darling. I'm always trying to hustle you. I don't know why. You're absolutely right; there's absolutely no need to decide straight away. But bear in mind that I love you.'

'Sure you're not just sorry for me?' I asked suspiciously.

'Sorry for you?' His voice swelled with righteous indignation. 'Of course I'm not. You brought this whole business on your own head, you pea-brain, and you've put a lot of people to one hell of a lot of worry and trouble and expense. My father damn

224

nearly *sacked* me. He said I hadn't done a full day's work since you disappeared, and probably wouldn't until I knew what had happened to you. That's how I managed to persuade him to give me a Sabbatical year. Sandy's left his home at a rather dodgy moment domestically, too, because I needed his help. As for your brother-in-law, God only knows what he must have spent looking for you.'

I cringed with guilt.

'It was only because your sister Anna swore you were alive. Luckily for you, Alan listened to her, and was rich enough to back her hunch. Ah, well done, Sandy. All serene?'

It was my turn to pull my forelock and eat humble pie. I said quickly, while Sandy disengaged himself from the rope and too softly for anyone else to hear: 'Thank you, Nick *darling*. I just couldn't bear to hear you being all sincere and chivalrous. Oh – and the answer is yes.'

Over Nick's shoulder I saw Sandy's look of alarm that changed to laughter as I was seized and hugged against the two-month-old growth of beard, and so great was my happiness that I never even wondered about lice. Gandhi cavorted round us distributing copious licks and wagging his tail; Jahanara chortled and all was laughter and merriment.

The only thing left on my conscience was that I hadn't told Nick about the baby boy left to keep the line of Akbar alive in the secret valley, partly because I simply couldn't explain how all my mother-love had transferred itself to Jahanara, partly because he might have felt obliged to organize a rescue party, or at least ask why I hadn't mentioned the matter before.

It sounds callous, but it's true that I've never felt anything for that baby; hardly even curiosity to know whether he lived or died. People who've fostered animals on other, unlike, animals, might understand my love for Jana and indifference towards my own baby. I understand now that it's mainly a chemical matter: if you haven't hugged, fed, smelt your offspring it has no more appeal to you than any other helpless young thing.

If Nick ever gets around to reading this, I don't think he'll be horrified, though he might have been at the time. He's a very practical person, when he's not blinded by chivalry. But I can see from the way I'm justifying and explaining that I do feel guilty in a way about that baby – guilty of not feeling guilty.

What I regretted far more than the baby, of course, were my sketches and those jewels. All I managed to bring home was the ruby collar and necklace, because I'd worn those non-stop ever since Khurram had presented me with them.

Alan spirited them through the Customs.

'You look far too big a bunch of crooks to take things like those in your luggage,' he said. 'Besides, you've got the dog to worry about – quarantine and all.' We were in the middle of a riotous celebration dinner at Claridges Hotel, New Delhi. 'Leave it to me,' he went on. 'I know a jockey who's out here for the flat-racing – he'll bring it back in his saddle as a favour to me.'

'And you call us a bunch of crooks!' said Nick indignantly. I knew, however, that he was glad to be relieved of the responsibility for getting the jewels home. He had rather puritanical views about smuggling.

'Be careful, Alan,' I urged. 'Don't forget they're Jana's birthright, dowry, and trousseau rolled into one, poor scrap.'

'Dear girl, it'll be as safe with my jockey as it would be in the Bank of England, which is where I suggest you keep them in future. You're flying home when? Next Monday? I have a little business to finish out here, but I'll take dinner off you on Tuesday week and bring the jewels with me.'

'And Anna?'

'Of course.' He grinned at Nick. 'Hindlegs on donkeys won't be safe when the sisterhood meets up again. I hope you've some decent port.'

Sometimes I dream of the valley. Not night-time dreams, because neither Nick's snores nor the noisy pillow-fights of Peter and Paul, our three-year-old twins, can wake me at night, and I never remember night-dreams, anyway.

But on clear, frosty days, especially in autumn, when the beech woods turn red-copper against a pale blue sky, I look up at them and remember the *chenar* trees planted by Akbar in the secret valley, and how the winding lines of irrigation channels used to puzzle me with their shadows, so that I drew them at every hour of daylight and every picture looked a different shape.

Then my mind moves past the neat terraced fields and stately trees, the flowering shrubs over the water, up the smooth sweep of track to the castle gates, and I hear once more the never-ending humming of the workers, and the quick double shuffle of their felt slippers moving to and fro across the courtyard. Through the great gates, past the guards with their waving black stings, and I am back in the throne room.

But this time the figure that sits so quietly on the smaller throne at the Queen's feet, as she judges, orders, counsels, reprimands, is not poor, heavy-lidded Azam, nor fidgety Khurram in his glittering splendour of brocade. It's a figure I know well, but have never seen. That stiff little bundle, swathed in silk surcoat, long wrinkled tight trousers and ridiculous slippers with upturned, embroidered toes, is my son.

His face is smooth and pale, like those of the valley people; his eyes darkly rimmed with kohl. He wears an overlarge, sprawling turban pinned with a great turquoise, but from beneath it a lock of hair has escaped, and – this is where I always rouse myself from the day-dream and busy myself with some unnecessary task, for I cannot bear to watch that figure any more – this stray lock is exactly the same washy red-gold as my own hair.

You mustn't try to find him, Jana darling. You're bound to feel curious about your birthplace, and you might even get some crazy longing to rescue this poor puppet-brother of yours, and bring him to life in the real world, but you must take my word for it that the only thing that would make him really unhappy would be removal to the twentieth century when he's been brought up in the sixteenth. The two don't mix.

Ten to one, the Chinese will soon quietly annexe the little kingdom, and that'll be the end of it, but on the other hand, it may bumble along undiscovered for several hundred more years if we, who know of its existence, leave it in peace.

I want you to promise that you will, too.